THE FOURTH WAY

WILLIAM HATCHETT

THE FOURTH WAY

NEWPULP

NEW PULP PRESS

Published by New Pulp Press, LLC, 926 Truman Avenue, Key West, Florida 33040, USA.

The Fourth Way copyright © 2017 by William Hatchett. Electronic compilation/ paperback edition copyright © 2017 by New Pulp Press, LLC.

This is a work of fiction. Names, characters, places, and incidents either are the product of the author's imagination or are used fictitiously, and any resemblance to actual persons, living or dead, businesses, companies, events, or locales is entirely coincidental. While the author has made every effort to provide accurate information at the time of publication, neither the publisher nor the author assumes any responsibility for errors, or for changes that occur after publication. Further, the publisher does not have any control over and does not assume any responsibility for author or third-party websites or their contents. How the ebook displays on a given reader is beyond the publisher's control.

For information contact:
Publisher@NewPulpPress.com

ISBN-13: 978-1945734199 (New Pulp Press)
ISBN-10: 1945734191

Printed in the United States of America
Visit us on the web at www.newpulppress.com

THE
FOURTH
WAY

1

Conservatives
They left their clothes on the beach and went for
swim when John Major was in charge. We stole them.
Now watch the bastards drown!
                                        - The New Labour papers

Emma Henderson liked having sex in toilets. Next to attending parties in sweaty Soho basements (which she could not do anymore) it was her favorite activity.

She sat astride her chauffeur, her back against the door; he was pounding into her in a kind of frenzy.

"Oh! Sean, Sean!"

He exploded. She felt him sliding away.

"Is that the best you can do?"

He felt the reproach like a stab.

She pulled herself off him and, with dignity, smoothed down her black Prada skirt. She had not been wearing underwear – it was in the car.

"I'm not finished," he said, pathetically.

Emma pushed up the back of her hair.

"We're going. You will follow me, in five minutes."

It was a ladies' lavatory, so there was no problem – for her. Sean heard water swish into the washbasin. She would be dabbing her lips, putting her face back on. A little later, he heard her kitten heels click across the tiled floor.

She was waiting for him on the back seat of the Jag – composed but in a terrible mood. Sean knew better than to say anything. He slid the car out of the car park and back onto the M40. They were on the Westway by seven o'clock. Emma loved driving back into London at night. It was one of the few advantages of going to her constituency in Middlewich by car.

She was forty-four years old and the Member or Parliament for a dull town in the west midlands. Emma was a minister in the Department of Trade and Industry. One would have called her a rising star, except that her universe, New Labour, elected with great hope and promise in 1997, was fading.

The prime minister, Tony Blair, now in his second term, needed people like her. She was a product of the Home Counties and Oxbridge, smart, clever and attractive - a blue-eyed ingénue sometimes attracting the moniker blonde bombshell. She wore expensive, and sexy, clothes. The late nights and the poor diet of politics could have played havoc with her body if she hadn't spent so much and time and money on making sure that they didn't.

They passed the Arc – Emma loved that building – and swung down through Mayfair. Emma lived alone in a flat off Kensington High Street. The flat, she told people, was handy for the Commons. It was also convenient for her favorite shops – Harrods and Harvey Nicks. Emma, although she concealed it well, was posh for New Labour. On the outside, she could be warm and charming but underneath one sensed something hard and cold. This accounted for a nickname sometimes used by her friends and associates, the Ice Maiden.

The food of Middlewich sat heavily in her stomach. She was looking forward to plundering her fridge, with its chilled Belgian truffles and delicacies from Marks & Spencer. After the chauffeur, Sean, had penetrated her gated compound, she dismissed him. She was eagerly anticipating kicking off her shoes and having a warm bath.

It was more than two hundred miles up to Middlewich and back – too far. Emma was not sure how much longer she would carry on with this life. Her position was low in the ministerial pecking order – at trade and industry she gave out licenses to mobile phone companies. Admittedly, the perks were good but she wanted something more – a job with one of the real departments, like the Home Office, the Foreign Office or the Treasury. She wanted to be on TV more. And she wanted to be on Desert Island Discs (she had already chosen her eight records).

~ ~ ~

That morning, Rick Gilliver woke up early. He usually did. It was ten to six. He lay in bed, listening to Farming Today, turned down to a faint volume, worrying. His alarm would not go off for another hour and a half. It was Friday. Later, he would have to take his daughter, Gina, to school.

It was far more complicated than that. Usually, he would put his head round her door at quarter past seven to wake her up. She would ignore him. Ten minutes later, he would try again. She would say something rude to him; he would retaliate. This morning, they would scream at each other. He would actually stamp his foot, like an infant having a tantrum. "You will go to school!"

Rick was a journalist on a trade magazine, Planning Today. He had to be at a press conference that morning, in central London. He kept telling Gina "I can't be late!". But it made no difference.

Gina was thirteen. In the mornings, she applied her make–up slowly, while TV cartoons played in the background, or soft music thumped from her ghetto blaster. Rick had little idea what music she was into. Three years before, it had been S Club Seven – her world had been painted in simple, primary colors. But

S Club had been disdained by Gina before the rest of the United Kingdom had abandoned them; she had moved straight from their innocence to the tortured complexities of Nirvana. At her request, Rick had painted her room dark purple.

Rick had custody of Gina on Thursday nights and every other weekend. During her grunge phase, they had spent a year driving together to Camden market, in north London. Rick waited, feasting his eyes on strangeness, while Gina went into shops that looked like fairground booths, booming out deafening music. Style-wise, she was not something as simple as a grunger. She looked down on kids who thought that just wearing a hooded top and baggy jeans – the uniform of grunge – were enough. At 12, she looked like a student at some esoteric fashion college. Her forearms were coated with bangles; she jangled as she walked. But to Rick's surprise, she quickly lost interest in grunge – Nirvana soon went the way of S Club Seven.

Now, he could not answer the question "what kind of music does your daughter like?". He suspected that it was something to do with drum and bass or hip-hop. But these forms of music were largely a mystery to him. Their practitioners seemed to combine frightening lucidity with social withdrawal. Presenting a silent, scowling face to the outside world was valued, as was wearing "the right kind of trainers". Of course, once you had badgered your parents into buying the "right" trainers, you risked becoming a figure of ridicule, because, in the fickle worlds of hip-hop and skate boarding, they would not be "right" for very long.

"Come on Gina, for God's sake! I've told you, I can't be late!"

"Shut up dad!"

"Don't tell me to shut up!"

And so on. The thing that scared Rick was that, weirdly, these arguments were rather like the ones that he had once had with Gina's mum Carol. They had split up two years before.

"Look dad," he heard through the door, "the more you tell me to hurry up, the more it's going to wind me up! OK?"

"Right!"

That was the last straw. Rick pushed through the door, like the villain in a Victorian melodrama. Gina was peering, wide-eyed, into her mirror. Her little TV was on – the one he had bought her from Dixons the week before, as a peace offering.

"Gina, I'm sick of this! I've told you …"

He stood there, ranting. Gina just stared at him. Her cheeks were glazed with foundation. She looked like a make-up demonstrator in a posh department store in Oxford Street, except that she had the black-rimmed eyes of a Panda.

"Shut up dad!" she said.

Rick was clenching and un-clenching his fists. He was going to have a coronary if their relationship went on like this. He expressed his fury by slamming Gina's door, a peculiar role reversal, and stomping downstairs. He waited in the car, glancing at his watch, pale with anger.

~ ~ ~

They drove in silence to the local railway station Gina got out of the car and waited by the door. She was wearing purple and black tights and a black skirt. Her green sweatshirt bearing the school's logo (it was not a coat of arms and there was no Latin motto) was covered by a pale blue hoodie. Her long hair, tied in a bunch at the back was some undefined color between yellow and red. There were huge silver hoops on her ears.

The final indignity was that she demanded money from Rick, as she glared at him through the open door. And he gave it to her. A crumpled five-pound note.

"Thanks dad." She managed to include both scorn and vulnerability in the two words. Someone underneath those clothes was the little girl who had loved Barbie dolls. The one who had gone with him to see S Club Seven, at a concert in Hyde Park. Now, whenever he heard their cheesy hit "Reach for the Sky" he remembered that day and it made his eyes go watery.

He watched her clomp into the station entrance.

"Love you darling."

Sometimes she would echo "love you too" back at him. But not today. She looked witheringly in his direction without saying anything and disappeared into the station. She would be late of course. Rick had recently discussed with her teacher Gina's 84.7 per cent attendance record at her school. The teacher told Rick that she had a whole drawer filled with over-sized earrings, seized from Gina – enough to open a stall in Camden Market, he had joked. Camden Market! They didn't even go there anymore. There were even cooler places, but Rick did not know where they were.

Rick turned the ignition key of his blue second-hand Mondeo. He would have to drive back to the suburb where he lived, park the car outside his house, then catch the bus to central London Inevitably, he had not had any breakfast. He could feel the digestive juices eating at his stomach wall. He was sure that he was getting an ulcer.

He waited to pull out, cursing, as a long line of cars drove by. There was no way he was going to make the press conference in time. He turned on BBC Radio 4's Today program. It was wall-to-wall speech for new junkies – Gina would not let him listen to it when she was in the car – and beat a furious tattoo on his steering wheel, cursing silently.

2

Both assassination and ennoblement are effective as a means of disempowerment. Assassination is quicker, but should be used sparingly. Misguided fellow travellers, meddlers and senior party figures who are now a threat to us need to be watched

- The New Labour papers

Doctor Keeley dressed with special care that day, the 17th of July 2003. He was wearing, the papers later reported, a Barbour jacket and cap and a striped shirt. His socks were beige. These were not his working clothes – he was off work, with stress. Dr. Keeley was a renowned international expert on the effects of electromagnetic fields on biological systems, based at the Royal Free Hospital in Hampstead, north Lodon. In his pocket were his house keys and a mobile phone. Keeley was a thorough, meticulous man.

Mrs. Keeley later said that he had been surprisingly relaxed, almost cheerful, considering what was going on at work. After lunch, he emailed some friends from his study. At three o'clock, which was his normal time for a constitutional, he went out for a walk. Their small, modern house was only a couple of minutes walk from Hampstead Heath. If Keeley had followed his normal pattern, he would have strolled from through the North End of the heath and returned via the Vale of Health

His wife remembered asking what he wanted for supper – Keeley did not express an opinion. She recalled saying goodbye to him and her husband muttering something inaudible as he went through the front door. He did not stop at the newsagent to buy the Guardian on his way to the heath. This was surprising, as he had been following the news of the Iraq war carefully. Perhaps he had intended to get one on the way back.

Keeley said hello to one of his wife's friends at the end of his road. She commented later that he looked quite relaxed – not stressed or unhappy. Although there was a pale sun, it was a cool, windy day. Sometimes, Keeley liked to cook. As he walked, he put together a menu in his mind. He would prepare something really nice for his wife, to compensate for how irritable he had been lately. In a minute, he would phone her to tell here not to bother to make dinner.

He started up a familiar track. Thinking what wine would go with the food, he nodded acknowledgements to the usual dog walkers, enjoying the breeze on his face and the emerald grass. The path led to a beech copse. Keeley was halfway towards the trees when he noticed that two men were walking towards him. One was tall, the other short. They were wearing dark coats, despite the sun. The head of the stocky man was fashionably shaved.

They reached him. His instinct was to run, but it was too late. The squat leading man grabbed his forearm.

"Let's go for a little walk, shall we?"

"I'm sorry ..."

The grip tightened. Keeley could smell stale spirits on the short man's breath.

"It's a bit public here. We just need to have a talk with you, in private ... Dr. Keeley."

The tall man had spoken. He was smartly dressed and carrying a black leather briefcase.

"You're looking very tired. Must have been working too hard, is that it? We might be able to help you there."

"What are you talking about? This is outrageous ... you can't ..."

"Yes, we can," the tall man said.

Keeley looked around breathing hard. There was no one to be seen, for miles.

"Let's go shall we."

One on each arm, they dragged him down the slope, protesting, to a place where they would not be seen.

~ ~ ~

The next evening, a Friday, Emma Henderson, wearing a white toweling robe, caught Keeley's name on her living room TV She had just come out of the bath. The news went on and on. There was not much actual detail – the story was padded out with hinted conspiracy. She listened while dripping water onto her leather settee.

"A body matching the description of Dr. David Keeley – the mobile phone expert at the center of the Digitrunk row – has been found in north London. prime minister Tony Blair has already announced that there will be a full judicial enquiry into his death.

"The body was found at 9.20 on Hampstead Heath, a short distance from a public footpath. Dr. Keeley, 54, is a leading expert on the effect of electromagnetic fields on the brain, based at the Royal Free Hospital, in north London.

"Next Thursday, he was due to give evidence to a select committee at the House of Commons. The committee is investigating how the Digitrunk communication system was adopted by the Home Office for the UK emergency services, although it is now thought to be unsafe.

"Dr. Keeley left his house at about three o'clock. His wife said that he was depressed and in a disturbed mental condition. She reported him missing that night." Blah, blah, blah ... she was only half listening now. Dr. Keeley's body was found lying on the ground. His left wrist had been slashed and he had bled to death. He had removed his glasses and wristwatch. A police spokesperson said that early signs indicate that he had taken his own life."

Good! That was all OK. Her pulse started to slow down. Through a blind trust, based offshore, Emma owned shares in Techtonic, the company that had developed Digitrunk. As minister, she had made sure that Techtonic had won an £11bn Home Office contract to "roll out" a new radio network for the emergency services.

Like mobile phones, the Techtonic system was based on microwaves. But the waves were pulsed and the transmitters were extremely powerful. Techtonic had erected them on schools and housing estates all over the country by giving money to education authorities and residents' groups. Some called it bribery. It was the fastest way to get the system up and running.

Now, protestors were saying that kids would get brain cancer, that policemen using handsets would hallucinate and that Digitrunk would knock out defibrillators in ambulances.

A recent article by Dr. Keeley's, published in The Lancet on the dangers of the new system, had been inconvenient to Emma, to say the last. Techtonic's shares had started to tumble the day after it was published. She had been able to sell the shares before they hit rock bottom, but, still, she had lost her shirt on the investment. Now, the clamor for Digitrunk to be scrapped was intensifying. Parents' groups were signing petitions and MPs were asking awkward questions of the minister in Parliament. She, of course, responded that "according to international guidelines", Digitrunk was "perfectly safe". Yeh, like British beef was "safe", said the protestors.

A select committee enquiry had recently begun. Emma was to give evidence to it herself. She would be asked, by sarcastic MPs, how the government had made such a monumentally stupid blunder, why it had poured billions of pounds down the drain, and so on.

Keeley had been called to give evidence to the same committee the following week. The papers had been hyping up his appearance for days. They were getting hysterical about the Digitrunk scandal, saying that it was "New Labour's smoking gun". Why the hell had Blair's party invested in a communications system that damaged kids' brains?

Well, Emma thought, Keeley's moment of glory wasn't going to happen. He was lying on a shelf in a mortuary. She smiled to herself. She decided that she would get back into the bath and luxuriate. She would take a Valium and let the soft, warm water caress away her aches and pains.

~ ~ ~

Three months later in October, Emma was coming down the M40 in a Jaguar XJS from her constituency. It was a Sunday night, the end of a grey, squally day. It had been a tiresome weekend – meeting boring people and shaking their clammy hands. Her weekly surgery was held in a drafty, ill-lit room over a shop. In Emma's jaundiced view, the people of Middlewich, her constituency, had been cast adrift from civilized life. Their speech sounded like sheep bleating; they thought that prawn cocktail-flavored crisps were a luxury food item and that Michael Ball was an opera singer. Even sweaty and energetic sex with Sean, her driver, had not made up for the appalling experience of her weekend.

On the way north, they had made love in a car park close to Junction 4 and again in a public lavatory when they had arrived in Middlewich. She had not allowed Sean to stay in her room at the Post House Forte outside town (Middlewich did not have a hotel). But she had called him up in the middle of the night, requesting a "back rub". After they had had sex, Sean had insisted on telling her about his childhood.

She was sitting in back, cocooned by Verdi. They had just passed through the Chiltern gap. The huge escarpment cut through chalk hills always cheered her up. It was a sign that they were close to London. Thank God.

Her mobile rang. He looked at the number. She did not recognize it.

"Sean, turn down that racket would you. Thank you."

It was an unknown voice, saying that the prime minister was about to come on.

"Hi." The voice was friendly and relaxed. "It's Tony here."

"Oh!" She had to be careful. It might be a disc jockey or an impersonator.

"Listen, Emma ... I've been er following the Digitrunk thing."

Everybody had. It was a hot topic of conversation for the chattering classes.

"I think you have done very well."

"Oh, thank you." There was a pause. Compliments were nice. However, they generally followed by a sting in the tail.

"To get to the point, I'm having a reshuffle Emma, as you know, next week, and, well, I've got some good news for you."

She took a deep breath. This was it, she thought. The Foreign Office or the Treasury.

"I'd like you to be the new minister for London."

"Oh." Her breath came out in a sigh. Tony heard the sound.

"It's a very important job, Emma."

She felt semi-detached for the rest of the conversation. London! How could he? Tony just wanted to shift her from the DTI, now that the Digitrunk pressure was easing off. She had acquitted herself well at the select committee. With wide blue eyes, she had told MPs that she had had completely confidence in the safety of Digitrunk when the Home Office contract had been awarded. One always followed the advice of one's civil servants and the experts at the National Radiological Board. Of course, if there were legitimate concerns ...

"The thing is," said the prime minister, "I'm a bit concerned about the London mayoral elections. Tim Barstow hasn't been performing very well.

Tim Barstow was the current minister for London. He was an enthusiastic but ineffectual character, an intellectual, with a permanent grin on his face that looked like a smirk.

"Tim has had problems. I don't think that he has been ... incisive enough, if you see what I mean. We need to make sure that the Labour candidate wins the mayoral elections next year, Emma. And I think that you are exactly the right person for the job. You have er ... street appeal."

"Have you told Tim yet?" She was studying her crimson fingernails.

"No, it's my next call." He paused, waiting for her response.

"Your first engagement will be a press conference next week. I want you to make a major announcement."

"Oh."

"So would you like the ..."

"Of course I would." She had cut the PM off. She felt herself blushing.

"I would love the job. I am immensely flattered that you have asked me."

"No need to sleep on it?"

"Of course not."

They chatted for another couple of minutes. Emma asked after Tony's wife, Cherie. She did not have a partner. Her husband, who had been a senior executive with a commercial television company, had been killed in a tragic accident at their house in Hertfordshire, just before she had been selected as an MP. They talked about some mutual friends.

It was a pleasant conversation. Afterwards, she began to feel cheerful. The new position was a move sideways, another minister's job. But it could be more high profile. Emma had been born in London, in Putney. She had never had a London accent and she had lost her posh vowels when she was at Oxford. Politicians had to be classless these days. Being London minister could be rather fun, she decided. She knew one of the cast of EastEnders. She could invite him to her first press conference.

"Ma'am?" Sean's voice, with its Irish lilt, interrupted her thoughts.

"Yes, what?"

"Was that the prime minister? Only, when I heard you say Tony, I thought ..."

"Sean!" It was her harshest voice. "Shut up. I have made this clear. You must never, ever, listen in on my personal conversations. Do you understand?"

"Yes, ma'am."

"Good. Now put the Verdi on again, would you."

"Yes, ma'am."

Soon Rigoletto was flooding through the car, like a velvet ocean. Emma felt her whole body tingle. Emma Henderson, minister for London. The post would mean a new office, in the deputy prime minister's kingdom near Victoria station, Eland House. Eland House was a gigantic glass ziggurat, with a huge atrium inside, close to Victoria Station. The building was more air than substance. It was ostentatious and over-sized as the deputy prime minister himself.

Emma felt sure that she would be able to charm the deputy PM. He would instinctively dislike her, an upper middle class southern woman. It would be an interesting challenge.

Tony's words and the new job were like a hit of cocaine. She started to feel sexy again. They had not made love since Junction 11, outside Banbury. Sean was a boring as a breezeblock, but still ...

"Sean ..." Her voice insinuated itself through the lush chords of the Verdi aria. It reached her chauffeur's attentive ears in the front of the car.

"My shoulders are feeling awfully tight. I wondered ..."

Could he pull over at the nearest exit and give her a back rub? Of course he could.

~ ~ ~

Rick Gilliver was late. He was always bloody late. Ahead of him was the headquarters of the Office of the Deputy prime minister. He was here for a press conference held by the new minister for London. Emma Henderson was going to make some kind of announcement.

There was no safe way to get to the front door, especially if, like Rick, you were too impatient for pedestrian crossings. There were three lanes of speeding traffic between him and the giant glass building. It was just a question of jumping off the pavement and hoping for the best. He did.

Luckily, the press conference had not yet started. Rick squeezed his way past other better-paid and better-dressed journalists. Those who worked on the broadsheets were nearly all from public schools and Oxbridge - peas from the same pod. Self-confidence had been bred into them – even the ones who were seemed modest. They knew that they were the ruling class.

Rick had been educated at a comprehensive school and a minor university. He tried not to think that he was locked out of the secret club that the broadsheet journalists belonged to. But somehow, he knew he was. They had a way of putting you down, even if they didn't mean to.

"Excuse me."

He had just crawled over the lap of a fierce looking woman with black curly hair. She was from the Times. Rick was wearing black jeans which looked like proper trousers and a blue jacket which he had bought, with Gina, from a shop called TK Maxx in Croydon. When he had become so shabby that he embarrassed her, he would allow Gina to pick some new clothes for him. Now this jacket needed replacing. Rick hated buying new clothes. The experience gave him a panic attack.

He saw someone he recognized – Huw Evans, editor of Planning Weekly, another trade magazine. It was a well-respected title. Rick's magazine, Planning Today, was a new kid on the block.

"Ladies and gentlemen."

Emma's smooth amplified voice brought all eyes to the front. She was wearing an expensive, tailored jacket, in a fierce New Labour shade. Her blonde hair shone like glass; her face, caressed with expensive oils, was glowing. The woman from the Times was affronted by how well the minister looked. Emma had their attention. There were a couple of cameras at the back. She would be lucky to make more than a few seconds as the end of the TV news. She knew that.

"Thank you very much for coming here, on such a cold, wet day." There was a murmur of appreciation. The Deputy PM would never have said anything like that. He hated journalists. He always looked as if he wanted to hit them.

"We are here to celebrate a great city, London." Emma scanned the front few rows looking for familiar faces. She found them. There was that bitch from the Times – she would ignore her – the worried frowner from the Guardian, Roger Coverington; the extremely posh, red-faced man from the Telegraph (she could never remember his name); that weasel, Howard something, from the Mail. He would try to trip on higher taxes and unnecessary regulations.

The people further back didn't really matter. They were probably from boring trade magazines. Really, she was here for the cameras. However, she knew that they would only use the footage if this was the dullest day in London's history. It was a tricky occasion. She had to breathe some life into her portfolio without making her predecessor, Tim Barstow, look like an idiot.

She was going to announce a major program of housing and investment for the East London corridor, which was why Rick was here. The brown land east of Dagenham would soon be covered with more churned up mud. New Labour's favorite architect was sitting to her right. He was an unctuous, grey-haired charmer with an East European accent. In the green room, he had grasped Emily's hand and congratulated her on her "smashing" jacket.

The problem was, nobody gave a stuff about the boring East London corridor. The journalists were far more interested in the coming elections for the Mayor of London. There were strong rumors that New Labour was going to let the present mayor, Ken Livingstone, back into the party so that he could stand as their candidate. Livingstone, a maverick socialist, had been kicked out of the Labour party three years before. If he were readmitted, Emma would have to endorse his candidacy, even though she, and Tony, hated him like poison. That was the speculation.

She had finished her spiel. It was question time.

"Howard Harris, Daily Mail. Ms. Henderson ..." His brow furrowed with concentration. "The mayoral elections. If Labour lets Ken back in and if he stands as mayor next June, will he enjoy your full support?'

Emma smiled. She was skilled at answering tricky questions – reconciling contradictory points of view, defending propositions in which she did not believe – in other words, speaking bullshit. That's why she was a good politician.

"There are lots of ifs in that question, Howard," she said. "As you well know, whether or not Mr. Livingstone is allowed to rejoin the party is entirely a matter for the national executive committee and no decision has yet been taken. In any case, we are not here to talk about Ken, but a major program of redevelopment for London. The fact is ..."

Rick studied the minister, as her mouth moved and sounds came out. He cast his eyes over her shining hair, buffed up at Toni and Guy's, and her crimson jacket. He wondered what she was wearing underneath her smart business suit. He knew that it would be something expensive and made out of silk. For a politician, he realized, she looked almost human. In fact – and this discovery alarmed him – she was sexy.

Rick had seen photographs of Emma in a feature in Hello magazine. In the main picture spread, she had been reclining on an expensive settee in her casual clothes – well-fitting Levis, a white football shirt and a faded denim jacket. As portrayed in Hello, Emma lived in a fresh, white and pink world – an innocent, newly plucked English rose. The sycophantic caption explained that she was a Fulham FC supporter. It was the closest that rich people got to football.

"Thank you minister," said the man from the Mail. He looked disappointed.

There was a silence.

"Any more questions?"

Emma's piercing blue eyes scanned the room. Rick felt himself putting his hand up. It was an almost unconscious action. He had not meant to.

"Thank you. The man in the er ... blue jacket."

Rick waited, while the microphone worked its way down the row. It was always a frightening few seconds. Journalists from the nationals hunted in packs. They were as quick and vicious as jackals.

"Rick Gilliver. Planning Today."

"Go ahead, Rick."

He asked a complicated question. It covered sub-regional development frameworks and the need for cross-boundary liaison mechanisms. Afterwards no one spoke.

"Thank you." She smiled. "That was a very good question. Unfortunately, I er ... can't answer it, at least in the detail that it deserves. I've only been in this job for a week you know."

The room filled with laughter. The journalists were on her side. It was a breath of fresh air, they were all thinking – new minister admits that she is not infallible. The deputy prime minster, with his convoluted sentences, would never have admitted that.

He would have baffled them with convoluted nonsense, his syntax as tangled as a fur ball.

A man next to Emily, with a sharp, narrow face, whispered something into her ear. She murmured into the microphone.

"Oh, I see. Rick?" She looked ahead, squinting in a delightful way. "Perhaps you would like to come up to the front. It seems that we might be able to help you."

Help me? Really? Rick grinned. The woman from the Times frowned, as he slid past her, disgusted that this little oik had won the minister's attention.

He made his way to the front.

3

Email

What a brilliant idea! The more we can remove the human interface between news gatherers and the news, the better. The key newspapers are safely tucked away in Canary Wharf – that means fewer boozy "off the record" lunches. We should disseminate information by website and email as much as possible and avoid meeting people. The more electronic we are, the more control we will have over the human factor.

- The New Labour papers

Rick's magazine, Planning Today, was situated at the top of a flight of steep, rickety stairs in Charterhouse Street, next to Smithfield meat market. Style magazines used to predict that Smithfield would be the next Covent Garden. It hadn't happened. In the small hours, refrigerated lorries parked by the market, purring like cats, waiting to carry sides of beef up to Scotland. Later in the morning, shoals of white vans congealed around the entrances. Men in stained white coats lugged bits of dead animals into them and the gutters ran red with blood and entrails. Lovely.

The magazine had been started by two former ad sales women, Joan Hudson and Olive Wilkins, with big ideas and some venture capital. Joan was thin and choleric, her business partner, Olive, was large-boned and sanguine. They had kitted out the office with shopping mall furniture – pine tables that wobbled and shelving made out of bendy red tin.

Joan Hudson, who was a chain smoker, lived in a glass-partitioned room, a kind of fish tank, at the end of the office. She lurked in her rank-smelling den peering out, like a malevolent conger eel. Olive came in less often. She worked mainly from home. When she did sweep into the office, she would deliberately double-park her car. If she were clamped, a hapless lackey would be instructed to deal with the consequences.

Quite often, Joan and Olive held meetings in the fish tank with mysterious men in suits who smelled of aftershave and who were never introduced to the rest of the staff. Joan would frown and scowl through the proceedings, itching for a cigarette. Olive would radiate bonhomie. Joan and Olive's company, Hudson and Wilkins Ltd, intended to launch more magazines, for the moment, Planning Today was their flagship.

Although Rick had become familiar with planning, his relationship with the subject was ambivalent. In all honesty, its practitioners, most of whom worked for local government, tended to be dull. Even the odd and eccentric ones lacked interest. He had drifted into the magazine, after an English degree and a post-graduate journalism course at the London College of Printing. Still, at least he was the editor.

Back from the press conference, he walked across to his desk, out of breath from the stairs. The eel was watching him from her tank. He could feel her nasty little eyes. He smiled at his assistant editor, Karen.

"Everything OK Kaz?"

Karen nodded, looking vacant. She floated through life on a cloud. Rick suspected that someone had forgotten to connect some crucial wires in Karen's brain. Everything for her was either "nice" or, in some cases, "really nice". If she felt that something was not nice, she regarded it with deep suspicion and ignored it. She felt instinctively that Rick was not nice. It was no use sending Karen to a press conference. She would simply smile through the proceedings and come back staring ahead blankly from her bovine eyes.

Two other people worked on Planning Today (or Planning Yesterday, as Rick called it), Simone, the production editor, and Nick, the editorial assistant. Nick was inexperienced, but keen to get on. He wanted to believe that journalism was exciting and that it meant something – so did Rick. Simone was a babe. Rick had always fancied her. But he had never plucked up the courage to tell her.

Rick's desk had an Apple Macintosh computer (he loved Macs. He would hate to use anything else), a phone, a forest of yellow post-it notes and bulging filing trays. Karen sat opposite him. Sometimes she would place a vase of flowers in the space between them. Often, Rick would knock the vase over and be forced to apologize.

He slumped down into his red office chair. However many times you adjusted it, it was always uncomfortable, like perching on a ledge. Why did office chairs have wheels and levers? Chairs were not supposed to have wheels, or levers. It was ridiculous.

It was quarter to one, almost lunchtime. Karen was a punctilious observer of lunch breaks. She would leave her desk at shortly before one and always take at least an hour. No one knew where she went. Thursday was never a busy day for Planning Today, because the magazine had gone to press the previous evening. It was a time for sorting things out, deleting junk emails and having long conversations with your friends.

Because the piece that he was about to write would not appear until the following week, Rick had the luxury of taking some time over it. Slowly, he pulled his reporter's notebook out of his jacket pocket. He sighed.

The intro was always the hardest thing to write. Once he had cracked it, he would be flying.

"It's a tough job dealing with Dagenham," he started. "But someone's got to do it." Rick said that Emma Henderson, who was ambitious and appealing, in a Daily Mail kind of way, would put more oomph into her post than her predecessor, Tim Barstow, England's Olympic grinning champion. But it would take more than a pair of shoulder pads and a winning smile to make people interested in the development of east London.

He said that it would be interesting to see how Emma would handle Ken Livingstone, who was a consummate politician, if he was adopted as Labour's mayoral candidate.

He was finishing off the piece when Karen came back, just after two. She was carrying a copy of the Standard, London's daily paper. Rick knew that she would spend the first hour of the afternoon reading it. Once she had told him that this was "research", but this was scarcely credible. The Standard tended to concentrate on bitchy gossip about film stars' shoes, rather than planning or local government.

That afternoon was no different to scores of others. They were two people thrust together into a claustrophobic space who had nothing in common and little to say to each other. Rick started to work on a feature on the new planning bill for next week's issue; Karen subbed the letters page. At three o'clock, she made some milky Earl Grey tea. Rick declined her offer of a cup. He detested the stuff. It reminded him of musty country houses and wet Labradors.

Karen went home at five. Rick turned off his Mac an hour later. As he did so, Olive glared at him through her glass wall. Why did she always make him feel guilty that he was not prepared to work through the night to make her more money?

~ ~ ~

A moment after he had turned off his computer, his phone rang. The voice was faint, as if the person was trying not to be overheard, but it was confident.

"Hello, is that Richard?"

"Yes." The greeting sounded strange to Rick. Nobody used his full name, except his mother.

"I have something to tell you."

"Oh yes."

Lots of people thought they had a tale to tell. They were usually weirdos who believed that their water was being poisoned by aliens or that they were being brain–washed by radio waves.

"It's about New Labour."

"Really?"

Rick's interest increased slightly.

"The thing is ... I can't tell you about it over the phone."

Uh oh, here we go again, thought Rick.

"Why not?"

"I just can't."

"I suppose you can't tell me your name either."

"Of course not. I'm a civil servant, I can tell you that. You can call me Adam."

Rick sighed. People often insisted that they had a big story. Usually, it was a fistful of nonsense – a feud with their neighbor, or a workplace grievance. Drunk people at parties were the worst. Then there were the carefully Sellotaped letters, addressed in capital letters and containing newspaper clippings with weird, paranoid underlinings. Something in this person's voice, however, made him a little bit interested.

"Well, Adam, we'd better meet. Are you doing anything later?"

"No."

"Well, how about meeting in a pub, somewhere near here?"

"Where is that?" Adam sounded faintly irritated.

"I'm in Smithfield, close to Holborn Circus."

"I see." There was a pause. "OK then." It was clear that Adam did not like going out of his way. But, in this case, he was prepared to stretch a point.

They made the arrangements. Rick did not need an excuse to go for a drink. He had a pint or two on his way home most evenings. This side of journalism appealed to him – clandestine meetings with contacts on the trail of murky and wicked deeds. One day, he hoped that he would uncover a really big story that would get him a job on a proper paper.

~ ~ ~

He had chosen the Cheshire Cheese off Fleet Street because it was close to his office and because of its interesting associations. In the old days, reporters from the national papers would mingle here with barristers and loose-lipped clerks from the Law Courts, trading drinks and cigarettes for scraps of information. Those days were gone. The great newspapers had left Fleet Street in the 1980s, like liners sailing out of a harbor. Their departure had sucked the glamour and vitality from the street, leaving it with the atmosphere of a provincial shopping mall. Now the pubs and wine bars were usually empty. The newspapers' offices were like ghostly hulks.

Rick was a cyclist. He had ridden his mountain bike to work that morning and locked it to a parking meter outside the office. He rode to the pub via Ludgate Circus. At five to seven, he was sitting at a corner table, guarding his pint of Samuel Smith's bitter, wondering whether it would hold out until Adam arrived. The bar was deserted. It was hard to imagine nicotine-stained hacks had once jostled here on their slow homeward journeys. But the poets and drunkards of Fleet Street were gone. And they were not coming back.

Just then, Rick saw a man who looked like a civil servant. He was in his mid-thirties, with a dark Next suit and short hair, shaved neatly at the back. He was carrying a high-tech silver metal briefcase. He was wearing a small stud earring. That probably meant that he was gay. The man ordered a Pils, without a glass. He carefully placed the briefcase on the floor, next to his expensively shod feet. Rick walked over to the bar.

"Are you Adam?"

The man looked him up and down.

"I'm sitting over here."

The man nodded.

Adam worked in the Office of the Deputy prime minister. His job involved planning, although he found this subject just as unappealing as Rick did. He was thirty-six years old and slightly jaded. He lived in Brixton. Rick gleaned these facts in the following ten minutes. Also that Adam had gone to a private school and a good university. They were a mismatched couple, opposites in almost every respect. Rick looked at his pint. There were bits of sediment at the bottom of the glass. Adam took that as a sign that he was in a hurry. Actually, he wasn't.

Adam explored the room with his eyes. He looked nervous.

"Look, I only phoned you because I know something important."

Rick was suspicious. Adam had probably discovered a mistake in his tax code.

"Oh yes," he said, noncommittally.

"You remember John Smith?"

Rick did not respond.

"You know, the leader of the Labour party."

"I know who he was."

"Did you know that he was murdered?"

Rick hesitated.

"No he wasn't. He died of a heart attack."

"Do you know what caused that heart attack?"

"Natural causes."

"That's what they wanted you to think. I happen to know that there was nothing natural about it."

"Why are you telling me?"

"Because I read your magazine."

"Seriously?"

"Oh yes."

Rick felt flattered. Planning Today readers were a rare breed.

"Do you get it every week?"

Adam nodded

"Admittedly, it's not your usual kind of story. I just thought ..."

Rick saw an imaginary front-page in his mind's eye. "John Smith was murdered. Exclusive."

"Have you contacted any other journalists with this? I mean, on the nationals."

Adam looked down at his glass.

"They weren't interested. They thought that I was mad. Some of them were quite rude."

"I see." That was par for the course.

Rick saw that his beer was nearly finished. Suddenly he felt thirsty.

"Would you like another drink?"

Adam shook his head. He was a one-bottle man. Rick came back from the bar with a pint and a bag of crisps. He knew that Adam would be far too fastidious to accept a crisp.

"So what's the story then?"

Adam leaned forwards. "I'll tell you. Just listen. About ten years ago, I was living where I am now with two housemates, John and Graham. Graham worked for the Treasury. He used to knock about with this woman, Emma. It was a few weeks before we twigged that she was Emma Henderson. You know, the Labour MP?"

"I know her."

"Quite often, Emma and Graham used to go to the Think Tank night club, up at the Elephant and Castle."

Rick knew the place, because he had been there. It was a huge, multi-floored warren. The club played thumping music that only made sense when you were on drugs. The club's name was also a brand used to sell T-shirts, CDs and other merchandise to blissed-out punters.

"Anyway, one night, I think it was in May 1994, a black Jaguar pulled up outside to pick Graham up. I was looking out through the curtains. A really mean-looking bloke in a black bomber jacket got out first. He had a diamond-shaped scar on his right cheek and scary eyes, like a Rottweiler. He looked up and down the road, to see if the coast was clear. Emma got out and rang the doorbell. She was wearing a short black skirt that barely covered her arse ..." Adam's face showed distaste. "She was carrying a silver briefcase. This one." He felt for the object beneath the table.

A customer had come into the bar. He had the cropped hair of a convict or squaddy and a fierce scowl. Adam glanced at him anxiously before continuing.

"The car must have come back at, what, four in the morning. Emma and Graham came into the house. I heard them in the kitchen, making coffee. I could tell from Graham's voice that he'd been taking Es. He had this funny high-pitched laugh?"

"Go on."

"Well, my bedroom was next to Graham's. And the wall was as thin as paper. I know it was wrong of me, but I could hear most of their conversation. Emma must have been really off her head because I could hear her boasting. I heard her say that John Smith was history. She said that by the following Wednesday the boring Scottish bastard would be a goner.

"She told Graham there were these blokes who did special jobs for her. She called them the E Squad. They had tried to push Smith off a mountain in the Highlands the month before, but it hadn't worked. Emma said that Smith used to buy malt whisky from this little off-licence up at King's Cross. Well, they were putting stuff in it, I think it was atropine, and it was making Smith ill - sweaty and short of breath. He had already had one heart attack, six years before. There was going to be a gala dinner the following week, she said, and they were going to finish him off, by spiking his drink with something a bit more powerful."

Neither of them spoke.

"Why were they going to do this?"

"After Smith was out of the frame, Emma said that it was a dead cert that a New Labour candidate would get the Labour leadership. Of course, New Labour would put the frighteners on the other contenders. I could hear her laughing. Then they had sex. I lay there until dawn, listening to them humping. She was moaning like a porn star. I couldn't believe what I'd just heard. I mean, you don't just kill the leader of the opposition."

Rick's mouth was starting to go dry.

"The following day, I went into Graham's room. I found Emma's silver briefcase under the bed. She must have left it there by mistake. I took it and hid it."

"Wasn't that a bit mean of you?"

"I never liked Graham. He was a creep. He was always badmouthing me to my friends."

"What was in the case?"

Adam looked evasive. "Papers. They describe New Labour's strategy to win the '97 and '01 elections – lists of names, instructions. I haven't really read them properly."

"So what happened next?"

"Emma Henderson must have freaked out when she found that she had left her briefcase in Graham's room. The next night, her men came back. There was the one with the star-shaped scar and two others. They turned the house over. The scar-faced one, Trevor they called him, pinned John up against the wall. John was petrified."

"Did they find it?"

"Of course not, I'd taken it to work with me hadn't I? It's here." He nudged the case under the table.

"Listen, I'd like you to pick it up, when we leave. I don't want the thing."

"It's an expensive case. Are you sure?"

"Just take it." Adam's lower lip was flecked with spittle. "Look, they killed John Smith and they killed Graham. They're murderers."

"They murdered Graham?"

"The week after our house was trashed, he fell under a tube train at Brixton station, didn't he? The inquest said that it was suicide. But there's no way he would have killed himself."

Adam took a final sip, finishing his drink. "When they made Emma Henderson minister for London, it made me really angry. She's such an evil bitch." Adam spat out the plosive consonant with hatred. " That's when I decided to contact the press, or at least, Planning Today."

Thanks for the compliment, thought Rick.

"Well?" said Adam.

"Well what?"

"Would you like to take the briefcase? It's all in there."

Adam nodded.

"I suppose so." How could he refuse?

Rick reached down for the sleek case. As soon as his fingers touched the cold plastic of the handle, he knew that he was committed.

"What are you going to do?" said Adam.

"I don't know. I'll read the documents first and we'll take it from there." Rick thought of something that he had once read in a thriller. "If you need to phone me, it's best to use my mobile. It's harder to trace."

"Why would I do that?"

"If you need to meet me again."

Adam looked at Rick as if he were a medical specimen. "I won't want to meet you again. And I never want to see this fucking thing again. As far as I am concerned, it's over. Just do what you have to do."

"I understand. But please, take my mobile number."

Adam sighed. Rick scribbled the digits on a piece of paper.

The other man in the bar had removed a Standard from his pocket and was studying it. There was a strapline beneath the masthead – "Johnny walks out of the jungle". It was something to do with Johnny Rotten appearing on a crappy reality TV show. Adam watched the man's lips move as he read. He placed the scrap of paper in his jacket without comment. After a brief, cursory handshake they both left. This time, Rick was carrying the silver case.

It was a perfect size for the pannier at the back of his bike. Rick cycled down Fleet Street and over Blackfriars Bridge. As usual, he took his chance with the kamikaze roundabout at the Elephant and Castle, weaving unsteadily towards the south London suburbs.

4

Foreign policy
Schleswig Holstein and all that. Sorry, it's not my
subject. Suggest that we shove our head up America's
arse and follow wherever they go.

- The New Labour papers

If you cycle, or walk, down Walworth Road from the
Elephant and Castle and you have sharp eyes you will
notice something peculiar. Number 150, part of an
anonymous-looking Georgian terrace, used to be the
headquarters of the Labour party.

That modest town house was connected with the
party for years – the words Labour and Walworth Road
became interchangeable. It seemed appropriate that
Labour was associated with a working class street in
south London, where you could buy cheap electrical
goods, chipboard furniture and expensive trainers. The
pulse of Walworth Road – noisy, brash and multi-
ethnic, with its low-rent Irish pubs and its garish
market, East Street – ran through the party's veins.

In 1996, the building was named after the recently
deceased leader, John Smith. There was a touching
little ceremony and a discreet stone plaque was placed
next to the front door. It said John Smith House, in
faint gilt letters carved from white marble. The naming
of the building had seemed like the right thing to do at
the time. There were pictures in the papers.

When a reborn Labour party, New Labour, was
elected in 1997, it was a dead cert that Walworth Road

would have to go. It was far too rootsy and proletarian and there was nothing working class about Tony Blair. Also, bigger premises were needed. The party upped sticks and moved to a soulless high-rise building called Millbank, down the Thames Embankment from the House of Commons. A new term now gained currency for the Labour party, or at least for its decision-making infrastructure, Millbank.

Something peculiar now happened. Some people in New Labour decided to remove the reminder of John Smith from Walworth Road. His gravitas and his under-stated dignity, his trade union associations and the credit that he could take for modernizing the party were just too much for them to bear.

They did not make a big song and dance about it. There was no ceremony or press release. The John Smith plaque was simply scraped off the wall. Only a person who travelled up and down Walworth Road regularly, like Rick, would have noticed it had happened.

They placed some new-looking bricks where the plaque used to be. It was easy to see where John Smith's name had once been. Perhaps, Rick thought, they had been deliberately careless, like thugs who leave scars, in order to frighten people. Or perhaps they had merely been too arrogant to care. This, in a way, was even more frightening. He could not make up his mind which explanation was more probable. Either way, he concluded, the removal of the plaque was an act of political revisionism.

~ ~ ~

Rick cycled down Walworth Road that night, after meeting Adam. He glanced at the clean bricks and they set him thinking. New Labour had airbrushed John Smith from its former headquarters. What did that tell you?

There was not too much traffic. He took a left turn down Albany Street, cycled down Southampton Way and climbed the long, painful hill that skirts Peckham Rye. He lived in Forest Hill, a suburb of London that most people had never heard of. His home was small and new, in a quiet little cul-de-sac. It was rented from a housing association. Rick had moved in just after his separation from Gina's mum, Carol.

He had nothing then. His ex had retained most of their possessions and their daughter. When he first moved in, he used to sit in the bare rooms, drinking cans of lager and sporadically decorating. He had no cooker and lived on boiled eggs and Pot Noodle. After that, the smell of gloss paint always made him feel sad. His daughter, Gina, now lived for most of the time with her mum in a neighboring suburb, next to Clapham. Rick was a part-time dad

He unlocked the front door and parked his bike in the cramped hallway. Upstairs were two bedrooms, one for him, the other for Gina, or at least for her things. Most of her short-lived enthusiasms were recorded there – Barbies, the doll's house he had made, Pokémon cards, Harry Potter memorabilia – like faintly visible geological strata.

Gina's 13-year-old self had not made much of an impression on the room, apart from make-up stains on her duvet cover and its appalling untidiness. That was because she was not there much these days. She was usually hanging out with her friends on Clapham Common. Rick's main job was to ferry her around in his car and to serve her pizzas. Sometimes, he would stand in her room, staring at the purple walls, wishing that she were there. But it made him upset. So he tried not to.

That Thursday night, he made himself a curry, using scraps from the previous weekend. Afterwards, he shifted into the lounge, with the silver briefcase. He removed the papers, which were held together by a plastic binder.

Rick sat on his settee. He read the New Labour papers while fondling his tabby cat, Sammy. There was a grubby title page, followed by about 30 A4 pages. On the title page was a date, October 1993. In places, additions and revisions had been made to the text, in blue fountain pen. He guessed that this was Emma Henderson's handwriting. He was reading the politician's own manuscript.

Introduction

The Labour party began in 1900. But it has only been in government for 23 years during this century. Quite frankly, it isn't good enough. How can we make sure that we win and, more importantly, keep on winning, into the foreseeable future? This document offers some tentative suggestions. What I describe here is an invisible infrastructure that will make us invincible and bury the Conservatives forever. You could call it the Fourth Way.

When we are in power (and we will be, I assure you) it is very important that we don't hurry. I would suggest that we could spend the first two or three years reviewing. After reviewing we can consult (wins brownie points). This can be dragged on for as long as necessary, especially for those policies we no longer favor and would like to kick into touch.

Near the end of our first term, after 2000, I would suggest a blitzkrieg of overlapping initiatives, each with different boundaries, delivery mechanisms and measurement systems. They will promote confusion while looking good, especially if we associate them with lots of vague and conflicting performance indicators. We will do blah, blah, blah by 2005. This will win us even more time. No one, apart from a few policy dweebs, will ever hold us to account for them.

The following sections are a brief guide to how we can ensure victory and then stay at the top indefinitely. Enjoy!

He could see from her comments that Emma Henderson had relished putting this together. Maybe she had only written it as a joke.

Constitution

There really isn't one. Only some unintelligible seventeenth-century gibberish and a homoerotic pantomime (men in tights, black rod etc.). Long may it remain so! We must keep this policy area as vague and confusing as possible, while promoting a vague idea of reform. Problem areas. Freedom of information. No way we can let that happen. Create bill with widely drawn exemptions? Human Rights. We're committed to adopting the European convention into UK law. Barristers will cream themselves with greed. But don't worry. It won't actually make all that difference

The House of Lords. I suggest that we deconstruct the upper house by abolishing most, if not all, of the hereditary peers and then fail to replace it! The situation can then be left in limbo. Obviously, in the longer term, a purely appointed upper house would be best. Parliament may not be very happy. I think that by 2006 or 2007 we would be able to get away with it.

It is extremely useful that our do-it-yourself democracy has few, if any, internal safeguards. As for the British public most of them haven't got a clue. Only those who go to public schools are taught about the Parliamentary system.

Countryside
We can't ignore it since, on a map, it's nearly all blue. Simply speaking, we have to win over the floaters and demoralize the Barbour-jacketed Tories. I suggest that we release a fast-spreading livestock virus into the countryside, just before our second election victory in 2001 – something potent that will knock the stuffing out of what is left of agriculture. Whining farmers – the few that have not killed themselves – will bleat on about being hard done by while they fill their pockets with compensation money. Stuff them!

Sammy was stretching, trying to escape. He walked across the settee.

Event management
We have to neutralize our opponents, especially those in our own party. MI5 are spineless public school types. Useless. Our own people will take over their role (assassinations, honey traps, blackmail etc.).

Some organizations we should infiltrate but otherwise ignore (Trots, animal rights people). They will simply make us look good, frothing at the mouth outside our conferences. Potential enemies in our own and other parties must be made harmless or taken out (see note).

Both assassination and ennoblement are effective as a means of disempowerment. Assassination is quicker, but should be used sparingly. Misguided fellow travellers, meddlers and senior party figures who are now a threat to us need to be watched closely and, in some cases, got rid of (e.g. JS).

Rick read the phrase again, added in blue ink (e.g. JS). He turned to the back of the papers and found the note that was referred to. It was a list of has-been politicians with rubber mouths, small-time media

38

magnates, trade union barons and nouveau-riche political groupies.

Three names jumped out at him, immediately – John Jenkins (socialist newspaper publisher from Manchester, jailed for rape in 1996), Reginald Harris (union leader, hanged himself after being found with a male prostitute), Christopher Phillips (millionaire, former Paymaster General), cocaine found in car when stopped by the police for speeding. John Smith's name was not on the list.

It was late and the light in the lounge was not good. Rick was squinting. He skipped a few pages.

Language

Language is power. It will form the skeleton and sinews of our success. We should adopt a vocabulary that suggests business-like efficiency, combined with social concern. For example, "rollout" (verb and noun), "toolkit", "empowerment", "cross-cutting", "capacity building", "joined-up", etcetera.

These words will be used in all speeches, consultation documents, white papers and press releases – e.g. "The DoH has announced the roll-out of a cross-cutting engagement mechanism for community capacity building". The fact that such a phrase means little, if anything, does not matter. 1) It sounds good. 2) Print has its own authority. 3) Most people are pretty stupid. They do not actually think about what comes in through their ears or eyes.

It is important that we spread our vocabulary as widely as possible. Gradually, it will seep into newspapers, magazines and even daily discourse e.g. "Mavis, have you rolled out my tool-kit yet?" (joking). This language will seep into the political culture. In time it will become the political culture. As I said, language is power.

The Language Generation Unit should develop software so that computers can generate policy documents spontaneously from key words - social exclusion, regional empowerment, whatever. (Suggest that Derek Foxton heads the unit. All speeches, press releases etc. must be cleared through him.)

~ ~ ~

He had read enough. Thursday night TV was dreadful. It had never been the same since they had moved Top of the Pops. He decided to go to bed.

The following morning, Rick took the bus to work, carrying Adam's silver briefcase. There was a route, the 63, that went from the end of his road virtually to his office. Most mornings, it was virtually empty. It was his own transportation system. Rick sat at the front upstairs, balancing the case on his knees. By the time the journey had ended, he had finished reading the New Labour papers.

Rick got off in Farringdon Road. He walked down Cowcross Street to Smithfield. Karen, of course, was already at her desk, looking smug. It was ten to ten so, theoretically, he was late. The eel gave him a filthy look, from her glass prison. He smiled at her. She looked away.

He sat at his desk. On Friday, he had to start writing stuff, so that Planning Today would not merely consist of blank pages. There was a diary in the magazine, a space for musings and the bin-ends of stories. It was called Off Limits. Rick liked writing it. Even planning officers had a lighter side. Rick used to enjoy trying to find their funny bones. He never knew if he succeeded or not. His readers were so inscrutable that they gave him little or no feedback, unless he made a mistake, when they heaped loads of sarcastic abuse on his head.

He had had an idea for Off Limits on the bus. He took the New Labour papers from the briefcase and opened them. He wrote the following: "Somewhere in southern

England (I am not permitted to tell you exactly where) is a top secret government agency, the Language Generation Unit. Its job is simple – to ensure that all press, releases, ministerial speeches, white papers and consultation documents contain the required quota of New Labour language.

"You will have noticed this lexicon of vagueness and euphemisms as you go about your daily business – *cross-cutting, capacity building, roll-out, engagement mechanism, tool-kit, community safety, social exclusion* and so on. You may even be fluent in New Labour by now, so effective has the unit been.

"The unit has been a great success. And you can see the result. These days, New Labour documents are generated spontaneously by the LGU's computers, from a few key words, like a silk worm spinning a cocoon. That is why they all read and sound the same.

"It's all top secret, of course. We should not have told you this much. And now we will have to kill you. Only joking!"

He felt pleased with himself when he had finished. Much of the piece was not his own work. But who was going to know? He did not want Karen to sub-edit what he had written. Whether out of indolence, stupidity or malice he never knew, she tended to shorten articles by removing the second paragraph – the words did not even touch the sides of her brain. So he put the article in a copy folder for the production editor, Simone. On Monday morning, Simone changed the word lexicon to vocabulary and removed the exclamation mark. They were not allowed in Planning Today. Otherwise, she left what he had written intact. She asked Rick whether the stuff about the Language Generation Unit was true. He merely smiled.

5

Soaps
Prole pap, de rigeur for those with the "common touch". "I never miss EastEnders". Poor production values, pantomime characters and crap stories. Try to familiarize yourself with at least one of them and maybe one or two actors. But not, please God, Emmerdale. Don't go there!
-The New Labour papers

Emma Henderson adapted easily to her life as a minister. It seemed to come to her naturally. As well as the extra money, she liked the media profile that it gave her, the party invitations and, best of all, the fact that a whole room full of people was paid to help her.

As minister for London, she merited considerable space, on the twelfth floor of Eland House. She had a great view, looking towards the sunrise and Battersea power station. The fusty reminders of the previous incumbent, Tim Barstow, had been taken out in cardboard boxes. Emma's friend Jamie, an interior designer who dabbled in Feng Shui, helped her to "sort out the space". He said that colors and vibrations would be tremendously important to the way that she did her job. She was a little sceptical. But she went along with it.

Central to the new decor was a large white settee from Heals in Tottenham Court Road. There were also paintings – not like Barstow's tacky crap – but expensive abstract ones, by contemporary artists. They were paintings that meant something, at least to people who knew about that kind of thing. Close to her desk was a small refrigerator and a drinks cabinet.

There was only one photograph on the wall, of Emma standing in the middle of a group of smiling constituents in Middlewich. She was smiling shyly. They looked proud of her and protective.

Outside the minister's inner sanctum was her private office. This was where her twelve staff lived. Her principal private secretary, a young ambitious MP, was the most senior. He was the minister's right-hand person, her bag carrier, her political antenna. The rest were all fast-track civil servants, in their twenties and thirties - her press secretary, Linda Plaskitt, who was also her political adviser, the deputy press secretary, the assistant of her pps, the diary secretary, the diary secretary's assistant, and so on.

Her private office organized her waking life. They stuffed and unpacked her red boxes, they booked train seats and hotel rooms. They dealt with her correspondence and gave her briefing notes. They ushered nervous delegations into her presence and sorted out her dry cleaning. Her pps made notes at meetings. Her press secretary whispered in her ear, telling her what to say. Her diary secretary was supposed to know where she was, every waking moment. That could be a little inconvenient.

It was a Thursday, exactly a week after Rick had written his diary piece on the Language Generation Unit. In fact, that week's copy of Planning Today was sitting on Emma Henderson's desk at this moment. The article had been marked with a post-it note, by one of the bright young civil servants, who knew that she was interested in that kind of thing. It said, "Read this!!"

She stood at the window. It was evening. She was enjoying the panorama of the smudged buildings and the purple and red sky, like a suppurating wound. One city was going home, another was waking up. She would usually have a g and t at this time often with her pps. It was when she felt at her most expansive, privileged and powerful. There had to be some compensation for working fourteen-hour days. This was it.

Tonight, she was going to a function at the Cafe Royal in Regent Street, the TV Tonite Soapstar Awards. It would be a swanky affair and some of her showbiz pals would be there. She would be photographed going in and coming out. She might even get into Hello magazine. She had one more little task do, before she called for her driver. To read that bloody magazine. Yellow highlighter pen guided her eye to the right place. Her pupils flicked over the print:

"Somewhere in southern England (I am not permitted to tell you exactly where) is a top secret government agency, the Language Generation Unit. Its job is simple – to ensure that all press, releases, ministerial speeches, white papers and consultation documents ..."

She started to feel wobbly. She sat on the Heals settee, the magazine in her left hand, the g and t in her right. The more she read, the weaker she felt.

The article described, breezily, exactly how the Language Generation Unit worked. Some of the phrases were awfully familiar. In fact, she had written them herself, ten years before, on a yellow legal pad, in a taxi stuck in traffic in Gerard Street. She read on. When she had finished the article, she sat quietly for a moment, thinking what to do.

The article meant, she realized, that someone had seen, or had access to, the New Labour papers. The magazine had four editorial staff. It should not be difficult to find which of them it was.

If anyone could link her directly with the papers, her career would be finished, she knew that – flushed down the toilet. She did want to become the political equivalent of Gary Glitter. She thought some more. Then she made a phone call.

~ ~ ~

Trevor Jones' office tended to be noisy, because it was above one of the dance floors in the Think Tank. After about nine, when the punters started to arrive, an insistent thudding began to vibrate through the building. The noise intensified through the evening. By one o'clock in the morning, the floor and walls of his office were quaking gently, like a ship's engine room. People danced to specialized kinds of vibration. Aficionados could tell the difference between techno and hardcore, the nuances of a hummingbird's heartbeat, as it blasted through gigantic speakers. But Trevor couldn't. For him, it was just an occupational soundtrack.

Trevor was the Security Manager at the Think Tank. He had insisted this title was placed on his desk. The nameplate was a symbol of authority, like having a whopping great bunch of keys dangling off your belt. His office was about three by five meters, with no window. It usually smelt of stale sweat and old cheeseburgers, depending on the time of night and how many bouncers, had been in there. There was a utilitarian desk, a telephone and a beige filing cabinet. There was quite a lot of paper work in Trevor's job – lists of staff, references, invoices – and he was not good at reading. Fortunately, he had help.

He was a compact, well-built man with a shaved head. His bulk was mainly muscle. Trevor kept his body tuned up in a gym over a pub in the Old Kent Road, where he pulled on tensioned levers and pummeled a leather punch bag. He needed to do that because, what with his managerial responsibilities, he was punching far fewer people.

It was six o'clock. Trevor had just arrived for a night's work. He hung his coat on a hook behind the door and placed his large buttocks on the flimsy office chair, farting noisily. His first task was to have a look at who was on tonight's roster of muscle. The roster was a childishly printed list of names. The names were mostly made up, for the purpose of evading tax and national insurance. He began to ring round, making sure that people could come in.

An hour later, he received a call. Usually, at this time, it would be the club's co-owner, Nigel de Vere. De Vere lived in a mansion, with a swimming pool and tennis courts, in East Finchley. He and a syndicate of upper class chums owned 90 per cent of the club. Emma Henderson had bought a 10 per cent stake, through an un-declared holding company, using some of the money inherited from her husband.

She and De Vere had been mates since the early 1990s, through hanging out in the same places. They had been lovers for a little while. They looked similar and some people thought that they were brother and sister. De Vere was a little rich boy who pretended to be a cockney wide boy, an impression assisted by a scar on his cheek, which looked like a knife wound. Actually, it had been caused by a childhood accident.

De Vere had been a big cheese in the rave scene in the late '80s, extracting more and more money from drugged up people in muddy fields. By 1991, rave culture had reached Woolworths. That year, De Vere sank his savings and a chunk of his father's money into a rambling old warehouse, close to the run-down Elephant and Castle area of south London, and converted it into a night club. The club, the Think Tank, was a huge success from the word go. Over the next decade it became a lucrative international brand, launching baseball caps, bottled water, a record label, even a magazine. It was a goldmine.

Most people in the media knew that De Vere and Emma Henderson were friends. She liked to be seen at the club, even after she became an MP. Sometimes, she even had her picture taken there. The gossip added spice to her image and it was quite good for New Labour, in a subliminal kind of way. Few people in the media would have suspected that Emma owned a portion of the club, salting the funds into an offshore account. Nobody had any inkling that it was the base for her covert operations and that she liked to take part in orgies there.

De Vere turned up at the Think Tank most nights, in a big luxury car, usually white, with a silicon-breasted lovely or two on his arm. He was treated like royalty. He would park his car in front of the club, watched by a queue of owl-eyed punters. Then a minion would take the car round the back. It was a piece of theatre. The regal party would sweep up to De Vere's office and hoover a load of charlie up their noses. Some kind of sexual act would usually then take place, often involving three or more people. There were mirrors and kinky stuff in De Vere's office. It doubled as an s and m sex dungeon. And there was a little bathroom attached to it.

~ ~ ~

The voice on the end of the phone in the security manager's office was unfamiliar. It was smooth and educated but there was something harsh, just beneath the surface.

"I don't know if you remember me, Trevor. It's Emma Henderson."

Trevor reached into his mind, like a rusty filing cabinet. He found what he needed. Ten years ago. Emma, the Ice Maiden. The MP. The E Squad.

"Yeh, Ms. Henderson. Course I do."

"Good. How have you been keeping, Trevor?"

Trevor started to tell her. She cut him off.

"Listen. This is really important. I don't know if you recall. But ten years ago, you did a little job for me. You went to a house in Brixton, in Mervan Road, to try and find some important papers, which I had lost. Does that ring a bell?"

Trevor frowned.

"You did not find them, I am afraid."

Trevor remembered. That geezer, he had done over at Brixton tube station. He had shoved him under a tube train. His head exploded like a fucking watermelon. He started to chuckle.

"Well, the papers have turned up again. Someone has them and it could be rather, embarrassing. We have to find out where they got them from Trevor. I want you to check the electoral register to see who lives in the house in Mervan Road now. You won't be able to do that until tomorrow, in office hours. If any of the same people are living there, you are to go back there, first thing on Monday morning. Do you understand?"

"Yeh, boss."

"You will bring them back to the club and hold them there. You will then contact me. Is that clear?"

"Hold them. Yeh, right."

"I am going to give you my mobile number and my private office number. If you phone the office, you may get my pps."

"Your pp what?"

"Never mind, just ask for me, Trevor, OK. Say that you are phoning about some flowers or something. You know the drill. Just like the old days."

"Yeh. OK." Trevor was feeling nostalgic for the time when he had been starting out as a professional bruiser. He remembered that guy they had dropped off a building on the Isle of Dogs and buried in concrete while he was still alive. His screams of agony.

"You will have to do this as soon as possible. You will report back to me as soon as you can."

"Yeh, chief. Electoral register, innit."

"That's right Trevor, you've got the idea. I know that I can trust you. And remember."

"Yeh?"

"I am the minister for London. And I don't want anybody to know about this. Is that clear?"

"Yeh, course." Trevor suddenly thought of something. It was important. "Oh boss. It's a good job that you mentioned that, that you're the Minister of London, right, cause it reminded me of something."

"Yes, Trevor, what is that?"

She had changed into a little black dress in her dressing room for the Cafe Royal do. Now, she was squirting jets of Chanel No 19 onto her neck.

"There's been this bloke here. He's been mouthing off. He reckons that he knows you. I wouldn't bother you with it, like, but he's a gobby little fucker. He keeps pestering Nigel. He says that knows you personally, so he wants to be put on the guest list."

"Oh yes, what is his name?"

Trevor was good with names, and faces. He matched and stored them carefully.

"He's a little Irish guy. I think he's called Sean. He's a chauffeur, he says, over Vauxhall way. Yeh, Sean. Tall, blond-haired geezer. Do you know him?"

Emma Henderson frowned. Why did her sexual liaisons cause so many problems. One shag and people thought they owned you. And there was always the danger that they would peddle their filthy stories to the tabloids.

"Yes I do. Or rather, I did, Trevor. It"s fortunate that we have spoken about this. I would like you to do another teeny weeny little job for me."

Trevor suddenly remembered the terminology of the E Squad.

"Code nine, boss?"

She reflected, like a Roman emperor in the Coliseum. It was life or death. Thumbs up, or thumbs down?

"Let me see. Code eight, I think."

That meant scare the crap out of him, but don't kill him. "Oh, and Trevor?"

"Yeh, boss?"

"Make sure that he can't drive would you. Ever again." She was reaching for her coat. It was hooked onto the back of the door, still in a dry cleaning bag. "If you do a good job, I'll ask Nigel to put something nice in your bank account. Does that sound like a deal, my darling?"

"Yeh boss."

"Good. Well don't let me down, will you."

The phone clicked. She did not say goodbye.

Trevor cracked his knuckles, smiling.

~ ~ ~

Trevor was connected to every bouncer in the club by walkie-talkie and it was quite easy to find Sean. As luck would have it, he was in the club tonight. He was on level three, edging towards a dancer who was cavorting in chains and leather in a cage, his white buttocks flashing through neat holes.

The drill was to tell Sean that he was wanted in the office for a "surprise". Sean was dead chuffed. He constructed a little fantasy in his mind, as he walked across the dance floor. Emma would be there. They would do some coke, then maybe go back to her flat. Perhaps their picture would be in the papers. No, Ms. Henderson would not want that. It was going to be nice though, whatever it was. He wondered if he would have sex with her again, tonight. He started to feel shy. In many ways, he was still a country boy.

He had taken a couple of Es and he was feeling full of love, even for the caveman who was leading him through the club. They walked trough the chill-out room and up some stairs. The offices were all on the top floor. The bouncer punched a four-digit number on a keypad. This opened a pair of silver doors. Now they were in the private part of the building. Sean felt important.

"We're going to Mr. Jones' office, first of all, yeh?" said the bouncer. "He wants to tell you somefink."

"Sure, grand."

Sean smiled. He was almost skipping. Three years in London, he had been. Whatever it was, it was going to make a really good story, back at the office.

Trevor Jones. Security Manager. They went through the door. Trevor was facing away from them, towards the wall. He swiveled on his chair, smiling.

"Sean isn't it?" He extended a white, pudgy hand. "Thanks for coming up, mate. It's really good of you. Take a seat." He gestured for Sean to sit, in front of the desk.

Sean had long thin legs. His loins were tingling, inside his tight leather trousers.

Trevor signaled for the other man to leave.

"You are probably wondering why Mr. DeVere, asked you up here." Pause. "A cunt like you."

"Sorry." Sean was a little perplexed. He looked at Trevor's face. There was a different kind of smile there now.

"I mean most people don't get that honor, do they, Sean?"

Trevor stood up. He walked around the edge of the desk, casting a shadow on the floor. Soon, he was almost behind Sean.

"Most little twats who are a bit gobby like you, we just fucking dump them in an alley. Know what I mean?"

Sean twisted his head, muttering something.

Trevor always liked this bit. The surprise.

"But you ..."

Trevor delivered a short jab with his right fist. It connected with Sean's ear, denting his head and whiplashing his neck. A blackness opened inside him. It filled with stars. He could not believe this was happening.

A forearm wrapped around his neck like a fat snake. Trevor pulled the arm tight with his other wrist.

"You had to shoot your mouth off, you cunt. You had to shoot your fucking little mouth off, didn't you?"

Trevor was pumping himself up. This was the killing phase, the red mist. He squeezed harder. Sean was choking. In about a minute, it would all be over. Suddenly, Trevor relaxed his grip.

"As it happens, I am not going to kill you, you cunt. This is just a warning. Don't you never tell nobody about that lady what you drove for. Do you fucking understand me?"

"What?" There were too many negatives in that sentence. Sean's heart was racing. His windpipe hurt like hell.

"You heard me. You just keep your gobby mouth shut. Put your hands on the desk!"

"What?"

"Put your hands on the desk!" Trevor screamed into his torn brain, like a drill sergeant. "Put your hands on the fucking desk!"

Sean started to whimper. A wet stream ran down one of his trouser legs. His hands barely made contact with the surface. They were trembling. He screwed his eyes shut.

Trevor reached onto the top of the filing cabinet, behind a pile of smeared grey folders. He retrieved what is known as a cob hammer – a squat, short-handled implement, used for bashing metal.

There was no warning.

He brought down the hammer as hard as he could, aiming at Sean's knuckles Sean watched his hands disappear. Pain was not the main problem, after the first few blows. The body can only take so much. He looked at the pulpy red things on the end of his wrists as if they belonged to someone else. Then he passed out.

Trevor summoned help on his intercom. He thought of something then. The little fucker might still be able to drive, even with stumps for hands. They spread Sean's legs out on the floor and he reached for the hammer. Sean came to. He squealed like a wild animal, until they sealed up his mouth with tape. There was blood on the walls and floor and Trevor's desk was fucked. It was a good job he had carpet tiles.

They dragged the body down the corridor to the service lift. Normally, the door supervisors would have chucked Sean into the alleyway behind the club, where they ejected people who were being objectionable, or who were wearing the wrong kind of trainers.

That was not really an option, in this case. Trevor called up a minicab firm he knew in Loughborough Junction. Sean was waking up, whimpering, so they gave him a little tap with a baseball bat. That fractured his skull. They shoved Sean into the boot. One of the bouncers got into the car with the driver, who was paid two hundred pounds, cash.

They drove through Hackney and then along the Lee Bridge Road. They took Sean's body from the back of the car, still breathing, and dumped it the depths of Epping Forest. Then they drove back to London.

~ ~ ~

Emma Henderson received a call on her mobile at eleven o'clock. She was sharing a table with the stars and production team of EastEnders – thespians who played villains, garnished with gold jewelry and a thin menace, stage school prima donnas in expensive perfume, all bosoms and flashing teeth.

"We done 'im, that Irish geezer. He won't be fucking driving no more, not even in one of them little Noddy cars."

Emma smiled, clutching her dinky little mobile to her ear.

"That is super news. Absolutely splendid. Well done."

There was a burst of applause. An award was being made. It was called RearEnders – soaps' best buttocks. That was of great interest to the minister. She switched off her phone. She bent forwards, to catch up on what she had just missed.

6

Investigative reporters
By-line freaks with bad haircuts. Tend to espouse
youthful causes as they grow old. Contemptible.

-The New Labour papers

Rick arrived at work precisely the right time that Friday – nine thirty-seven. He was late, which was a small victory, but no so late that the eel could criticize him.

The previous day had been quite productive, which had gained them some time on the magazine. This morning, he had a job to do. He wanted to find out more about the exact circumstances of John Smith's death - where he had collapsed, what hospital he had been taken to, and so on, to see if Adam's story panned out.

He needed to see what had been reported in the papers the day after Smith's death, the 13th of May, 1994. First, he logged onto the websites of the Guardian and the Telegraph.

He drew a complete blank. There was nothing. At first, he wondered whether something fishy was going on. Then he discovered the reason. The paper's websites had not existed in 1994 – well the Telegraph's had, but it was still rudimentary.

He phoned the British newspaper library in Colindale and arranged to go up there. It was a drag because Colindale was miles away, a distant outpost on the northern line. But they had almost every paper that had ever been published, going back donkey's years.

Karen was drinking coffee. She would still be subbing the same feature as the day before.

"Kaz," said Rick, "I've got to go up to Colindale, to do a bit of research. I should be back by three, unless I am abducted by aliens."

Karen blinked at him, with her large, stupid eyes.

"That's nice," she said.

It was a bright morning. He walked to Farringdon tube station, which was just round the corner from the office. From Farringdon, he took the circle line to King's Cross and then the northern line to Colindale.

It was a long journey but at least it wasn't the rush hour, so he wasn't pressed up against someone's armpits. The carriage was almost empty. After Hampstead, the train emerged into daylight. On either side of the track were chain-link fences and sun-dappled sycamore trees. Beyond them, miles of semi-detached houses extended to the horizon, like a sea of bricks. It was dull, comfortable suburbia. The world that he had grown up in.

Colindale was a newish station. The staff there had smart blue uniforms and were almost helpful. Next to the station was a model airplane shop, called Hannant's, and a greasy spoon cafe, Zara's.

The newspaper library is a huge ochre box, with elongated, metal-framed windows, like a 1930s power station. You don't need a special pass to get in, just a passport or a driving license.

Rick filled in some forms and made his way to the microfilm reading room. It was an eerie, dimly-lit place, with strange humming machines. It reminded him of a hospital radiology department. He placed a spool of film in a projector, so that he could scan through all of the Guardians published in March 1994.

The print blurred as he tracked back through time. Soon, he reached a headline published on the 13th of March: "Never did a more decent man rise to the top of British politics." Bingo. He stopped the machine.

It was strange how everybody had loved John Smith – not just his wife and daughters, but politicians of all parties, newspaper columnists, hospital workers, trade unionists, even the porter in his block of flats. No mud had ever clung to him. If he had a fault, he was a bit dull. There again, in the right company, he was said to be hilarious.

Smith, Rick now learned, was born in 1938, in central Scotland, the son of a Presbyterian headmaster. He went to grammar school and Glasgow University. After university, he diligently worked his way up from solicitor to QC. A committed socialist, he won a North Lanarkshire seat in 1970. He got into the cabinet in double quick time.

Dour and industrious, he looked like a country solicitor, although his daughters encouraged him to wear colorful ties. He was anti-Militant and pro-European, the ideal man to lead the Labour part after its hubristic defeat in 1992, when Neil Kinnock resigned. Smith carried on Kinnock's modernizing project, abolishing the trade union bloc vote, but he was more old fashioned – his feet were firmly planted in Old Labour.

Rick found out, from reading the Guardian and the Daily Mail, that he had attended a fund-raising dinner the night before he died. It was held in the Park Lane Hotel, Piccadilly – one of those ghoulish affairs, where famous people feed on their own celebrity, like sharks feasting on blood.

New Labour's A-list luvvies had paid £500 a head to meet and mingle. They were all there – the millionaire thriller writer, the alternative comedian, the hot-shot film producer, the left-wing playwright, the nasal-voiced novelist, the agony aunt, the barrister who wrote for TV. The French socialist, Michel Rocard, was guest of honor.

Smith arrived with his wife, Elizabeth, at seven thirty, sleek and confident in his well-padded dinner jacket. The scent of power was in his nostrils. Few doubted, as he pressed the flesh and quaffed champagne in the lobby with his guests, that he would be the next prime minister. But the thriller writer, to his credit, noticed that Smith was sweaty and peaky, and looked really tired.

In the dining room, Smith's wife told the person sitting next to her that she was worried that her husband was pushing himself too hard. He had thrown everything into the recent local elections, putting in 17-hour days. After suffering a heart attack in 1988, Smith had gone on a strict diet and begun a regime of hill walking. But now the weight was going back on again. And he was drinking.

Rocard made a functional speech, John Smith made a funny one. As always, the canny Scottish lawyer hit exactly the right note. There was nothing brash or boastful about him, but he had a commanding authority. When he said "the opportunity to serve our country, that is all we ask" people's eyes must have misted over. Dinner was mushroom and asparagus soup, noisettes of lamb and lemon soufflé. Then there was dancing. Smith had a few words with a Radio 1 disc jockey.

When he left at eleven-thirty, the party was still in full swing. He and his wife would have been driven by chauffeur back to their flat, on the 35th floor in the Barbican complex, close to Smithfield.

Labour's lost leader suffered a massive heart attack at five past eight the following morning, while he was in the bath. His wife first tried to summon a heart specialist who lived on the same floor. But he was not there. She dialed 999. An ambulance arrived at eight-fifteen.

In the ambulance, paramedics gave him two shocks from a mobile defibrillator and injections of adrenaline. One can easily imagine the panic, the sense of gravity, the frantic efforts to save him. There were further attempts at St Bartholomew's Hospital. But it was useless. He never regained consciousness.

He was pronounced dead at nine fifteen. An official announcement was made an hour and a half later, after attempts had been made to contact his daughters. Ironically, he had visited the accident and emergency department at St Bart's only two weeks before. He had said that it was a "scandal" that it was to be closed.

The news spread through the country like a cold draught. The suddenness was a shock. There was also an unnerving feeling that history had been cheated.

That afternoon, normal business was suspended in the House of Commons, for the first time since 1977. Many Labour MPs cried. The Tories put down their stabbing knives. Politicians showered flattering adjectives around like confetti at a wedding. Smith, they said, was hard-working, dedicated, loyal, honest and thoroughly decent, etcetera – especially now that he was dead.

The beleaguered Conservative prime minister, John Major, led the tributes. It was whispered in the lobby that Smith's death would gain Major, Margaret Thatcher's poodle, a little more time as prime minister – perhaps as much as a week.

Five MPs were in the frame to take over as leader of the Labour party, in a ballot of five million trade unionists and party members, the first to be held without a bloc vote. Shadow home secretary, Tony

Blair, was the candidate the Tories feared most. He had cut his teeth on law and order. He was young, articulate, a family man and ex-public school. Most people thought that he would walk it.

As reality sank in, bunches of flowers began to arrive at Labour HQ in Walworth Road. There was soon a heap of petals and messages in front of the building, a foot thick. One of the tributes was a spray of red roses from Emma Henderson, bearing a short, insincere note.

Reading the papers had brought the feelings of that day back to Rick, like a lump of ice in his chest. John Smith was such a lovely man – he was everyone's favorite uncle. He made his way to the tube station feeling sad, but also excited and a little frightened. He took the tube back to Farringdon, hardly noticing, this time, the world outside the train. He arrived at half past two.

~ ~ ~

From Farringdon station, he walked up Cowcross Street. There is a lot of history in this part of London. Most of it connected with violent death. Cowcross Street, for example, used to be a twisting track for medieval cattle drovers, taking their herds to Smithfield market. The name Smithfield comes from "smooth field". It was simply a patch of flat grass next to the city wall, ideal for selling cattle, holding fairs and jousting. Bartholomew's Fair was held on this site for centuries. Smithfield was a place of public executions. Thousands of heretics and witches were burnt to death here, or boiled alive – more than two hundred in the reign of Mary of Tudor. Cock Lane, nearby, was licensed for prostitutes. It is said, traditionally, to be where the Great Fire of London stopped, at a spot marked by a fat gold cherub. Giltspur Street was a route for knights, on their way to the

Smithfield tournament. Just to the south, on the current site of the Old Bailey, was Newgate Prison, which had an open-air gibbet. Death was a spectator sport once, as big as football is now.

In 1615, Smithfield was paved over. The selling of live cattle stopped in the nineteenth century when the Central Meat Market was constructed. Horace Jones' market building is a masterpiece of artistic engineering, like a Victorian railway station. It is an open structure, a vast roof supported by cast iron columns and piers, encrusted with Gothic details. Inside are the stalls of the meat sellers and their cruel hooks, an echo of Smithfield's gory history.

He walked through the market that afternoon and he sat down on a bench, to do some thinking. In front of him was St Bartholomew's Hospital, where John Smith had died. It had taken a wailing ambulance almost thirty minutes to get him there, through streets clogged with morning traffic. He would have died anyway. He had suffered a second heart attack on the way.

Smith had been a good bet to suffer a second coronary at 55 – overweight, over-worked and stressed out. But maybe he had been given a little shove. It would certainly have been easy to slip something into his champagne, or even his lemon soufflé. Rick was now almost convinced that it had been a political killing. But what do you do with a piece of information like that? Who do you tell?

It was a beautiful, golden afternoons. Bodies had hung near here from gallows, knights' lances had flashed through the air, prostitutes had screeched their bawdy cries, the ground thick with slime from slaughtered beasts, the air smelling of blood. In the old days, crime and retribution had been public spectacles. Now they were conducted in private.

It was now just before three o'clock. He decided to go back to the office, to put in couple more hours.

Karen looked up. He wondered what she had been doing all day. She smiled.

"Someone called for you Rick," she said. "Just after you went out."

He was out of breath from the steep, narrow stairs. "Who was it?" he said.

"I don't know. She asked me who had written that piece in this week's issue about the Language Generation Unit. She said that he wanted to congratulate them, because it was really funny." She looked at him. "I said that you wrote it, Rick."

"That's OK."

"She asked me where you live. I gave her your address. That's all right isn't it?"

Karen knew that she shouldn't have done that. Her eyes looked pleading and sad. Rick did not have the heart to call her a stupid cow.

"She sounded really nice, Rick," said Karen. "Maybe she works for one of the nationals."

"You shouldn't give out addresses, Karen," he said, "without knowing who people are. It's not a good idea."

Karen looked crestfallen. She would probably never take another message.

"Sorry, Rick."

"Never mind. It doesn't matter."

For a moment, Rick felt sorry for Karen. Now, he reflected, she had yet another reason to hate him.

~ ~ ~

There were few external signs that Rick's house had been broken into. In fact, none. He had not Chubbed the front door that morning. Whoever did it probably used a soft metal shim on the Yale lock. A professional.

He put his bike in the hall and headed straight for kitchen for a snack – a peanut butter sandwich. As usual, Sammy was waiting for him in the hallway, meowing pathetically. He needed feeding. Funny, he didn't remember leaving the cupboards open. Then he saw that there was paper scattered all over the kitchen floor – bills, postcards, letters. The intruder had even ripped everything off his notice board.

Living room. Same thing. Books all over the floor, snowdrifts of paper. The bedroom, ditto. He did a lot of work up there and had a desk, an Apple Mac, and a two-drawer filing cabinet, next to his bed. This had been the center of their operations, guessing that it was where the important stuff was kept.

Needless to say, every floppy disc was gone – even one that Rick had taped to the inside of his wardrobe, containing half a novel. That made his heart beat like a hammer, until he established that it was still on the hard disc of his computer.

He wondered whether to phone the police. But he decided against it. He didn't sleep very much. He sat upright in bed, with the light on. The silver briefcase was in his bike pannier and he left it there. He did not want them to find it anywhere near him. They didn't come back that night, or over the weekend. Each night, he slept a little easier.

7

Poverty
*I suggest that we drop this word. It's too scary
and, quite frankly, we can't do very much about it, like
the weather. How about using a term that is far more
neutral and ambiguous, like "social exclusion"?*

- The New Labour papers

Monday Morning. South London. Very early. There are
three men in the little white van. Trevor is driving.
Sitting next to him is Spoons. Crouched in the back of
the van, trying not slide around, is Spider.

Spider used to have a cobweb tattoo on his
forehead, hence his nickname. He has recently had it
surgically removed. The procedure left a scar of boiling
white flesh on his brow, up to the hairline. It is almost
as frightening as the tattoo.

Spoons also acquired his nickname in an unusual
way. He murdered his wife with a cutlery set, on New
Year's Day, 1992. He served 11 years for it, mainly in
category A prisons. It was while he was at Belmarsh
prison, in southeast London, that he met Trevor, who
was on remand.

All of them are wearing short black jackets, tight
faded jeans and woolly hats, the daytime mufti for
bouncers. Spider is thin and scrawny. Trevor and
Spoons are peas from same pod, thickset men with
fleshy jowls. The white Vauxhall Astra van is totally
legit. It is registered in the name of a blameless old
lady, who lives in Dorking.

They drove through Stockwell and turned left into Clapham Road. This was Trevor's patch. He had grown up on the Mursell Estate, one tube stop from Brixton. His mum was a single parent and a part-time prostitute. She had lost control of Trevor by the time that he was seven. He was one of those unpleasant little boys, who never grow out of torturing and killing things, but merely move on to larger quarry as they grow older.

Trevor and his mates spent most of their time hanging around the estate, occupied with turf wars. They got bigger and started using knives. He got his scar in a fight in Streatham. It was a jagged wound on the side of his face that gave him a new mouth. It needed sixteen stitches.

Trevor was sent to Feltham young offenders' institution when he was fourteen. It was not just for shoplifting but for terrorizing a Pakistani shopkeeper in front of his family. He came back with even more of a reputation.

Trevor had never been attracted by women, although he pretended to be aroused by the hardcore porn that circulated around Feltham. It was while he was inside that he had his first blowjob. It did his head in being a fucking queer. He left the youth who had pleasured him bruised and bleeding, a pattern that was to repeat itself.

One day, just after he came back from Feltham, Trevor was watching TV and eating a Pot Noodle. He was bunking off school. His mum, Tracy, was very thin. Her skin was almost translucent. The little blue marks on her face and arms were self-administered tattoos. Her forearms were covered with needle marks.

Trevor barely registered the fact that his mum was going out. She said something but he just grunted, not looking up. Then he heard the door close. She was wearing a tiny black skirt, even though it was cold. Tracy sold sex and blow jobs in and around the estate. What she charged depended upon the punter. But it was rarely less than ten quid.

Trevor was still watching TV, in the same position, when the police knocked on the door that evening. It was dark. He was pissed off with his mum for not coming back. The police told him that she was in hospital and they took him there. She had been found on Wandsworth Common, half beaten to death. She had come out of the operating theatre but she was in a coma.

He touched his mum's thin little body and he cried his eyes out. He wished that he had said goodbye. They had to drag Trevor away, the following morning, because he would not leave her. He became angry then, lashing out and screaming obscenities. It took three security men to get Trevor out of the ward and into a police car.

He was silent in the back of the car. They asked him if he was OK, but he told them to fuck off. Trevor went quiet after that. The anger was all inside him. He never cried for his mother again, even when they told him that she had died. But often he dreamed of her. In his dreams, he heard the door click shut, as she left the flat. Sometimes, he saw her in the hospital bed. He saw his mother's pale face with a tube coming out of her nose. Her chest was rising and falling but her eyes would not open.

The police took him to a council children's home. Social services tried to foster him, but it never worked out. Social workers never wrote down that Trevor was "nasty" or "evil", but that's what people said about him. He lied and stole without even thinking about it. He hurt anyone who tried to get near him. The harder they tried, the more he hurt them.

The council gave him a flat on a hard-to-let estate in Brixton when he left care at sixteen. It was soon full of stolen goods and drugs – conventional employment avenues seemed closed to Trevor. He didn't do drugs, apart from speed, because he didn't like to feel woozy. He would sell almost anything, apart from heroin.

After spending six months in an adult prison, Trevor sorted himself out. He had built up quite a reputation and he had started going to clubs. By talking to people, he got work on the doors.

Trevor found that he liked being a door supervisor and that he was good at it. He got fit by doing judo and pumping iron in a club in Clapham. The job allowed him to be sarcastic and to practice different ways of hurting people. In less than six months, he grew a corrugated stomach, broad shoulders and thick thighs that rubbed together when he walked.

In two years, Trevor was one of the best-known bouncers in London. He socialized with his colleagues in bars and gyms. They were a shaven-headed posse of squaddies and jailbirds, disgraced coppers, failed taxi drivers and small-town sociopaths. Trevor's mates worked the biggest and best clubs and did work on the side, including armed robbery and contract killing. They were fit for their purpose – gabby but tightly knit – the shock troops of the underworld.

Trevor was spotted by Nigel De Vere one hot sweaty night in Soho, in 1993, in a little drinking club in Brewer Street. De Vere used to enjoy hanging out there with low-life types, throwing his money around and practicing his cockney accent. He offered Trevor a job, that night, at his club at the Elephant, the Think Tank. Trevor, who was twenty, was delighted. It was, he told people, the biggest lucky break of his life.

Soon afterwards, he was introduced to Emma Henderson, the young blonde MP for Middlewich. He only attempted to have sex with her once. It was an open secret that he preferred boys. But she used to flirt with him. She loved his scar. Sometimes, when he was very drunk, he let her touch it. Through Emma, Henderson he got involved in other stuff – mainly bugging people, stitching them up and bit of killing.

He killed his first man when he was twenty-two. It was a West Indian, who had been getting lippy about the E Squad, which was Henderson's private army. Trevor stabbed the man through the eye with a skewer in a flat up at Chalk Farm. The body was never found. It was minced up and fed to pigs on a farm in Suffolk.

The E Squad was disbanded in 1997. Henderson was now a junior minister in the Labour Government and she didn't need it anymore. The following year, Trevor became head of security at the Think Tank. His function in this role was mainly dealing Es and humiliating and hurting people who did not comply with the club's somewhat ambiguous dress code.

He also provided some colorful muscle when De Vere was shooting porn movies, at his villa in Ibiza. Trevor did not say that he was gay, although he wore a diamond stud in his ear. He leered, like the other blokes, at the orange-skinned women with thongs and torpedo breasts who lounged around the pool. But everyone knew where his real interests lay. It was at this time that De Vere started to call him diamond. It was partly because of the earring and partly because of the scar on his cheek. Trevor loved that name.

~ ~ ~

Trevor liked the clarity of early mornings. He had picked up Spoons and Spider when it was still freezing cold and pitch dark. There were not many people about in Brixton at this time of day – down and outs, a few clubbers on their way home, the odd market trader. He passed Tesco's in Coldharbor Lane, guiding the little

71

Astra with one hand. Spoons looked ahead at the road, saying nothing. There was a copy of the Daily Star on his lap. The front page was mainly pictures. But there were words too – "Jordon: my night of lust with Andre", "Four die in rail horror".

Spoons had lost interest in the paper. As they passed the Universal Pentecostal Church he tossed it into the back of the van. There was a big banner strung across the front of the church. Black letters were picked out by orange Sodium lights. It said: "I will heal your wounds and restore your health says the Lord". Spider looked at Jordon, a tiny figure in a white basque placing a finger to her swollen lips. He started to feel something happening in his trousers. Trevor must be a mind reader. He turned round in his seat and accused Spider of wanking. They all laughed. Then they jerked off from the lights, turning right into Brixton Hill.

Trevor had checked the address in Mervan Road on Lambeth's electoral register on Friday afternoon and on a street directory CD. The information told him that one person who had lived there in May 1994 was still there. His name was Alan Baker. Trevor did a credit check on his name. He was a good risk with no bad debts and a high earner. Two other people also lived in the house now. They were both women, so it should not be too difficult to pick Alan Baker out.

"He'll be the one with the hard-on when we pull him out of fucking bed," he had told Spoons. He remembered visiting Mervan Road the last time. It was a quiet suburban street of bay-windowed Victorian houses. Some of them cost half a million quid. Why would someone that well off live in a dump like Brixton?

The white van pulled up outside the house. It was just before six o'clock. They put on gloves and ski masks to cover their faces. In a muffled voice, Trevor said that the job should be a piece of piss. The vans' doors opened simultaneously. They were all breathing heavily as they walked down the garden path. Their breath came out in white mist.

It was the usual routine. Spoons broke the door down with a metal enforcer and waited in the hallway. Trevor and Spider ran past him upstairs. The two women were in bed together. They screamed. Alan Baker, also known as Adam, was in a bedroom at the front of the house, all on his own. As Trevor later reported, his cock was as limp as a cold sausage. The man opened his eyes to see two huge intruders at the foot of his bed. He was too terrified to scream.

They ripped off the duvet. They told him to get his pants on and to grab his clothes and shoes. These they stuffed into a black bin liner. Alan was white with terror and shivering. In two more minutes, it was over. They bundled him downstairs, where Spoons was keeping watch through the door. They shoved him into the back of the van and threw the bag after him. Then they drove off.

Trevor was careful not break the speed limit. He headed through the Oval, towards the Elephant. Spider blindfolded Alan. He was moaning and complaining, so Spider sealed his mouth with gaffer tape.

There was a parking bay at the back of the Think Tank. It was big enough for about three vehicles. The rest was simple. They took Alan into the club and up in the service lift, to the top floor. He was trying to speak through the tape and tearing at his blind-fold. Trevor slapped his face, hard, and told him to shut the fuck up.

Where should they put him? Trevor had an idea. There was a walk-in wardrobe in Nigel De Vere's office, full of sex toys and rubber gear. It was just big enough to hold a person. They shoved Alan into the cupboard and threw the bag of clothes after him. They locked the door with a key from De Vere's desk.

De Vere would not arrive in the club for another twelve hours, but that didn't matter, as far as Trevor was concerned. Let the little bastard sweat it out.

Alan struggled and groaned at first, in a kind of frenzy. Trevor laughed. Kick all you fucking want mate, you're going nowhere.

He went down in the lift with Spoons and Spider. They were chuckling at the thought of their shut in that cupboard full of whips and dildos. They felt pleased with themselves. They went and had a greasy breakfast, at a caff called Ozzie's in the old Kent Road.

8

Think tanks

The purpose of a think tank is to encourage us to do what we wanted to do already and to show us how to do it. Initially, they will soften up resistance to "unthinkable" ideas – privatizing prisons, abolishing free healthcare. When the time is right, and public opinion has shifted, they will have already prepared the ground for some really wicked policies. Hey presto!

- The New Labour papers

The same Monday morning, Rick cycled to work. It was cold, but a pale sun was streaming through the London plane trees at the edge of Peckham Rye. The bumps in the road were clear and sharp. The silver briefcase was inside his pannier, wrapped in an orange Sainsbury's bag.

After the break-in at his house he had decided that he needed to tell someone what he had. It had to be someone on the periphery of New Labour, who was far better connected with the media mafia than he was. Someone who would be shocked by the Fourth Way and who would get things moving. He was just passing the BP petrol station near the end of Walworth Road, when a name popped into his head. Jez Parslow.

Parslow was director of the Strategic Policies Unit, New Labour's favorite think tank. He would be the perfect person to tell. He was bright. And he would know the right people – TV producers, editors, politicians. Telling him about the Fourth Way would be like jabbing a needle straight into an artery.

Rick had met Parslow when the Strategic Policies Unit had put out a document about planning and the green belt, the previous year. It was for one of the magazine's rare profiles, a two-pager. Rick had read up on the man from lots of clippings.

Parslow was New Labour to his fingertips. He had gone to a comprehensive school in London and studied politics and law at East Sussex University. After a stint in Washington, working for the Democrats, he had become a researcher for an Old Labour MP.

His next job was assistant director of the SPU. He had slid into the director's chair just before the '01 election. It was quite a jump. According to bitchy gossip, the fact that he was the son of a well-known TV journalist had not hindered his rise to prominence.

Parslow had a neutral accent and used the down to earth handle Jez, to reinforce the point that he was an ordinary bloke. Rick had made much of his "New Labour semiotics" in the intro to his article. He wore Armani suits (fashion conscious in a contemporary way) combined with black polo necks (casual, intellectual). Inevitably, he was an Arsenal supporter. It went with the territory, like holidays in Tuscany and the dinners in Granita.

Actually, Rick had liked him. Parslow had listened carefully to his questions and answered them thoughtfully. He had even asked Rick stuff about himself. He was earnest (a New Labour trait) with a "let's roll up our sleeves and get on with it" attitude. But he also seemed to have a sense of humor.

He had told Rick, for example, that the Secretary of State for Work and Pensions, Harold Johnson, was a "fuck wit," which could barely tie his own shoelaces.

Rick had not used that in his profile, "New Labour, new levers."

~ ~ ~

Rick cycled over Blackfriars Bridge. He thought that the view from the bridge was the best in London. It was a sparkling corridor lined with miraculous buildings – the Tate Modern, St. Paul's, the Oxo Tower. He had crossed Blackfriars Bridge in every conceivable weather condition and mood, sweating in heat waves, picking his way through ice, or battling against horizontal rain. The best days were when the sun lit up the pale grey dome of St Paul's, like a stage set. Every time he crossed the bridge, he felt a peculiar exaltation that he lived and worked in London. It made his flesh tingle. After the bridge, he swung into Sea Coal Lane, a medieval thoroughfare, now obliterated, except for its twisting route, by glass and steel.

It was five past ten when he arrived at the top of the stairs. He had crossed an invisible line. He was late. Karen was at her desk, looking smug. The eel gave him a horrible look from her fish tank. He smiled at her. She glanced away.

His first task was to look up the number of the Strategic Policies Unit in his contacts book. It was a small outfit. He was put straight through to Parslow.

"Hi." The voice sounded tired, with a hint of peevishness.

"Hello. Is that Jeremy Parslow?"

"Jez Parslow. Yes, it is. Who am I talking to?"

"My name is Rick Gilliver. I don't know if you remember me. I interviewed you last November, for *Planning Today*?"

Rick could almost hear the little cogs whirring in his brain.

"Oh hi, Rick. How can I help you?"

"Well, the thing is, I have something extremely interesting to tell you. It's a bit er... delicate. I can't really do this on the phone, you know."

"Try me." It was his don't-piss-me-around, I-am-extremely-important voice. Rick realized that he wasn't going to get anywhere, unless he gave Parslow something.

He took a deep breath. "I have in my possession a confidential document. It's a policy document. But not an official one. The contents are a bit shocking."

"In what way?"

"I can't tell you. I would rather show you."

"OK." It took Parslow only a moment to make up his mind. That was significant. But Rick did not pick it up. "When would you like to see me?"

"This lunch time?"

Parslow paused for effect.

"Well, I'm very busy. But, in the circumstances, fine. Why don't you swing over at about one o'clock?"

Those were the kind of phrases he used – swing over, ballpark, blue sky – sub-managerial jargon.

The rest of the morning, Rick worked through a sheaf of post-it notes and wrote letters and emails (in journalism, you are always apologizing for things that you have done, or have not done, and having arguments).

Karen seemed chirpy. Their tiff on Friday seemed forgotten. She spent the morning mailing out copies of Planning Weekly to contributors, with little notes. They said things like "thank you for your lovely article". Rick could not fathom her. She was an intractable problem, like a bag of cement tied around his ankles.

At twelve-thirty, he picked up his cycle pannier and went downstairs. His bike was locked to a lamppost, in front of a peculiar shop next door that sold vintage underwear and swimming costumes. God knows what it was doing in Smithfield, surrounded by wholesale butchers. The snooty bitch who owned it hated his bike being anywhere near her precious business.

She had once attached a snotty note to his saddle, beginning, "Dear bike boy ..." He had furiously pushed a reply through her door, "Dear knicker woman ..." He pointed out in the note that he was not a boy, he was 37 years old, and that he could attach his bike wherever he fucking liked.

He cycled down Fleet Street and the Strand, through Trafalgar Square and into Whitehall. As usual, there were armed police by the Cenotaph, looking warily towards the end of Downing Street.

~ ~ ~

The Strategic Policies Unit was located in a bog standard Georgian town house, in Horseferry Road. There was a small brass plaque next to the door. On the other side of the road was the Channel 4 building. It was all exposed pipes and meaningless buttresses and gantries, an office block pretending to be an oil refinery. This kind of architecture was supposed to be purely functional. Actually, it was fussily decorative, an update of Victorian Gothic.

On the ground floor was a reception area. It smelt of coffee and paper. Fresh reports were heaped up everywhere, waiting to be posted out. They were called things like "Joined-up solutions" or "Thinking out of the box". That's what the SPU did.

Jez Parslow's office was on the first floor. It looked over the street. You could see the Channel 4 building from his window. He liked that. It gave him a modern, thrusting backdrop, which was good for the cameras.

Parslow was a fresh-faced looking man in his late thirties, with a serious manner. He wore leather jackets to work. That Monday morning, he was trying to think out of the box. But it was a bit difficult with a raging hangover. All that Chablis last night. He should be feeling better by now. But he wasn't.

Parslow was one of the architects of New Labour. Culturally, he was at home with the party's obsession with presentation, its arm-twisting, its burying of bad news and "spinning" of good. Parslow was part of same social circle as Emma Henderson. They had dinner together occasionally and went to the same haunts – restaurants in Islington, the English National Opera.

Both basked in the success of New Labour. They were its golden creatures. Parslow was part of a new political generation. They were free of upper class associations and aspirations, possessing a middle class sense of duty, combined with its work ethic. The sons and daughters of university lecturers and trade union officials, they were a new ruling elite. They were bright, generally humorless and as sharp as knives – the subalterns and administrators of New Labour's political empire.

Rick was red-faced and out of breath when he arrived at the Strategic Policies Unit, his brain racing. He was a little more collected by the time he had been taken upstairs to Parslow's office. Parslow sat Rick down and offered him a coffee. Rick looked round. There were no family pictures anywhere. He wondered whether Parslow was gay.

The desk was uncluttered, with a blotter and some neatly arranged papers. Parslow knitted his fingers and looked serious, as if he was on one of those late-night TV shows that tries, a little too hard, to make politics interesting.

"Well, what have you got for me, Rick?"

Rick removed the creased Sainsbury's bag from the pannier. He realized that it looked ridiculous.

"Is it a pound of sausages?"

They both laughed.

"Not exactly."

He placed the New Labour papers on the desk.

"This is a document describing a secret strategy, the Fourth Way. It was written early in 1994, by a well-known Labour politician."

"Who?"

"I'm not sure, but I have an idea."

"I see."

Parslow's eyes widened.

"And?"

"Basically, it covers most areas of domestic policy – constitutional issues, drugs, asylum seekers, the royal family, the media, and so on. Although it was written ten years ago, it's virtually a template for all the things that New Labour have done in office."

"Can I have a look?"

"Of course."

Parslow began to leaf through the papers. He had long white fingers.

"What does this have to do with me?"

This was the good bit. Rick had prepared what he was going to say.

"OK. Imagine a political party that has no morals. A party that lies and cheats, as a matter of course, and is contemptuous of Parliament and democracy. A party that will stop at absolutely nothing to gain and retain power."

"Nothing unusual there. You have just described the British political system."

"What if it killed people who got in its way?"

Parslow raised his eyebrows.

"I know that all governments get rid of the odd whistle blower. They'll ruin them financially, or stitch them up for some crime, or shove them into a mental hospital. But this is different. Here we have a party, or a group within a party, which is advocating blackmail, perjury and murder. And which has been systematically using them."

Parslow was still glancing through the papers. He was listening.

"Where's the proof for this?" he said.

"Well, John Jenkins is mentioned in there."

"That newspaper publisher who was convicted for rape?"

"That's right. And the trade union leader, Harris. You may remember that he was against abolishing clause four and that he conveniently killed himself. Then there's Morris, the environment minister who did not like GM crops. He was sliced in half by a propeller. There are a whole bunch of other people in there who have died or who have disappeared, including John Smith."

"What about John Smith?" Parslow looked up.

"It is clear from these papers that he was murdered."

"Why the hell would anyone want to do that?"

"So that the right people could take over the party."

"The right people?"

"The ones who were in on the Fourth Way."

"I see." He was frowning, as if he had a piece of gristle beneath his teeth.

"Do you mind if I have a copy of these?"

Rick was ready for that. "No, of course not."

Parslow reached for his phone and dialed an extension.

"Well, Rick," he said. "It's bigger story than a planning story, isn't it? Not your usual kind of thing. Where did you get it from?"

"I can't tell you that."

"I understand, absolutely, protecting your sources and all that. Of course." He swiveled his chair. To his left, on the wall, was a picture of Tony Blair. The usual smile was pasted on, like a rictus.

"I am gobsmacked, quite frankly. If what you are saying is true, it's well... Who else knows about this?"

He looked into Rick's eyes. There were exactly the same age.

"At the moment. Just you, me and my source."

"I see."

They chatted, self-consciously, waiting for the photocopying to be done. The admin assistant came back in. She was young and dark-haired. Pretty. She was probably a politics graduate from one of the "good" universities, Rick speculated, in her first job. Parslow took one set of papers and handed another to Rick.

"That's the copy," said Rick. "Can I have the document that I gave you?"

"Oh, I'm terribly sorry, my mistake."

There was a strange look on Parslow's face. Rick took the manuscript covered with Henderson's fresh blue handwriting. Parslow smiled weakly as the original disappeared, back into the carrier bag. They shook hands. Afterwards, when Rick's back was turned Parslow reached down to turn off the little tape recorder that was hidden under his desk.

"Right, Rick. Thank you so much for coming and telling me about this. I am going to read through this lot right now. And I am going to talk to you later this afternoon. What time do you finish?"

"About five-thirty."

He paused.

"I have a meeting then. Tell you what, I'll phone you first thing tomorrow. Is that all right?" He grinned.

"Natasha will show you out, Rick. And we'll talk about this tomorrow morning. We'll decide what to do then, OK? Have a good night, mate. Mind how you go."

His smiled disappeared the second that Rick was gone. As soon as his door was safely closed, he picked up his phone.

Natasha, the admin assistant, exchanged a few words with Rick as she guided him back to the front door. True to type she had a Sloane ranger accent.

It took him longer than it should have done to cycle back to the office because he took a detour up Whitehall and into Covent Garden. That afternoon, there was the kind of golden light that turned London into an old master. He felt happy, knowing that all he had to do was to bash out some routine stories from press releases. Karen could write the product news.

"Nick should do that," she said.

"Nick is not here."

"Well, it's his job."

Karen should have worked for a railway company, or some other useless organization, with lethargic, poorly paid staff couldn't be bothered to do their jobs properly.

Rick gave a heavy sigh.

"I'm not happy about this," said Karen. "Why don't we get a temp in?"

He considered her suggestion. Why didn't they pay more than a hundred pounds for someone else to write three 50-word stories, so that she could go on reading the newspaper?

"Karen, we've been through this before," he said.

She looked as though she was going to cry. She thought that Rick victimized her because she was a woman.

"How long is it going to take," he said, "twenty minutes?"

"That's not the point, Rick. It's not what we agreed." Here we go, he thought. Rules and regulations. Standing order ninety-seven, as ratified by the executive committee. Please do not wash your balls in the hand basins. Her lower lip was trembling.

"Jesus Karen! It is the fucking point!" He slammed his fist down on the table.

Karen began to sob. She rushed from her chair, towards the toilet.

The eel scowled at Rick from her glass prison. Simone stopped chatting to her boyfriend on the phone. It was her job to follow Karen into the ladies loo and to console her.

Rick knew what was coming. He would be told by the eel that his behavior was "inappropriate" and forced to apologize. Karen would look superior. She would tell Simone, later, that Rick had a problem with women. Simone would humor her, although she knew that it was total crap.

That is exactly what happened. Sorting it all out took more than an hour. A pale and trembling Karen was allowed to go home early, like a swooning Victorian damsel. They almost ordered a minicab for her.

Rick did not leave the office until after six o'clock.

He now felt full of rage. With the eel, with the knicker woman, with Karen, with the little box he lived in, with his ex, Carol, with Gina and her inexplicable moods. In fact, with his whole stupid life. He did not know it, but things were about to get a lot worse.

9

Pop songs
Useful as anthems, but dangerous. Indie bands have street cred, but the singer will invariably be on heroin and badmouth you, once the novelty has worn off. Queen is favorite (royal associations, transvestism – always popular). Do not, under any circumstances, appear in a pop video!
- The New Labour papers

Emma Henderson was to meet Nigel De Vere at the Think Tank that Monday night. It had been arranged on the phone. That way, she could find out what Alan Baker knew, if anything, and decide what to do with him.

De Vere arrived at the club first. He squeezed his white A-class Mercedes into his spot at the back and went up to his office. It was six o'clock, far too early. The club was silent and empty, after the cleaners but before the punters.

De Vere arranged himself on the black leather sofa in his office and poured himself a generous Scotch and coke. For someone who was thirty-nine, he was not doing badly. He was a millionaire. De Vere was tall and thin. He wore Paul Smith suits and Italian loafers, his shirts open at the neck.

He had an Ibiza tan and usually wore something around his neck, a plaited braid or an amulet on a leather thong. That and his frazzly, sun-bleached hair told you that he had not earned his money from making cardboard boxes. He didn't do many Es these days, mainly coke and a little grass. Both made you as horny as hell and didn't fuck you up too much. That's why he liked them. He carried his drugs around in a little silver cigarette case.

He had lost most of his Eton accent by now, give or take the odd vowel. To people in the club, he talked estuary mixed with rapper slang. For meetings with bankers, solicitors and insurers, it was something more formal. His father, who was also a millionaire, despised the company that his son kept. But he was proud of his moneymaking acumen.

He swished the dark liquid around in his glass. There was a large mirror on the wall opposite the settee. Just thinking of all of the things that that the mirror had reflected gave him a hard on. Once, a long time ago, he had screwed Emma Henderson, on this very settee. De Vere had always been a heterosexual, even at Eton. He liked blonde beach chicks, with little dreadlocks, usually in twos or threes. Sometimes, he went for porn actresses. It was one of the perks of his job. His partner, Kristen, lived at the house in Finchley. Often, she joined in.

The entry phone on his desk chirruped. He stood up and tried to stop thinking about sex. It was the minister for London. He let her in.

She was wearing a midnight blue coat with a fur collar and a white silk scarf. She called it her Fred Astaire look. She hugged De Vere. His cheeks were freezing.

"It's like winter out there," she said.

"It is winter."

"Oh yes. May I?"

She took off her coat, draped it over the back of the settee and sat down. Revealed were black Moschino trouser suit and a plain white blouse. Ten minutes later, Emma was warm and relaxed. She was on her second whisky and coke.

"I hate my job sometimes, Nigel. It's such a bore. I've always envied you, you know."

"Have you?"

"Of course."

De Vere put some music on. It was trancy, with a hooky bass line. Emma closed her eyes, letting the sound massage her brain. She started to tap her court shoes on the carpet.

"What's this music?"

"It's a band called the Automatics. They're from Brighton. I've just signed them. You'd like the singer. He's really hunky."

She was not going to get involved. Bands were bad news.

"It's very, catchy."

There had been a pause as she searched for the right word. As usual, she found the wrong one. De Vere smiled. Sometimes, Emma was so 1960s.

"So how's the mayor of London thing going?" he said. He was sitting on a capacious black leather chair. He had taken his shoes off.

"Oh, you've been following that tedious business, have you?"

"A little bit, yes." Sometimes, De Vere liked to talk about politics.

"Well." The minister lifted her glass. Livingstone's going to win, hand's down. That's why we let him back into the party."

"Is that good or bad?"

"Good for him, bad for us."

"What do you mean?"

Emma considered her drink.

"Livingstone is on the up and up, we are going down."

"Do you think he will stand as an MP again and ..." De Vere paused.

"Be the new Tony Blair?" Emma laughed. "I fucking hope not. Besides, it's not very likely."

"Why?"

She gave a genteel little snort.

"Can't tell you darling."

"One of your wicked little schemes?"

"Yes. One of my best."

Emma smiled, looking into his face. Her expression was ambiguous. Nigel shrugged. Later, when they were high, he knew that she would tell him what the plan was. For now, he decided not to push it.

"Charlie?" he said.

"Oh, yes please."

Emma shifted her position on the couch. Her Moschino trousers were silky and beautifully cut. She had undone the top button of her blouse. She was tanned underneath. Nigel wondered whether it was real or from a salon. He tried not to look.

Cocaine was one of the rituals of their meetings, like the hug. De Vere produced his silver case and a little mirror from his pocket. He divided up two long lines of white powder with a razor blade.

The minister sucked the first line up her delicate left nostril, appreciatively. She liked feeling the mucus running into her throat from her nasal passages, that sweet juice.

"Mmmm ... very nice."

She watched the second line disappear up Nigel's nose. In a moment, both of them would be giggly and garrulous. The effect would evaporate quickly. Then they would have another line.

"By the way, Nigel." She had a surprisingly serious expression. "That guy Trevor picked up this morning in Brixton. Is he here?"

Nigel sniffed. "Yeh, think so. Do you want me to find out where he is?"

"If you wouldn't mind, my darling."

"No problem. I'll ask Trevor. Excuse me."

Nigel crossed to his desk. He picked up his phone to speak to Trevor. Emma could only hear one side of the conversation.

"Yeh ... so where is he ... where? ... in my what? ... my fucking wardrobe ... you!"

Nigel did not need to swear. He slammed the phone down with fury. He paced across the room. When he opened the wardrobe door, Alan Baker fell, full-length, onto the floor. He was twitching. He had removed his blindfold and ripped the silver tape from his mouth. A little mobile phone flipped onto the carpet from his hand.

He looked up at Nigel and at Emma. She did not say anything. Nigel screamed.

"Stay where you are! Don't fucking move!"

He crossed back to the intercom.

"Trevor. In here, now!"

It was quite easy to unravel what had happened. Trevor had simply forgotten to tell Nigel that there was a man held captive in his office. To make matters worse, there had been a telephone in Alan's trouser pocket, hidden in the black bin bag that he had flung into the cupboard with him. Trevor had not thought to look through the bag.

Alan must have heard everything and he could have texted anybody on his mobile, although there had been very little juice left in his battery. It was a royal fuck up. Trevor blamed Spider.

"I told him to search the bag. The little twat. I'm going to kill him."

"Shut up!"

Emma spoke for the first time.

"I don't care whose fault it was. We'll sort that out later." She looked down at the body. Alan had not eaten or drunk for more than twenty hours. He was asking them for water from his tight, parched throat. The words were unclear.

"We've got to find out who he has been talking to and what he knows. Correction, you have got to find out."

She glared at Trevor.

Nigel touched her arm.

"Listen, I"m really sorry."

"Don't touch me." She glared at De Vere. "Not as sorry as I am. Get this piece of shit out of my sight." She prodded Alan's chest with her pointed toe. "Go on, what are you waiting for?"

Nigel glowered at Trevor. Trevor knew that he had screwed up. Big time.

~ ~ ~

That evening, Rick was cycling home. It was cold and grey, but the rain had held off. Dusk was turning into darkness. He was halfway down Walworth Road, when he noticed his pursuer. A thin man, riding an expensive mountain bike, which was a little too big for him. There was a large scar on the man's forehead, like a scald. Each time Rick stopped at traffic lights, the man would pull up behind him, a carefully measured two meters.

He cycled through Camberwell Green and up Denmark Hill. That is when he realized that he was being followed. He speeded up a little, to try and shake the man off. Actually, he felt sorry for the guy. He was not in any physical condition for this kind of thing. He was breathing heavily, struggling to keep up.

Rick turned left at the lights into Champion Park. It was quite a steep climb. The thin man started to drop back. On the right was a large Salvation Army training hostel with thick, heavy towers in dark brick and windows like arrow slits. It was hideous. It always made Rick feel depressed that the human race could have conceived and built such an ugly thing.

The road went through a sharp right-hand bend and reached some traffic lights. There was a brilliant view here. It was the top of Dog Kennel Hill. South London spread before him, a jumble of council estates and Victorian terraces, scattered with orange and yellow lights, like fairy dust.

The thin man caught up and stopped at the red signal. He must have been relieved that they were on the brow of a hill. They now faced the incongruous prospect of racing together down Dog Kennel Hill, which is as long and perilous as an Olympic ski slope.

The lights changed. Rick pulled away. Right, you little bastard, he thought. He shifted up through three sets of gears and shot down the hill, like a bishop coming out of a brothel.

He had an idea. There is a set of traffic lights halfway down Dog Kennel Hill, at the end of a slip road for a supermarket. He would make a racing turn here and slalom into Sainsbury's. If the thin man followed him, he would have to take more drastic action.

It was a dangerous maneuver. The lights were green when he reached them, for the first time ever. Rick almost lost control of his bike, swinging round the bend in fifteenth gear. So did the thin man. He could have soared through the air like a stick and ended up decorating a rhododendron bush. He just managed to stay on his wheels.

Right, you fucker, thought Rick, we're going shopping. As he looked back, the thin man removed something from his pocket. It was a dark, not much bigger than his hand. The fact that it was a small caliber pistol, with a long silencer, did not sink in for a couple of seconds.

The thin man was now wobbling like a jelly, trying to steer as he held out his right arm to take aim. The affect was almost comic – at least until a 9mm round whistled past Rick's shoulder.

The thin man struggled to get his balance back. This won Rick some time. He shot into Sainsbury's car park like a frightened wildebeest. He flung down his bike, grabbed his pannier and shot into the shop. People must have noticed his odd behavior. But nobody said anything. Nobody ever does.

He was now in dreamtime. There was mood music, bright neon lighting. His heart was pounding through his ribs. Just inside the entrance was a security guard, in a brown uniform. Low-grade muscle on minimum wage. His presence reassured Rick.

He walked through the fresh produce, with its depressing displays of polished, chemically preserved vegetables. In this harsh fluorescent light, the customers looked like that too. It was the early evening clientele. Housewives were foraging for courgettes, after school runs in their people carriers.

Surely, he wouldn't be followed in here. He reasoned that the thin man would wait outside, for as long as necessary, and then take a pop at him on the car park. He had not counted on Spider's low intelligence and the fact that he was now as riled as a wasp in a pub garden.

When he reached the end of the aisle, he looked back. The thin man had come inside! His face was red and he was talking, intimately, with the security guard. It was funny how these people all seemed to know each other. They must have gone to the same school. The thin man could probably make sure that the CCTV footage would be disappeared.

Rick turned right at the end of aisle one. He decided to make his way to the deli counter and take a gamble on aisle twelve or thirteen. There was no way that the thin man could cover all of the checkouts and exits. He had blown it.

He really liked the deli counter in Sainsbury's. But, usually, he was far too impatient to get one of those little raffle tickets and queue up for something. He looked longingly at the stuffed olives, roll-mop herrings, pates and salamis, realizing that he was famished. It was his downfall, that little lapse of concentration.

The thin man was making his way purposefully up aisle fourteen, like a panther scenting blood. By the time Rick had realized, it was too late. His pursuer was only four meters away. And closing. His options were now limited. The best escape looked like his usual exit route, the booze aisle. He walked briskly through French sticks, croissants and cream cakes. The thin man followed, pretending not to run, his hand welded into his pocket.

It was next to the spirits and liqueurs – stuff that Rick never bought – that it happened. The thin man looked up and down the aisle. It was clear. In slow motion, he removed his hand from his pocket and raised his arm. Rick froze like a statue. His hair became brittle. The blood drained from his face.

Fortunately, the thin man was an unpracticed assassin. Four bullets missed Rick by a wide margin. Instead, a shelf-full of Famous Grouse cascaded into a miniature Niagara, covering the floor with whisky. He looked directly into the thin man's scarred face. His whole life flashed in front of Gulliver's eyes. The council estate, exclusion from school, his first convictions.

Suddenly, all hell broke loose. Someone had set off a shrieking alarm system. There was an announcement, "Code forty-seven in aisle fifteen", and a sound of running feet. A herd of brown thugs was stampeding down the aisle. The thin man was frozen now, as Rick had been earlier. He really was useless.

Like a flying gorilla, one of the security guards launched himself into the air from a highly polished Doc Marten. He made a game-saving tackle and felled the thin man like a tree. The two bodies didn't stop. With a splintering crash, they reduced a wall of lager to a pyramid of glass, cardboard and foam. The thin man was pinned to the floor, protesting his innocence in a voice that sounded like a rusty hinge. Lager was his nemesis.

Rick did not hesitate. He slipped down the aisle to the nearest checkout and legged it. People were already milling around the entrance, in confused, curious groups. His bike was still where he had left it. He cycled calmly away, knowing that the thin man had two security guards sitting on his chest.

He was able to think now. His first realization was who had stitched him up – Jez Parslow, the little bastard. His second was that he could not go home. At least, if he wanted to stay alive. He pondered on what to do as he rode down towards East Dulwich railway station, at the bottom of Dog Kennel Hill.

He stopped out the station, his heart pounding like a jackhammer. He pulled his phone out his pocket. There was a text message on it. The phone must have bleeped and he had never noticed. The message had been sent at 9.03 that morning.

It said: "Help!!! Locked in. Danger." Rick frowned. He checked on the phone who the text was from. It was Adam. Shit! They had caught him. Could you find out where people were, from their mobile network? Rick did not know.

He sent a text back. "Don't worry." There was not much else he could do.

Where was he going to go?

Carol, his ex, would not be much help. They weren't talking at the moment. Stacia Shipley's name popped into his head. She was a woman who came in to do subbing shifts at Planning Today. They were quite good friends.

He phoned her. Luckily, Stacia was in. Rick did not give her the whole spiel. She said that he could come over to her house. No problem.

He left his bike locked to a lamppost in front of the station. Four hundred quid's worth. That was the last he ever saw it. He removed the pannier, still with the precious silver briefcase inside.

He was on the platform, waiting, the phone bleeped and a text message came back from Adam.

"I am in a cupboard."

"What?" thought Rick. A deep furrow was etched across his forehead. The line seemed to get deeper every day as the rows with Carol and problems with Gina intensified. It really bothered him. That was it. The text broke off. The time was now 19.03.

He sent one back "Hang on will rescue." It was a ridiculous optimistic message, he realized.

The train to London Bridge station was virtually empty. He phoned the T-Mobile network and asked them whether text calls could be traced to locations. They said yes, sometimes, but that they were only allowed to give the information to certain authorized persons, such as the police. Rick asked how he could get permission to access the information. The operator became suspicious and evasive. He gave up.

He was still arguing with the operator as he passed through the automated ticket barrier at London Bridge station. He liked this station. It was slick and new and not so big as to be intimidating.

Rick descended on an escalator into the underground, where the station's newness ran out. He took a dirty old northern line train to King's Cross then changed onto the Victoria line, heading for Walthamstow, where Stacia lived.

Since it was Monday there were no tipsy early evening office workers on the tube. The bleak carriages were almost empty. He kept looking at other people, wondering whether he was being followed.

Just before he reached Walthamstow Station, another text arrived. The time was 19.45. It was the last message that he received. It said simply "Livingstone. Millennium Wheel. Danger."

10

Integrity
Insincerity is the oxygen of politics. However, if you don't believe anything, you can't be insincere can you?

- The New Labour papers

Alan Baker was tied to a chair in Trevor Jones' office. He was held with thick black electrical cable. It was wrapped around his wrists and secured his arms to the back of the chair.

They had given him something to eat and drink, a can of Red Bull and a sticky chemical-laced muffin. It was the only stuff that Trevor had in his fridge.

The end of the cable trailed across the carpet. Trevor bent to pick it up. There were red welts on Alan's cheeks – Trevor had been lashing him with cable as well as thumping him. His left eye was one large bruise, like an over-ripe Victoria plum.

Trevor whipped him again. Jagged strands of copper at the end of the flex clawed Alan's right ear, like a snake's fangs. The searing flash merely topped up his pain level. His body was one dull ache from his neck to his abdomen, especially his ribs, two of which were cracked.

"So, who is this Rick Gilliver?"

Alan was whimpering.

"He's a journalist, I told you, on this magazine, Planning Today."

"Planning Today?" Trevor looked incredulous. "What the fuck is that?"

"It's a trade magazine ... we get it in the department every Friday. I ... Ow!"

The cable claw burned into Alan Baker's head.

"When did you see 'im?"

"I told you. About ten days ago, in a pub."

Alan remembered the night. There was no atmosphere in the Cheshire Cheese. He felt cheated. It should be Rick here, not him. That was the whole reason he had given him the suitcase.

"Is he the only one you gave the document to?"

"Yes. Look ... please don't."

Trevor leaned over him, leering menacingly. His eyes were bulging.

"Why?"

"Because ..."

"Because what?"

"Because I have told you everything."

Trevor fingered the cable.

"You've told me fuck all, my friend." He edged forward.

"Now ..."

"Trevor." The smooth voice was Emma Henderson's. She slid off the edge of Trevor's desk, where she had been sitting. She was wearing faded blue Levis and a black and white Fulham FC football shirt. The jeans fitted her beautifully.

Alan's telephone was in her hand. It was the latest Ericsson. Rick's mobile number was stored in the phone's address book. It might be useful later. She slipped the little phone into her pocket.

"I don't think that there is any point in going on with this, interrogation."

She looked into Trevor's eyes.

Trevor caressed the flex.

"I think that we have the information that we need, don't you?"

Trevor shrugged.

His face registered a question.

"What shall I do?"

Emma looked cross. "Just use your imagination Trevor!"

He smiled.

"Eight or nine boss?"

"Nine." Emma said the word with distaste. She walked out of the office and left him to it.

Alan began to squirm frantically, as Trevor moved up behind him, just like Sean had done. Trevor wrapped the cable around his victim's neck, twice. Then he began to pull.

~ ~ ~

Walthamstow is a satellite suburb, northeast of London. Young professionals move there when they can no longer afford London prices. They tell their friends that interesting things happen there. But they are lying. If London were a bonfire, Walthamstow would barely register as a pilot light.

Stacia Shipley had lived in Walthamstow for about a year. In the late 1980s, she had been in a band which was quite successful. In those days, she had lips like a bee sting and vertical hair. It was rarely the same color for more than a few days. Magenta and lime green were her favorites. These days, her hair was dark, but it still stood up on end. She mainly wore black. Stacia was a more restrained version of her previous self. But she was still funny. She had been born in New Zealand. But you could not always tell from her accent.

Her house made a strong impression. She had not just knocked down the living room wall, like most people. She had taken the shell of a three-bedroom Victorian villa and converted it into a high-tech loft. There was no hallway. A visitor walked straight into a large airy space, combined from three rooms. The walls were white. An exposed metal staircase led to a gallery, where there big green plants and a pale blue Conran settee.

Stacia worked downstairs. Her desk looked over a small back yard, which she had added a pond to and filled with interesting plants.

Rick liked her house very much. Although he was not into minimalism, he liked its sense of order – perhaps imposed because her life had been chaotic before. On a previous visit, he had wondered how she could afford all this. Perhaps it had something to do with an advance from a record company. He never inquired too closely.

He knew that Stacia made a good living as a freelance writer and graphic designer. She was great with Apple Macs. Something he used to phone her up and ask her questions, when his computer was making him go mad.

It was pitch black now. Rick stood on her doorstep, looking and feeling terrible. He pressed the bell. Stacia was wearing faded combat trousers and an orange tee shirt, not too far in color from her hair.

Her face was pale and she wore lots of make-up. Stacia was nearly always cheerful. She was now. She was very small. She barely came up to his shoulder.

"Jesus," she said, "you look fucking awful. What happened?"

"It's a long story."

She motioned him inside. Her house was like a big, light cave. The time he had been here before was Stacia's house warming party. Warm would be the wrong word for the house now – it was cool and very controlled. But he found it comforting.

He placed his pannier on the carpet, sat down and buried his head in his hands. He started to tremble.

Rick felt the urge to cry. But he knew that he would not.

"All you all right, Rick?" She was standing in front of him, with her hands on her hips. She looked small and fragile. "Would you like a drink?"

It wasn't a difficult decision. She poured him a large vodka, with a splash of tonic. Vodka was his favorite spirit.

As he took a first sip, he realized that there was music playing in the background. She must have turned the sound down when he rang the bell.

"Well, Mr. Gilliver," she said. "What an earth has been going on?"

He told her the entire story, from his meeting with Adam. He even told her about the rage incident with Karen that afternoon. It seemed like a million years before. Stacia had worked with Karen and knew how infuriating she was. They used to laugh about it together. Rick told Stacia about the peculiar text messages from Adam how worried he was about his safety.

"What are you going to do now?"

"Could I have a bath?"

"Of course. Afterwards, I mean."

He shrugged.

"I have no idea."

After his bath, they drank vodka and listened to music – it was a Beck CD. That night, Adam slept on the settee. He felt groggy and warm, his fear smothered by the vodka. He realized that night how much he liked Stacia. Not many people would welcome someone into their house in these circumstances, in the middle of the night.

She was up early the next morning. That day she was working for a firm of architects in the West End, producing some glossy brochure for them.

She padded down the stairs at about seven o'clock. Her face was paler in the mornings, her hair standing up. She went into the kitchen and made herb tea for herself, filter coffee for him. He got up and they had breakfast.

Her kitchen was the only other room on the ground floor. It had a big stripped pine table, granite work surfaces and cabinets with pale green doors. The back door was glazed. It gave a glimpse of flagstones and herbs in pots. Stacia's cat, Jagger, came to join them. He was big, grey tomcat.

As he ate his Marmite on toast, Rick realized that he felt content. One of the reasons was simple. He wouldn't be going to work today. Nearly always he was running somewhere, worried about something. His old life had suddenly been taken away from him. But for how long?

He liked looking at Stacia. He liked talking to her. It had only taken her a few minutes to change from her disheveled morning self into a happy, positive person.

"Well, I've got to go," she said.

"Oh." He was disappointed.

She looked surprised.

She said that she would buy him some clothes – he would need them – and that she would make a nice dinner. Rick felt happy. No one ever cooked for him. He said that he would help her.

"OK."

He felt, for a moment, like giving her a kiss. He wished her a nice day. She looked back, framed in the doorway. Then the door clicked shut.

Stacia's workspace was unusually tidy. In Gilliver's experience, creative people were often neat. The incompetent tended to have clutter around them. It went with their tantrums.

Rick had had asked Stacia if it was OK to use her computer, which was a G4, and her text scanner. She said to do whatever he wanted.

He was gazing out of the window, wondering how to get started, when he heard a thump. He was a bit worried. Then he realized what it was. A newspaper dropping onto the floor. Having your paper delivered was a unusual luxury for London. Perhaps living in Walthamstow wasn't so bad.

Rick could see the newspaper from where he was sitting. He went to fetch it. At the bottom of page three was an interesting little story.

Millennium wheel booked for London mayoral debate

London's leading mayoral candidates have been offered a platform in the Millennium Wheel, for tomorrow's Big Wheel Debate. Each candidate will be filmed by TV cameras, describing their plans for the capital city.

The event is to go ahead tomorrow morning, despite increased fears of attacks on the capital from Al Qaida terrorists. It was the brainchild London minister, Emma Henderson.

Ms. Henderson said: "This is a great way to give the candidates a soapbox, to put across their ideas and visions. It will also send out a clear signal to the terrorists that Londoners have absolutely no intention of giving up their daily business."

The candidates set to appear in the debate are current mayor of London, Ken Livingstone (Labour's candidate), Thomas Dawkins (Conservative), Sally Green (Liberal Democrat), Kevin Williams (Socialist alliance), John Foster (UK Independence party) and Montague de Lorean Mousetrap (Monster Raving Loony).

He remembered the last text message from Adam, the one about the Millennium Wheel and Ken Livingstone. Suddenly, it made sense. She could kill the mayor using an explosive device, taped to one of the wheel's viewing pods. Cast adrift from its mount, Ken's pod would drift down through the spokes of the wheel. It would shatter on the embankment, like a Christmas tree bauble, or drift down the Thames – a cracked Perspex egg, smeared with blood.

The following evening, the same piece of film would be shown on television over and over again. Digitally captured images would be blown up to a huge size in all of the papers. Perhaps there would be a picture of white faces peering out, as they plunged to their doom.

In his imagination, Rick heard Emma's voice. She would say on the news how tragic it was, in her silky, patronizing voice, but that we must not stop the elections, because "that's what the terrorists would have wanted". Politicians always said that.

In a Commons statement, the minister for London would pay tribute to Ken Livingstone – "a tireless champion for the people of the capital. We did not always agree, but I had great respect for his commitment to the people of London."

She would try to appear said, but in the photographs her expression would look more like a smirk of triumph.

Rick's first job was to scan in the New Labour papers, page-by-page, typing in hand-written additions, that the scanner could not understand. It took almost an hour. When he had finished, there was a new electronic version of the document on the desktop of the Mac. He thought of making this into a pdf file. But he didn't know how, so he left it in Word.

His next task was to set up a directory of people to email the document to as an attachment. He started with Stacia's address book and added names of his own – news and features editors on national papers and trade magazines, TV producers and researchers, politicians, friends who worked in the media and Private Eye, the satirical magazine.

He wrote an email, explaining who he was and what he had found, hinting at the role of Emma Henderson. He said that his life had been threatened. He said that there was a plan to attack Ken Livingstone, during the following day's mayoral debate. He did not give precise details. Rick said that the information was not libelous. For one reason. Because it was true.

At the end of the message, he gave his mobile number. Finally, he sent the email to every person on his contacts list. Later, he would phone the people he had emailed and start telling them his story.

Finally, he had to phone in sick. Getting the timing right for a sicky is important. You have to phone after people are wondering where you are, but not so late as to suggest dishonesty, or indifference.

At precisely twenty past ten, he told Karen that he had been struck down by a tummy bug. It must have been a dodgy curry. He tried to do this in a weak, brave voice. Karen's voice sounded tight. He could tell that she was seething underneath.

"What am I going to do, Rick?"

"You're the assistant editor. Listen ..." He took her through what stories to write, the main elephant traps that could trip her up on that week's issue. The thought struck him, at that moment, that he had never trusted her to do most of this stuff before. And that his contempt for her must be de-motivating.

"Will you be in tomorrow?" she said, almost pleading.

"I don't know. Have to see how it goes."
"Rick, you have to. I don't know if I can ..."
"Goodbye Karen." He put the phone down.

11

Tabloids

Potty, botty, totty. That's the level one is dealing with. A puerile baby world, on the threshold of consciousness. Unfortunately, the tabloids are important. If people want to have their genitals tickled and bright dangly things bounced in front of their eyes, there's not very much we can do about it.

- The New Labour papers

Rick started phoning people at eleven o'clock. The problem was, nobody was really interested in what he had to say. When he got through, he was met with indifference and incomprehension, even from the people he knew. He grew tired of hearing his voice giving the same repetitive explanation of the New Labour papers. It sounded mad.

Only one person that Tuesday morning would listen to his story, a reporter on the Newcastle Journal, who was bored and who had nothing else to do. The reporter humored him, half mockingly. They went through the whole thing – who had been killed and why, how New Labour had slithered its way through two elections and how its wheels had been oiled by Emma Henderson.

The Geordie reporter said that it was a fantastic story but that it was the most libelous thing he had ever heard. The conversation ended.

He gave up trying in the middle of the afternoon. He felt tired and dispirited. But he knew that the email he had sent out would have consequences. People would be talking about it. Sooner or later, tentacles of rumor would entangle Emma Henderson's group of friends. The minister for London would start to feel vulnerable.

He thought about Adam, wondering what he should do. He phoned Adam's mobile a few times. He left some voice mails and he sent text messages. But there was no reply. Adam had gone cold.

At four o'clock, he paid a visit to Stacia's little corner shop, to buy an early edition of the Standard. There was a whole two-page feature in the paper about tomorrow's Big Wheel Debate, with profiles of the candidates and descriptions of their policies. There was a story saying how innovative the debate was and how it had all been Emma Henderson's idea.

Rick made a cup of tea and a peanut butter sandwich. He watched some TV, but the programs were all crap – Australian soaps and crass word games. He wasn't very good at doing nothing. He decided to play around on the Internet.

One of the bookmarked sites was Stacia's own website, www.staciashipley.com. It was colorful and well designed but tasteful and business-like, just like she was. He was still sitting in front of the computer when he heard her key turn in the front door. He felt guilty and furtive, because he was on the net, as if he was doing something wrong.

Stacia was as fresh and cool as a walk on the embankment. She was weighed down with carrier bags. In them were vegetables and groceries from Berwick Street market and his new clothes, from Gap in Oxford Street – two pairs of combats, three polo shirts and a dark green fleece, with a hood.

Rick was really touched. No one had ever bought him clothes before, apart from his mother. And no one had ever bought him clothes that he actually liked. She noticed that the computer was on.

"What are you doing?"

"I was visiting your website."

It sounded a bit rude. She gave him a funny look.

"Do you like it Rick?"

"Yeh, I love it."

~ ~ ~

Later, Stacia cooked a vegetarian couscous and salad for dinner. Rick put some music on. He was surprised to discover that Stacia liked opera. He opened a bottle of rioja. Stacia told him about her day, the humorless people that she was working with and their weird office politics.

She asked him about his day. He explained the scanning and emailing, his fruitless phoning of newspapers. Then he told her his theory that Ken Livingstone would be murdered in the Millennium Wheel.

"I used to work for Ken," she said.

"Really?"

"Yeh, when he was leader of the Greater London Council."

"What was he like?"

"He was a great guy. Really casual. He only used to wear a suit and tie when he had to meet people. He was dead friendly and easy to talk to. Had a temper on him though."

"What do you mean?"

Stacia smiled. He did not pursue it.

"Listen," she said. "I have Ken's email address and his mobile number in my Filofax. Have you told him about all this? I mean, that someone is going to try and kill him?"

"No."

"Don't you think that you should?"

"Yeh, why not. I'll do it. Where is your Filofax?"

"In my bedroom. I'll go and get it, shall I?"

He looked into her eyes. Should he? Why not?

"Can I come?"

"Of course."

He followed her up the stairs to the heavenly sound of the aria Vissi d'arte from Tosca, by Puccini.

~ ~ ~

Much later. Two o'clock in the morning. Bedding in lazy drifts. Stacia's white body, her smudged eyes. He ran his fingers down her vertebrae. She turned round. Now he could look into her eyes for as long as he wanted.

Stacia told him about the time when she had been in her band, Razor Blade. She had lived in a decrepit block of flats off the Cut, near Waterloo. She told him about her friends – Keith, the Asian skinhead, Sniper, Mad Dog and Sniveling Bob, a man who blew his nose on crisp packets.

The band played loads of pub gigs and made one vinyl album. That was just before the lead guitarist in her band, who was her lover, had killed himself – ironically, by cutting his wrists. The band had split up shortly after that. Afterwards, she had moved to Stoke Newington with Sniper, the Scottish punk. He had turned out to be a psychopath.

Rick told Stacia about his dislocated childhood. He told her about his university days in Warwick and his band, the Magic Mushrooms, about squatting in Kentish Town and meeting Carol, just before he had got into journalism. He told her about Gina and how they were going through a difficult patch, what with her turning into the teenager from hell.

Stacia laughed.

It was a thick duvet. Rick felt flushed and sweaty. He knew that he was drinking too much.

"I'm sorry," he said.

"Don't be stupid."

She looked him.

"I've got really unhealthy. I never used to be like this."

"You know why, don't you?"

"Because I'm an alcoholic?"

"It's not just that. Your whole diet is all wrong. Your body is full of toxins."

He had tried before to live without coffee, alcohol and chocolate. But their psychoactive properties were indispensable. Usually, the experiment lasted until his next deadline. Eating junk made him feel depressed, so he ate more. The same as most people.

He looked away, confused. Stacia read his mind.

"I didn't mind did I?"

"Yes, but ..."

"Are you saying that I would sleep with anybody?"

"They would have to have a pulse."

She threw off the duvet. Rick decided to try and improve his diet. Tomorrow.

~ ~ ~

Bob Clack's office was similar to Richard Gilliver's at Planning Today, only far larger. It had more desks, more computers, more harassed men in their shirtsleeves, more cool, well-coiffed women, more glass cages.

Clack was senior reporter on the Sunday World, a down market, kiss n' tell tabloid. His newspaper took up an entire floor of a large open-plan office in London's docklands. He was a stout, middle-aged man, with thinning grey hair. He was portly and somewhat shorter than the proportions of his limbs would have suggested. In some ways, he looked like a puppet.

Clack was a damp man – his thin strands of hair, his palms and his lips were permanently moist, even on cold days. He was friendly and self-confident, but there was something vaguely unsavory about him. He had the air of a person who spends his time sniffing dustbins in rancid alleyways and listening to private conversations in darkened rooms. There was a reason for this. He did.

Sexual entrapment was Clack's specialty – kinky vicars, three-in-a-bed sex romps, pedophile scout masters, that kind of thing. The previous year he had exposed two premiership footballers, a brothel-keeping estate agent and a Church of England bishop.

Tuesday is the first day of the week for the Sundays. Clack was at his desk at nine, sorting through his emails. Most of the messages were get rich quick junk, ways to enlarge your penis, deranged pleadings from weirdos and scam merchants. The spam thing was getting ridiculous. The email from Richard Gilliver was the eighty-seventh that he opened that morning. It had been forwarded to him by his news editor.

Clack saw two words, Emma Henderson, and became interested. He read the email, opened the attachment and printed it off. His was licking his wet lips as the New Labour papers came off the laser printer. Clack had good instincts and they had been honed by years of experience.

The senior reporter knew a lot more about Ms. Henderson than most people did. In fact, he had been thinking about her a lot recently. Two weeks before, he had been phoned by a man with a cockney accent. The man said that his sister was a cleaner at the Think Tank nightclub at the Elephant. She had got hold of a videotape. It was porn. But there was something interesting about it. One of the people in it seemed to be that politician, Emma Henderson.

"Really, are you sure?" said Clack. It was a busy Thursday afternoon. He was tired and his nerves were frayed. He had run into this kind of story before. Nearly always, they were garbage.

"Course I'm sure. It's 'er, Emma 'Enderson."

"How do you know?"

"I know that she has sex in the club sometimes, in the manager's office. There's this one-way mirror and he's been filming her, hasn't he? Only she don't know about it."

"Yeh?" Clack was not convinced. Listlessly, he arranged to see the video. He said that he would send a bike round to pick it. The man was not sure. Clack reassured him. He said he would give him a receipt for the video. If the story were pukkah, he would be looking at a big check. At least five figures.

He watched it that evening in the news editor's office with an "expert", the editor's PA. She had chatted to Emma Henderson at a garden party, the previous summer.

The tape was disgusting. The lack of a sound track made it particularly squalid, as did the banality of the setting – a black settee, office furniture. The three participants did not seem to know that they were being filmed. It was like CCTV, shot in some depraved car park.

The editor's PA fled from the room after about two minutes. Even Clack was shocked and he had seen some sights. There seemed no doubt that Emma Henderson was in the video, being serviced by two well-muscled young men, with greased, orange bodies. They took it in turns to have sex with her. The film ended with both men ejaculating. She grinned idiotically.

Clack and the news editor composed imaginary headlines Yes, yes, yes minister, cum cum, and so on. None of their usual hand-me-down adjectives – depraved, sordid, wicked, disgusting – seemed at all adequate somehow.

"Fuck me," said Clack.

~ ~ ~

The following week, Clack firmed up Emma Henderson's connection with the Think Tank. He established that the minister was still seen there, occasionally, at show biz dos. She had been photographed outside the club with Nigel De Vere, a couple of months before.

He had some digital shots taken in De Vere's office by a photographer smuggled in by the cleaner who had obtained the tape, to see if the settee and decor matched those in the videos. They did. But that proved nothing. The woman in the video could still have been a double.

There was only one way to nail Emma Henderson. And that was to photograph her at it, through the one-way mirror. They would need De Vere's help. Normally, Clack would have thrown money at the guy. Trouble was, he was a millionaire.

Clack would have to put pressure on him. He would threaten to expose the club as a brothel and drugs den, to make De Vere co-operate, as well as offering him money. Only when there was irrefutable proof, would the money for the original video would be handed over.

That was as far as Clack had got, when he received the email from Rick. Now the story was even better. Henderson was not just a pervert. She was also, potentially, a murderer. It was bigger than Profumo, bigger than fucking Watergate. That's what he told his news editor, at the editorial conference that Tuesday morning.

12

Livingstone, Ken
Don't be fooled. He's a reasonable fantatic. Stalin in a cardigan. He wants power, he's as slippery as a condom and he'll use exactly the same techniques as us to get it. Creating a mayor of London could create an opening for him. Watch carefully.

- The New Labour papers

Rick did not so much wake up that Tuesday morning as never get to sleep. He felt dreamy and sated from love making, physically content, but also knackered. It was a strange combination.

It was six o'clock. Light was slanting through Stacia's Ikea blinds. He had not woken up with a woman for a long time. Stacia was breathing softly, lying on her back. He wanted to touch her small white breasts, to caress her sleep-softened face. But he did not. He just lay there, looking at her.

She stirred and murmured something. Her eyes half opened and she reached for him.

Afterwards, he got up to make some filter coffee. He knew that he shouldn't drink the stuff. It was poisonous. He needed to attach jump leads to his tired body.

Stacia had to go to her job in the architects' office that morning. She left him on the doorstep with a deep, lingering kiss. He felt as though he had been filled with helium.

He pottered around for a bit. At nine o'clock, he made a phone call.

"Hello."

"Hi, my name is Rick Gilliver. Is that Ken Livingstone?"

"Yes. How did you get this number?"

"From someone who used to work for you."

"Who?" There was an edgy pause.

"Stacia Shipley."

"I see. Well, what do you want?"

"You know the Millennium Wheel debate later this morning?"

"Yes."

"Well, I think that someone is er ... going to try and kill you."

"Sorry?"

"I think that your pod on the wheel will fall off. The person behind it is Emma Henderson. I have also emailed you, this morning, a copy of the New Labour p ..."

"Thank you. Good bye."

It was a pity that you could not slam down mobiles, Ken thought. Fucking nutter. There were far too many of them these days.

He was in his bedroom in Cricklewood, selecting a jacket for the debate. Since he only possessed two "good" jackets, the choice was not too difficult. He wondered whether he should wear a tie. No, he decided. For this job, he could be informal.

Over breakfast, he made some notes on a scrap of paper, folded it and tucked into the breast pocket of his shirt. He was looking forward to going up in the wheel and talking about London.

~ ~ ~

After the call, Rick felt stupid. He debated whether to phone Ken Livingstone again, but he decided against it. Fuck it, he thought, unworthily, let him die then. He knew that it would take about an hour to reach the wheel and he wanted to be early. It was a five-minute walk from Stacia's house to the tube station. He caught the Victoria line to Green Park, then the Jubilee line to Waterloo.

The Jubilee line was the newest addition to the underground. It had been intended for the ill-starred millennium celebrations. At first, the line had been the system's glory, designed by famous architects, its stations, in muted silver and grey, were awe-inspiring. Now, the fashionably exposed concrete was streaked with mildew, the pipes were tarnished. The Jubilee Line was a ramshackle mess, held together with yellow and black hazard tape. London Transport had claimed the line as its own.

Rick turned left out of the tube station and made his way to Waterloo Bridge. It was a grey, blustery day. He joined the network of ramps and underpasses that begins at the Hayward Gallery and walked along the South Bank. He was wearing the green fleece and the combats that Stacia had bought him. His hands were thrust into the patch pockets and the hood was up. He felt like one of those white middle class kids who pretends to be an LA gangster.

It would be great to come here with Stacia on a Sunday, he thought. That was his favorite day for visiting the South Bank. He liked exploring the bookstalls in front of the British Film Institute. He could spend hours there. He liked the clunk of the skateboards, the way that the sooty arches of Hungerford Bridge boxed you in, the melancholy buskers and the snatches of pretentious conversation. The South Bank was a perfect remnant of the 1960s, seedy, exotic and a little dangerous. If they ever tried to re-develop the South Bank, he thought, they would only ruin it.

Looming ahead of him, by Westminster Bridge, was the Millennium Wheel, the London Eye. Audacious and beautiful, it was a perfect alignment of form and function. The wheel's main structure was a thick white column, anchored by steel guy ropes. It was as massive and unapologetic as something that the Victorians would have built. The wheel was so huge that it made County Hall, behind it, look like a doll's house. It was a paradox – an ephemeral object made solid, a still thing that was actually moving. The wheel's thirty-two aerodynamically designed pods nudged through the air so slowly that, at first, you barely noticed that they were moving.

He had been up in the wheel once, with Gina and her in-laws. She had been sulking that day. He had wanted to point out landmarks to her, like a typical dad, but she had not been interested.

It was half past ten. The South Bank had been closed off, by the wheel, for the filming of the mayoral debate. There were outside broadcast vans trailing thick cables like jungle vines and men in puffer jackets looking busy and bored at the same time.

A little group of mayoral candidates stood with plastic cups of tea in front of a catering truck. One wore a well-cut grey suit and a blue silk tie. You cold see, from his highly polished brogues, his greased grey thatch and his sharp creases, that it was the Conservative candidate, Gerald Dawkins. He was an unsavory character, Rick thought, a market trader dressed up to the nines, selling bullshit. Women were said to find him attractive. God knows why.

Standing behind him, was Ken Livingstone. He was as familiar from the constant repetition of his image as a member of your own family. Livingstone was ignoring the attentions of a figure in a jester's hat, carrying a large cardboard fish. That would be the Monster Raving Loony. One of their policies was to turn the river Thames into a fish farm.

Rick was separated from the candidates by two sets of metal barriers, guarded by policemen with machine guns. He could not get close, even with his press card. Should he make a fuss? Be carried away protesting? He decided not to. It would be unseemly and, anyway, it would not make any difference. He cut through County Hall and made his way onto Westminster Bridge, to see what happened.

Nothing happened. One by one, the candidates entered the pods, as the wheel turned with agonizing slowness. Ken was the last to get in. Rick watched the mayor's silhouettes, making expansive gestures as he laid out his stall for London. Rick remained on the bridge with a crowd of people for an hour.

Afterwards, he did not want anyone to see him. Shoulders hunched, he made his way down Westminster Bridge Road, feeling utterly miserable. He was passing the bus stop in front of St. Thomas' Hospital, when his phone chirruped.

"Hello."

"Hi. Is that Rick Gilliver? Bob Clack here, Sunday World."

Rick did not say anything.

"I got your email, Rick, and I'm quite interested. How much do you know about Emma Henderson?"

That she murdered people? The thing with journalists was not to give them too much.

"I don't think we should talk on the phone," he said. "We should meet somewhere."

"Name a place, Rick."

His mind went completely blank, as if he was a Japanese tourist, just off the plane. Clack jumped in.

"Do you know the Hippodrome night club, in Charing Cross Road?"

"Yeh."

"I'll meet you there, in about an hour?"

Rick wasn't doing anything else and he did not need to think. He just said OK.

It was just like Clack to choose one of the tackiest place in London. Rick was there first. Clack was easy to recognize – a perspiring man in a belted raincoat, prizing himself out of a black cab, ostentatiously removing notes from his wallet.

When they shook, Clack's hand felt as wet and nerve-less as a sponge. They walked down Cranbourn Street, towards Leicester Square. There weren't many tourists about. A fitful wind tossed leaves around a deserted miniature fairground.

They went into Yates's – a pub, cafe hybrid full of backpackers – and sat at the back. Clack ordered two coffees. Rick felt strange, as if he were a character in a film. It felt nice not to be at work though. He didn't have to shave.

"Tell me more about Emma Henderson." Clack's pupils moved rapidly, as if he was scanning a page proof. Rick explained how he had been phoned by Adam and given the New Labour papers and how someone had tried to kill him, in Sainsbury's. He told Clack that Adam had been kidnapped and taken somewhere. He had no idea where.

"Where are the New Labour papers now?"

"They're hidden at my girl friend's house."

"They're not in her knicker drawer are they?"

"No, why?"

"It's the first place they'll look."

It's the first place you would look, thought Rick.

"So who else did you email them to?"

Rick went through the list – the Daily Mail, The Guardian, The Observer, Private Eye ...”

“OK. I get the picture.” Clack took a sip from his latte. “You will need to give me the original document, Rick. Is that all right?”

“I hadn't really thought about it.”

“We'll keep them secure for you, locked up in our safe in the office, with the pictures of the Queen Mother. They'll be sound as pound, I assure you.”

Rick shrugged.

“You're thinking about money, aren't you?”

Rick was not thinking about money.

“How does five grand sound?”

He did not say anything. He was shocked.

“OK, ten grand. But that's tops. I've spent far too much money on this fucking story already. We'll give you half when you hand over the document, the other half when the story is published. I don't think it will be this Sunday. Probably next. We'll have to move fairly quickly, because there may be other people onto this.”

Ten grand. Suddenly, Rick started to smile. That was six months' salary. The eel would continue rotting in her fish tank. He would be at Stacia's, surfing the net and watching daytime soaps.

“Which charity would you like to give the money to, Rick?”

“What?”

Clack winked. “Only kidding.”

Clack said that the next stage was to work on De Vere. They would get his office wired up and bug his phone. They would get Emma Henderson over to the De Vere's office and record the two of them talking. They would also take pictures of her having sex with someone, if that was humanly possible. It was short notice, but he was going to try to set this up the following night.

The sting would give them more evidence. With audiotape, pictures and the New Labour papers, the case against Emma Henderson would be solid. It would be the Sunday World's biggest ever story.

Rick would need to listen in on the recorded conversation, because of his "special knowledge", and to help out with factual background to the story. The Sunday World could take him on, as a consultant.

"How are you fixed, Rick, for money I mean?" Clack's fat little hand was reaching for his wallet. "Have this to be going on with."

He removed two hundred pounds, in twenty-pound notes.

"If you need to stay in a hotel, just let me know. We'll get it sorted. My feeling is that you won't need to. From what you've told me, every journalist in the fucking country knows what you have and your phone number. I don't think that Henderson would dare to touch you. But if you fancy kipping in a hotel for a bit, with your lady, just let me know."

Rick thought about it.

"Oh and one more thing, Rick."

"What's that?"

"You don't talk to any other print or broadcast journalist about this, right? You are now the property of the Sunday World. Every inch of you. We fucking own you. Is that understood?" He made eye contact. "Deal?"

He stretched out his clammy hand. Monogrammed links secured his cuffs.

"Yeh, it's a deal."

They shook hands for the second time.

Clack smiled. He placed a grubby note on the table, next to the empty cups. Before they left he placed his arm around Rick's shoulders and gave him a fatherly squeeze.

13

Influence
First, find out what a person wants most. It could be sex, it could be fame, it could be the love of their child. Then threaten to deny it them. They will do whatever you want.

- The New Labour papers

Spider was a twat. He had always been a twat. He was a twat at Stockwell Primary School, when he told the head master that he and Trevor had set fire to that Indian gentleman. He was a twat when he joined the army at seventeen. He was a twat when he had a cobweb needled onto his forehead in Wandsworth prison, in Biro ink. "Is that the man you saw on the night in question?" "Yes sir. It was the man with the blue cobweb tattooed on his head."

Now Spider was shivering in a cold, wet alleyway. He was only wearing jeans and a T-shirt. He had been socializing in the Think Tank when Trevor had tapped him on the shoulder and said he wanted to have a word with him, outside.

"You fucking little idiot."

Trevor loomed above him, in the narrow space. He was in his work gear. Black shoes, black trousers, white shirt, black jacket, with silk lapels.

"Trev, leave it out ..."

Whack. Trevor's thick-soled shoe made contact with Spider's scrawny chest. One of his ribs gave way. He started gasping. His lungs had been tarred up and squeezed out by twenty years of smoking Marlborough Lights.

"You cretin. Trying to kill someone on a bike, in a fuckin' supermarket. What was you thinkin' of?"

A noise like a rusty harmonium was coming from Spider's throat, with each breath.

"I was tryin to make things right, Trev."

"Yeh, for the fact that you left the mobile phone in that gobshite's pocket. You made me look like a fucking amateur, Darren. I do not like that."

Trevor drew back his right foot.

Spider squirmed, trying to make himself small. A light rain was falling. Trevor did not want to get his jacket wet, or he probably would have spent more time at his task. He settled for a short hard jab. It shattered the cartilage in Spider's nose.

"Trev, we went to fuckin' ..." Spider's voice sounded nasal. It was quite comic.

... school together, Trevor finished Spider's sentence in his mind.

"I know we did, you little fucker. That's why I'm going to do this wivout fuckin' hurting you."

"No, Trev, please ..."

Spider's eyes went big. He stopped squirming.

Trevor put his hand in his jacket pocket and removed his piece - a silver 0.25 Beretta. It was a small, neat little thing, like a toy really. But very effective at close range.

Spider knew it was all over. He remembered their first day at primary school. Trevor had thumped him in the mouth and made him bleed.

"Trev, mate, please ..."

One shot. One hole between the eyes. It was a clean kill. Just a flattened nose, the bashed-in rib cage, the entry and exit wounds and some blood dripping from the mouth. The gun would have to be disposed of.

Trevor regretted the loss of his weapon. He had never killed anyone with it before. It was just one of them things. He also regretted having paid for Spider's operation to remove the tattoo and that he had given him a job at the Think Tank, as a door supervisor.

Spider was too small to be a credible bouncer. He tried to build himself up, with weight supplements. But it didn't work. He was too slow for bookwork. And he embarrassed everybody, boasting and trying to pull women. He was too cocky and he got nasty when he didn't get his way. Trevor had a last look at Spider's flattened face and the scar on his forehead. It was the crust on top of a saucepan of boiled milk. Waste of money, that fucking operation.

He disposed of Spider himself. He bundled up the skinny corpse in black bin liners. The next morning, he drove out to Kent, in the white Astra. Trevor knew some blokes in the building trade out that way. Spider's body was cut into pieces and thrown into some footings. His remains joined the foundations of a new supermarket, on the outskirts of Sevenoaks. It was an Asda.

~ ~ ~

Two men in a hotel room. One, short and perspiring, is mopping his forehead in the bathroom. The other sits on the bed. The one on the bed is wearing headphones. He is listening to a crackling sound that also comes through a small loudspeaker.

It is a Thursday night. Outside, red lights shine from tower cranes. Building sites and half-finished office blocks are simplified by the dark.

"Is it working, Rick?" The short man comes out of the bathroom, toweling his hands.

Rick looks up. "Yeh, I think so." The hissing turns into a clear signal.

They had chosen the Docklands Marriott Hotel because it was right distance from the Think Tank. It was also close to the Sunday World's building. They were using a radio microphone, hidden in a picture frame in De Vere's office. There was also a telephone bug. They could switch from one to the other, as required.

When Clack had phoned Nigel De Vere, asking him to rat on Emma Henderson, he had expected to be given a hard time. In fact, it was ridiculously easy. De Vere told him that she was an evil little bitch. He had made the porno tape as an insurance, to stop her from stitching him up at a later stage. The Ice Maiden's associates tended to end up either feeding fishes or holding up buildings.

At first, De Vere said, it had been useful and fun knowing Emma. She had sorted out the Think Tank's entertainment and fire safety licenses, by greasing palms at the council. But she was really straight. And, since her promotion to minister, she had become an arrogant cow. De Vere said that he would be only too pleased to help the Sunday World in any way he could –"I was naive, says duped millionaire". He said that it would not be right for him to take any money. Clack was delighted by that.

De Vere phoned Emma Henderson and asked her to come over to the Think Tank at nine o'clock that night for a "surprise". That was normally code for sex or drugs.

Clack stood at the foot of the hotel bed. Rick was concentrating. He had a reporter's pad on his knee, ready to make notes from the conversation. He did not need to, because everything was being recorded.

A mile and half away. De Vere leans back in his office chair, his feet on his desk. Emma Henderson is stretched out on the black leather settee. She reaches occasionally for a tumbler of whisky and coke on a glass-topped table. Also on the table is a small mirror, smeared with white powder. A vague thumping noise throbs through the floor. The club is open for business but it has not really got going yet.

Emma is only partially dressed. Her blouse is open to the waist and she has no bra on. She is wearing black stockings but her white silk thong is lying somewhere near De Vere's feet. After smoking some ganja to loosen her up, she has just been made love to by an energetic young boxer, who uses Trevor Jones' gym in the Old Kent Road. His name is Vincent.

The Sunday World's photographer has taken more two hundred needle sharp images with his Cannon digital camera, from behind the one-way mirror.

For publication, the newspaper will make the pictures look blurry, as if they had been taken on the hoof. A good shot to use, the photographer thought, would be the boxer from behind. They could crop off his buttocks. The picture would show the minister's face tilted back in ecstasy, just before her orgasm.

They also had some images of the Middlewich MP snorting lines of coke, before the sordid sex session. A picture like that was priceless in terms in syndication, especially as Emma Henderson was an outspoken opponent of hard drugs.

As he talks, De Vere tries not to look at the poster on his wall, which shows the club's logo in day-glo colors. He also tries to keep his eyes from Emma's small brown nipples.

Clack had told De Vere that the microphone hidden behind the mirror would pick up anything, from a whisper to a scream, anywhere in the room. De Vere is trying to make his words sound natural, a bit like acting. Don't push it, take your time, Clack had said.

Feed the rope out slowly and Henderson will hang herself.

"Fuck, fuck, fuck ..." The minister had spilled some of her drink on the table. Her hands were trembling. Clack and Rick heard the words distinctly. Rick wrote fuck x 3 on his pad, in shorthand.

"Sorry, Nigel. What did you say? No, we didn't blow the pod to kill Ken. Couldn't you see? God knows who Alan Baker told about the Millennium Wheel thing, when he was locked in your little torture chamber. Where is he, by the way?"

De Vere tapped his cheek. The gesture indicated that the corpse had been disposed of in such a way that it would never be found.

"Are you sure darling? That's good. You know Trevor used to be really reliable. He must have got rusty over the years. He was a rotten fuck though. Not like you, Nigel."

There was a curious expression on her face. She placed a fingertip near the top of her neatly trimmed pubic hair. Nigel had a ridiculous hard-on. He smiled weakly. He still had work to do. But would she think it suspicious if they did not have sex? He took a deep breath.

"So how are you going to deal with Ken now?" He regretted the question at once. It was too direct. Emma looked at him, quizzically. Her face was innocent. It was strange how their eyes were exactly the same shade of blue.

"I don't know ..."

Burn him alive. Chuck him off the top of the glass onion, City Hall? What was going through her mind?

"Are you still going to ...?"

"Kill him?" She paused. "Haven't decided yet. Murder is such a crude weapon. And now I've bloody well got this do deal with."

Rick heard a noise. It was a thump as she banged a rolled up magazine down on the glass table.

"Have you seen Private Eye? There's a nasty little article in it. It strongly suggests that I am the author of a document called the New Labour papers. It also implies that I have ordered the blackmailing and killing of political opponents."

"Well, you did, didn't you?"

"Of course. You don't get to be a minister by being nice darling. Look at poor old what's her name."

"Estelle Morris?"

"Exactly."

She placed her glass firmly on the table.

"So what are you going to do?"

"I'm going to sue Private Eye for every fucking penny I can. It's a shame that Carter Ruck is dead. He would have loved this one, the little snake. I am also going to make a statement in the House of Commons, on Monday. There is no real proof. Someone may have a copy of a document, which allegedly has my handwriting on it. But that is not going to get them very far, if it ever gets to court. Especially if we can get hold of the document first."

"How did Private Eye get hold of the story?"

"From Richard Gilliver."

"Who is he?"

"He is the editor of a tedious little magazine. He's the person that Alan Brown texted from your cupboard."

"How are you going to deal with Gilliver?"

The minister looked at De Vere, her eyes wide and blue. "What is this, Nigel, twenty flipping questions?"

"I'm sorry. I'm just interested.'

She looked into her glass. "I've been thinking about this. Gilliver has a child, a thirteen-year-old. We could kidnap her and hold her, unless he hands over the document and promises to keep his mouth shut. We can always arrange an accident for him, when things have quietened down."

"What if he goes to the police?"

"I don't think that he would risk it, do you?"

"I don't know."

Rick's face was burning. He had just heard the story – "Minister's evil plan to kidnap child". The problem was, he was in it.

De Vere had stood up. He was crossing from his desk, to pour himself another drink. He had finished reading the article that she had shown him in Private Eye. It was stained with whisky and cocaine.

"There's something in this that I don't understand."

"Yes?"

"What is the cyber project?"

She sniggered. "Nigel my love, I'm exhausted. No more questions, OK?"

"Nigel, my sweet?"

"What?"

She looked at him. She touched a moist fingertip to her mouth. "Aren't you going to make love to me?"

Nigel considered his options. He decided that he would just have to. Oh well. Slowly, he undid his belt.

~ ~ ~

Rick relaxed his shoulders. Clack was standing next to the hotel room's wall-length window, watching the dark. Canary Wharf, a pinpricked rectangle tipped by a gun-sight, dominated the view. It was Thatcher's monument – an ugly monolith, devoid of grace or imagination. A train was shuttling down the Docklands Light Railway, like a luminous blue bobbin. There was a large gin and tonic in Clack's hand. It was tough work, this surveillance. But someone had to do it. He was delighted with what they had, on tape and on camera. His news editor would be ecstatic.

They could hear rustling through the radio mike, as Nigel De Vere removed the rest of his clothes.

"Fucking little bitch," said Clack, advancing towards the bed. "Don't worry about your kid, Rick. We'll get her and your ex out of their flat tomorrow, and put them somewhere safe. Of that I promise you. I didn't think that she was that nasty."

"I did." Rick had taken his headphones off. He was massaging the back of his neck. "Do you thing we've got enough?"

"What do you think?" said Clack. "She as good as admitted that she has killed people and she said that he was going to kidnap your daughter. But it's the pictures that will nail her. If we've got the boy shagging her and her snorting coke she'll be out of office before you can say Basil Brush."

Clack phoned the Sunday World photographer on his mobile. The photographer said that the minister was having sex again, doggy style on the desk. Should he take any more pictures? Clack said yes, just for your own collection, winking. The snapper laughed. "OK boss," he said.

During their conversation, there was a light tap on the door. It was Stacia, carrying her overnight bag. The room had been booked for the night. She and Rick were to stay there. In her bag was a small bag of skunk.

Clack made his excuses and left, after assuring Rick that Gina and Carol would be safe. As he backed into the corridor, he winked, leering at Stacia.

"Have a good night Rick, mate."

"Yeh, thanks. I'll talk to you tomorrow."

The door closed.

For a moment, Rick wondered whether Clack, the perv, had rigged up a hidden camera in the room – "Sex-starved journalist's secret love nest".

Stacia seemed happy and relaxed. She had spent the evening in the bar, drinking vodka and fending off the attentions of predatory commercial travellers. They stood by the window, looking at docklands. Even at night, it was a frigid landscape, soulless, like an architect's drawing.

Rick took some miniatures from the mini-bar. Stacia went into the bathroom. He heard running water, then Stacia's voice.

"Come here, Rick."

She was naked. A lighted spliff was resting on the edge of the bath, filling the room with sweet smoke.

Hotel bathrooms are always over-supplied with mirrors, something that Rick had never liked – before.

Stacia sat on the edge of a hand-basin. As they made love, he watched, dispassionately, reflections of themselves.

After they had finished, they drank the miniatures in bed and ate Pringles. They looked at some soft porn on the pay-for-view channel and giggled. All the really sexy bits had been edited out. It was just like the Sunday World – emasculated nonsense.

14

Cyber project
Imagine if we could grow a politician. We could
give them the right face, and hair, and fill their head
with our language. He or she would always use the
right words and hit the right emotional register. I
believe that this may now be possible. An MP that we
started now could be foreign secretary by 2005 and
prime minister by 2009. Think about it.

- The New Labour papers

Prae Wood, near St Albans, was a rambling Victorian
building, with bay windows and stone walls,
standing in half a hectare of grounds. It looked like a
children's home or a cottage hospital. Once, Prae Wood
had been the headquarters of Section Five of British
Intelligence. Kim Philby had worked there, heading the
Iberian section. Now, a large sign announced its new
function. It said, in white letters, Department for the
Environment, Food and Rural Affairs – Agricultural
Technology Division.

In fact, no such division existed. In Philby's day
you could walk in off the pavement. The building was
guarded by a man in a wooden shed, next to the gate.
Now, in the age of New Labour, Prae Wood was
surrounded by a three-meter-high fence, topped with
barbed wire. Lethally armed men, with dogs, patrolled
its perimeter.

Most mornings, there would be a little gaggle of
protestors outside – eco-warriors with dreadlocks,

wrapped up in duffel coats. They believed that unholy experiments in biotechnology were being concocted behind the barbed wire – killer seeds with terminator genes that did not germinate, mice with wings, crops that glowed in the dark. In reality, something far more sinister was going on.

Derek Foxton flashed his pass and drove beneath the barrier. It was too early for the crusties with their pathetic banners. They were probably still in bed, or collecting their Jobseekers' Allowance. Lazy bastards. He drove his white Saab 9-5 to the rear of the building and parked it, efficiently. The car's sleek body was covered with miniature droplets. It was a grey, drizzly morning. Foxton's music stopped with the ignition. He had been listening to Bartok's third piano concerto.

He zapped on his car alarm, entered the building and murmured hello to Bob at the reception desk. Foxton checked his watch, as the wrinkled old man inspected his laminated card with its small photo, for the millionth time.

"OK, Mr. Foxton, sir, you can ..."

He was already striding down the corridor, towards his office.

Derek Foxton was not in Who's Who and never would be. But if he had been, his entry would have been bland. Born in 1955 in Chester-le-Street, attended St Asalph's Preparatory School, Durham, and Fettes College, in Edinburgh, the same school as Tony Blair. First class honors, Oxford University, in politics, philosophy and economics. Masters degree, Berkeley, in computing science. Here, the Who's Who description would have become vague, saying that he was a civil servant and that he did not belong to any clubs.

Although Foxton and Blair had been in different years at Fettes, Scotland's grandest public school, they had known each other. In those days, Foxy had always been tinkering with electrical things, making amplifiers, synthesizers and primitive computers. He was almost unnaturally clever, people thought, a tall, rangy boy with long brown hair. His clothes were permanently spotted with acid burns from chemical experiments. He smoked cannabis – all the interesting ones did – but he was never caught.

In May 1997, in the first euphoric weeks of New Labour, Foxton had received an important telephone call. It was Tony Blair's closest confidante, the new MP for Lancaster south, Geoffrey Juniper.

Juniper said in the call that he wanted Foxy to head up the Language Generation Unit. The language what? Juniper explained that it was a secret government department, vaguely attached to the Cabinet Office. It had begun in the 1940s. Its job was to create words and phrases, to buttress up whichever party was in power, and to brief politicians, civil servants and journalists in their use, so that they gained popular currency.

The unit had plodded along for decades, staffed by Oxbridge classicists, giving themselves something interesting to do. It was harmless and vaguely useful. Harold Macmillan indulged it. Although it was never officially credited, a bright spark at the LGU had come up with his catchphrase "you've never had it so good". This had undoubtedly helped Macmillan to win the 1959 general election.

Macmillan's successors, Harold Wilson and Ted Heath, largely ignored the LGU. Wilson was vaguely paranoid about it, as he was about most things. Officially, the unit did not exist. That's why Foxton had never heard of it. So where was it based? What did it do now? These were good questions, Juniper said.

The blessed Margaret Thatcher, he continued, had seen the value of the unit but had never fully exploited it. In the late 1980s, she increased its staff and moved it out from Westminster, to more spacious accommodation, in Hertfordshire, liberated by the thawing out of the Cold War. The unit was given a bigger budget and powerful new equipment. Thatcher was removed from Downing Street in November 1990 and her heir, John Major, became prime minister. Major was a nice man, a grey, well-meaning ditherer. The LGU's computers were never taken out of their boxes.

"Here's the thing," said Juniper (he had already told Foxton that he could call him Geoffrey). "To ensure our success, we will virtually need to invent a new language. That's where the LGU will come in. All speeches, press releases and consultation documents will have to go through the unit's computers to give them the right kind of spin. It will all be done using PCs and email. That way, we will have a complete grip on all of our linguistic output. Language and ideology are indivisible, you see. Control one and you control the other. In other words, language is power.

"When I say we. I mean you. I want you to head up the unit. You can beef up the IT side, develop new software. We thought that you would be the ideal chap, because of your unique er ... knowledge and your capacities."

"I see." Foxton was sitting in the hall, in his flat in Hornsey. He had a really boring job, working for a merchant bank. "Well, I. It's ..." He wondered how much a job like that would be worth. A lot probably. He said yes.

~ ~ ~

Seven years later, in February 2004, he walked into his Prae Wood office and hung up his coat. There was a black, ergonomic chair, a large desk, with a keyboard and monitor, two white filing cabinets, a few pot plants.

Tony Blair and his brood smiled from the wall, in a family group. Through the window, you could see a rectangle of grass, some conifers and a chain-link fence.

The LGU had expanded considerably since 1997. It now had more than thirty staff – linguists, policy wonks, technicians. They were well paid. Their Audis, BMWs, Volvos and Rovers filled the car park. The unit was equipped with the latest computers and connected by high bandwidth telephone lines to all government departments, quangos and agencies, from Cornwall to the Shetland Islands. The LGU was hard-wired into the political system. It had become the throbbing brain of a finely tuned electronic nervous system – in effect, a political machine.

It was eight-thirty. Foxton opened his briefcase. He removed his palm-top and connected it to a wire that trailed across his desk. He phoned an extension, to talk to a colleague, Chris Drake. Drake was on the morning shift. He would have started work half an hour before. Drake was a short, stocky man with lank hair, a graduate of Reading University. He was a carefree soul but his job had given him a worried frown. Like his boss, he was an oddball and a bit of a genius.

"Hi Chris," said Foxton, "how's it going?"

"Fine. Everything's hunky dory."

"How was the handover?"

"It was OK. There's only one thing. He's a bit knackered and I don't know why. But all the systems are working perfectly. Why don't you come and have a look?"

"OK, I will."

At the end of another corridor was a large, well-equipped Laboratory. Here, clever people were working on something even more secret than generating words and weaving language. Something that even Tony Blair did not know about. It was Prae Wood's most important task. The cyber project.

On one side of the room were a settee, comfortable chairs and a low table. A door led to a small kitchen. On the other, were control panels and banks of screens. You could tell, from the room's hushed, calm atmosphere and its stale air, that the cyber project was a 24-hour operation.

Foxton crossed the room to where Chris Drake was sitting, in front of a wide monitor. The screen showed the interior of a house. It was a modern kitchen in bright colors, yellows and blues.

"What's he doing at the moment?" asked Foxton.

"He's still having his breakfast."

A piece of buttered toast floated up to the base of the screen.

"Do you want the sound on?"

Foxton nodded.

They heard the mastication of jaws, a slithery, crunching sound, like the inside of a termite's nest.

"It's not pretty is it?" Chris turned to face Foxton. "At least it works though."

The angle of vision shifted. They were looking towards the right-hand side of the kitchen now, at a tall woman in her thirties. She had dark, straight hair and a pale complexion. She was dressed for a business meeting. A bit frumpy looking, Foxton thought. But sexy.

"I've already told you, Barry," she said, irritably. "I've got a really important meeting tomorrow night. We need to find someone to look after Frazer. I told you yesterday."

"OK. OK."

It was clear that an argument was looming. The woman's nerves were frayed. She was barely controlling her temper. Through the screen, they saw a disc of pale brown liquid. It was tea. It came up to meet a mouth. There was a disgusting guzzling sound, as if they were sitting inside a drain.

Most people would have thought it impossible to watch the world from inside another person's head. But this, in fact, was one of the lesser achievements of the cyber project.

~ ~ ~

The name of the person who they were looking through was Barry Triffit. Foxton had selected him from a number of candidates on Labour's back benches, after the '01 election. It needed to be someone pliable, who could be molded. Triffit was ideal. He was as dull as a bowl of vegetable soup.

He had been MP for Northampton since 1997. In the previous four fears, he had done nothing of note. He had conscientiously obeyed the whips, voting with the government every time, even when it was being cynical and power-crazed. His maiden speech had been judged by those who had witnessed it as the most boring in living memory.

Triffit reminded one sketch writer of a boy scout with a degree in politics. The MP listed his two main interests, without a trace of irony, as pensions and the footwear industry. He was a thickset man, with heavy jowls and thin dark hair, which he wore in a fringe, like a dilapidated curtain. Grey and beige were his favorite colors.

He had joined the Labour party when he was in his early twenties. After studying sociology at Birmingham University, he worked for the GMB union, as a policy researcher. He lived in Camden and became active in the Labour party there. Labour selected him for its Northampton constituency in 1996, just before the general election. Northampton was a good seat for him, because his hometown, Kettering, was only twenty miles away.

Triffit was a proud Blairite foot soldier. He promised his constituents, on election night, that he would be a breath of fresh air, blowing through the pensions and footwear industries. He would be a champion for freedom of information, devolution, a national minimum wage, the reform of the House of Lords, and more. He was on his way.

He was kidnapped in Northampton town center in February 2002. The MP went to Tesco's on a Friday evening and came home, vague and confused, in an ambulance on Monday morning. They told him in the ambulance that he had been mugged in the car park, knocked out and left unconscious. His wallet, containing his ID, had been stolen, so it had taken a long time to identify him. Triffit was in no position to contradict the story. He could not remember anything after getting out of his Ford Focus. He and his wife, Suzie, always referred to the two days as his "lost weekend".

In reality, he had been grabbed from behind in a car park, injected with a powerful anesthetic, bundled into the back of a car with diplomatic plates and driven down the M1 to Prae Wood.

First, Foxton made an incision and peeled back a flap of skin from the top of Triffit's head. Then he drilled a hole through his skull, the diameter of a small coin. He removed some brain material, using a technique similar to liposuction. This created a space for a nifty piece of kit that he had invented, a neuro-linguistic programmer.

Foxton used microsurgery to wire up the programmer to Triffit's optic nerves and to his brain. He was no surgeon, but he had read some books. His subject was anaesthetized with gas, and strapped into a dentist's chair, his head tipped back, under a spotlight. It didn't really matter if he something went wrong and he died, because they could always get another Labour MP. There were plenty of them.

When the programmer was connected, Foxton placed a plastic disc over the hole in Triffit' skull and sewed the skin back in place. There would be a small scar, just beneath the hairline. Triffit would be told in the ambulance that it had been caused by his accident.

Foxton was pleased with what he had done. He wiped his hands on a stained white tea towel. He smiled at Chris Drake, who had handed him the instruments during the procedure. Triffit's life functions were all normal.

"I feel a bit like Dr. Frankenstein," he joked.

"You look like him," said Drake.

The concept was beautifully simple. The neuro-linguistic programmer would shape how Triffit expressed himself and, consequently, how he saw the world. The programmer could be updated, by radio transmitter, as New Labour's concepts and terminology changed, so that he was always "on message".

Controllers would run the MP from Prae Wood at all times, splitting night and day into three eight-hour shifts. The controllers watched what Triffit saw through his eyes and heard what he heard, not through his ears but by means of an internal microphone. A controller could over-ride Triffit's speech with his or her own – the words would come out in his flat Northamptonshire accent – and could direct the movements of his body.

In most cases, this should not be necessary. Triffit's mental concepts, his linguistic patterns and all of his behavior would now be imbued with the spirit of New Labour. That would mean that he would never walk through the wrong lobby and vote against the government, never swear in public and never punch anyone on the jaw. He would be as pious as a vicar, with a strained sense of humor.

There was also a failsafe mechanism. It was a knob calibrated from mild headache, through flaming migraine, to epileptic fit and then brain hemorrhage. Triffit would have to be terminated if his secret was ever about to be discovered. Foxton was gambling on the fact that he would be able to retrieve the body before an autopsy was carried out. When the neuro-linguistic programmer had been slid out of his brain, only an innocent cavity would remain.

They tested the MP on Sunday afternoon. Later, they would wipe these memories from his mind – officially, he was in a coma for the weekend. Emma Henderson was in the control room when they tested him, giggling and hugging herself with glee.

She had a go at being a controller. She got Triffit to take his penis out and play with it. Then she made him get down on his knees and lick a toilet pedestal.

She said that Foxton had succeeded beyond her wildest dreams in achieving her ambition of "growing" a politician. The cyborg was perfect. She wanted one for Christmas.

"He'll make perfect lobby fodder," said the MP for Middlewich. "Any chance of you knocking out about four hundred more for the back benches?"

Foxton did not realize that this was a joke. "Could do, but it would take ages and we would need more than a thousand controllers. We would need something like a call center to run them from."

"I see." Emma Henderson smiled. "Well, never mind. This one will be perfect for the time being." She was beaming. "Foxy, you are now looking at the next prime minister. Or deputy prime minister. He'll make a lovely assistant with a bit of buffing up and some new clothes."

Barry Triffit had come back from the WCs. His penis was hanging from his trousers and he had an idiotic grin on his face."

"Hmmm," said Emma. "What should we do with him next? Ah, I know. I have an idea."

Foxton's body stiffened slightly.

"Oh come on Derek," she said, as she undid her black Gucci skirt, "what's the point in having a new toy if you can't play with it? Lighten up sweetie."

She looked into Foxton's eyes. "You don't have to watch. OK."

Foxton shrugged. He looked confused.

"That's much better," she said. "Now, where was I?"

15

Executive
The big one! Remember this is where power should be. Effectively it's the Cabinet (which, for public consumption, has only one voice), and the prime minister's Office (which should be greatly expanded). Our leader should be a president not a prime minister. Not difficult, because Parliament is a poodle.

- The New Labour papers

Emma Henderson stood at the dispatch box, with a single sheet of paper in her hand. Her heart was beating fast. The foot thumping and cheering from her own benches had died down. But sneers and jeers were crossing the floor from the other side. The Tories were trying to put her off.

She did not feel nervous, now that it was happening. She just had to remember to breathe properly and to speak slowly.

"Thank you Mr. Speaker. With your permission, I now wish to make a statement about a series of allegations that have been made in the media ..." Her own side was urging her on, like a football crowd. They were loving it. A sneering "shame" or a "resign" would occasionally be lobbed over from the opposite benches. She could feel the wind in her sails. She took a deep breath.

"In these stories I have been connected with covert and illegal activities that allegedly took place before and immediately after the 1997 general election. There can only be one explanation. I believe that these malicious falsehoods are being spread by those who are jealous of this party's ... "

Conservative arms began to flail. The boldest were standing up, baying like ruffians at a hunt ball. "Order! Order!" The Speaker glared to either side, his face was puce. "You will give order!" For the minister, the turmoil was like an electric current. Her moist eyes darted around. "Oh yes! Oh yes!" She flourished her piece of paper.

"These wounding stories have already caused embarrassment and distress – not just to myself, but to my family and my colleagues. They are designed to damage..." "The Tories were going ape shit." "Order! Order!" "... to damage this party and to spread political mischief."

"These lies may be little more than the warped fantasies of small-minded and devious people. However, I have a duty to take them seriously. Oh yes!" Cheers and stamping emboldened her. She felt like a center forward, jinking through defenders, in front of an open goal.

"In the interests of decency, of democracy and of open debate I must stop this disease now, before it spreads. I have therefore, this morning, instructed my lawyers to serve writs for libel upon the main source of these spurious allegations, Private Eye magazine."

She surveyed the chamber – the green benches were boiling. Millions of people would watch this on television tonight, including Tony. She tried to look serious. This was the more in sorrow than in anger bit.

"There are times, Mr. Speaker, when the truth must not lie down. It must not be trampled into the mud, by the forces of cynicism, spite and envy. That is why, with regret, I have decided to take this step. Thank you."

She had wanted to end on a low note. There are no questions after statements to the house. The Tories clamored. Labour MPs gloated. The Speaker moved on to the next business.

She had had copies made of her speech. She made sure that they were distributed to the lobby journalists and around the Commons. At lunch–time, someone she knew came over to congratulate her – a tall man in a brown jacket.

"Well done, Emma. May I call you Emma?"

She smiled.

"Of course you may." She looked into the white, podgy face. "And you are?"

"Barry Triffit.

He paused, searching for recognition. "MP for Northampton."

"I see."

Triffit clasped her hand, a little too long. She noticed that the backbencher's shoulders were sprinkled with dandruff. His hair was greasy and his tie was dowdy. In fact, everything about him was wrong. How on earth could she have had sex with him? He needed a major makeover.

"Thank you so much," she said. "It's super to have so many people behind me, I can tell you. Now, if you will you excuse me ..."

That afternoon, the minister held a press conference, at Dean's Yard, next to Westminster Abbey. The setting gave it a religious aura. It seemed appropriate.

She was sober and matter-of-fact. She paraphrased her Commons statement and answered questions. She said that she had been shocked and hurt by the libels. OK, on one level it was merely the rough and tumble of politics, but she could not allow her family and her friends in the Labour party to be dragged through the gutter. Money was not important. If damages were awarded, she would donate them to charity.

The press conference was over in twenty minutes. It was a great success. She got the whole front page of the following day's Daily Mail – "Wounded minister lifts 'shield of truth'." There was a large photograph of her at the dispatch box, with a grave but defiant expression. It was brilliant. She would have that front page framed, for her toilet.

The other broadsheets gave the story less space but a similar slant. Only The Guardian, hinted, carefully, that the minister for London might have a case to answer.

~ ~ ~

It was a complete fluke that Bob Clack had a personal connection with the protestors at Prae Wood. But there were always incredible coincidences in his business. Often, that's all stories were – coincidences. Clack's niece, Shirley, was at Reading University (Nice girl. Nose ring. A bit wild.) She was studying environmental science. Her boyfriend, who was also on the course, was into the animal rights movement. He had a pal, called Robin Atkins, who was even more into it.

Robin had been of the crusties demonstrating against biotechnology outside Prae Wood. Since the place was impregnable, they had come up with a cunning way to get inside. Robin had science A-levels and a good degree and he looked quite presentable with his long black hair tied back in a ponytail. He had applied successfully for a job as a lab technician. He had been working inside Prae Wood for six months.

What Robin told Shirley – Prae Wood's secret – was so amazing that it almost made Clack fall off his bar stool.

Shirley said that Robin was willing to spill the beans to the Sunday World about what he knew. Actually, Robin had told her that he despised the paper, like all the tabloids. It was cat litter. But Shirley knew that her uncle had well-developed skills of persuasion.

Through Shirley, Clack arranged to meet Robin, in a pub on the outskirts of St. Albans. He drove out there in his Renault Clio, feeling excited.

It was Tuesday night, the day after Emma Henderson's Commons statement. That morning, Clack had bashed out the bare bones of his exclusive. It was an everyday tale of how a perverted politician had boasted of murdering and blackmailing people, while snorting cocaine with her teenage lover. And how she had planned to snatch an innocent child from her mother.

As well as the sex pictures and stills from the porno video, there would be blown-up illustrations from the New Labour papers, showing Emma Henderson's handwriting, and a transcript of her conversation with De Vere. This would be available for Sunday World readers to listen to, by phoning a premium rate number.

There would be a background feature, charting Emma Henderson's career from ruin, to rehabilitation and back to ruin, a story based on interviews with Alan Black's flatmates and an article about the modest and unlikely hero of this saga, Rick Gilliver.

Clack's news editor was pushing him to get it all finished by Friday, for publication at the weekend. You couldn't sit on something like this, he said. Rumors would start to leak out of the building and, the next thing, there would be a D notice or an injunction slapped on them. Even worse, another paper would get hold of it. Clack did not want to rush things. He wanted to hold off for another week. But now his niece had added a new chapter.

He pulled into the pub car park. It was one of those 1930s, redbrick establishments found on ring roads all over England. A pub for commercial travellers and for Sunday lunches with the kiddies.

The large, barn-like bar was almost deserted. There was only one young man in there, so it had to be his contact. Clack looked conspicuous in his fawn raincoat, with his red face.

The young man had a ponytail was and wearing a beige fleece. He looked up, with a sour expression.

"You Robert Clack?"

"Yeh, that's right. You can call me Bob." The journalist extended his hand. The young man ignored it.

"Whatever. Listen, let's get this over with."

"I've only just got here." Clack was offended. He would wade through a river of shit to get a good story – in fact he had once – but he did not like people who were rude.

"Would you like a drink, Robin?"

The young man nodded towards his full pint of Guinness.

"Mind if I have one?"

Robin shrugged. Which fucking charm school did you go to pal, thought Clack. He walked to the bar. He came back to the table with a double whisky – and a pint of Guinness. Robin glared at him.

"I know you didn't ask for it. We can just watch it evaporate OK. I thought that would be rather amusing." Robin almost smiled.

"You don't like me, do you, Robin? Now why would that be? Let me see. It's probably because my paper exploits women as sexual objects. Because we ridicule people who care about things. Because we don't give a toss about the environment. Because we have crap adverts for china Elvises. Because we take revenue from wank lines. Because our readers are morons. And because, despite my expensive watch, I am obviously working class. Am I right?"

Robin shrugged.

"Robin, my friend, you are absolutely correct, in all regards. The Sunday World is garbage, an embarrassment. Don't think that I am proud. Here I am, a grown man, writing about women with plastic knockers and kinky vicars. But, in this case, my friend, you have possibly the best story since Cain murdered his brother. Or was it the other way round? You need me. And I need you. It is as simple as that."

"I am not your friend."

"I apologize. OK?"

Robin took a gulp of Guinness. Things got better after that.

Clack started asking some basic questions. When had Robin started working at the lab? Why? What was going on in there? He had not wanted to get out his notebook – this was just a preliminary foray. But he couldn't help himself. And Robin, once he had thawed out, did not seem to mind.

"So, you are telling me that they have this MP. They have hollowed out his skull and they are controlling him, like a puppet. I have heard some pretty strange things in my time, Robin, old pal, but that takes the biscuit."

"So you don't believe me?"

"I'm not saying that. It's just a bit ... weird."

"I've got a mate at Prae Wood, Dennis Johnson. He is one of Barry Triffit's controllers. Dennis usually works the night shift, from midnight until eight in the morning. Triffit is always in bed by eleven, with a library book and mug of cocoa. He's that boring. There is sod all to do. Dennis was getting bored out of his skull.

"A few days ago, Dennis had this cool idea for a little experiment, to make things more interesting. He woke Triffit up and he got him to take a delivery of some ganja and a bunch of CDs. He got Triffit to put on some music and roll up a spliff, in the middle of the night. The next thing, Triffit was stoned out of his gourd."

"What happened?"

"What do you think? He ate the contents of his fridge and two packets of biscuits. He put on a Prodigy CD. Then he woke up his wife and they had incredible sex, on the living room carpet. Three times."

"Wasn't she a bit surprised?"

"At first, yes. But Dennis said that she got into it, after a while. Must have, because they did it again the following night. And again after that. Normally, they only had nookie about once a year, at Christmas. Dennis got off on it, too."

"Isn't it against Triffit's principles. I mean, the sex and the drugs?"

Robin smiled. "You'd think so wouldn't you? But Dennis says that the dope seems to over-ride the neuro-linguistic programmer that's been rammed into his head. It seems to reverse everything that a tight-arsed Labour MP would normally do."

"I see." Clack was perplexed. It was getting far too complicated – "Evil experiment MP is drug-crazed love puppet'. "How does Emma Henderson fit into all this?"

Robin had started on his second pint of Guinness. Clack knew he would. "Well, this programming thing was her idea, apparently. It's called the cyber project. She intends to groom Barry Triffit to be the next star of the Labour party. And she wants him to be the next prime minister, after Blair. I know it sounds ridiculous."

"From what you tell me, Robin, it's all going a bit wrong."

Robin chuckled. "Not necessarily. Maybe New Labour needs a ganja head as their top banana. I'd vote for him."

"I know you would."

Clack was driving, or he would have had another whisky. He sighed. There was a lot more work to do now. A whole new section to the story. But would the Sunday World's readers be able to get their heads round it? Would his news editor, for that matter?

"Dennis has this plan, Mr. Clack." Robin's voice interrupted his thoughts.

"Oh yes, what would that be?"

"He's going to jam the Prae Wood radio signal that controls Barry Triffit, using a pirate radio transmitter."

"What will that mean?"

"Well, tomorrow night, Triffit has been booked to go on one of those dull political programs on TV, Round the Houses, it's called. It goes out live. Dennis is going to immobilize the Prae Wood system, before Triffit goes on. That will mean that New Labour will have absolutely no control over their cyborg. We will."

"What will happen?"

"I don't know. But it should be quite interesting."

Clack's brain was working again.

"This Dennis, will he talk to us?"

"Yeh, probably. Off the record."

"Will you talk to us?"

"I just have, haven't I?"

"No, I mean properly, with a reporter, about what you have found out about Prae Wood?"

Clack knew that Robin would. There was almost no person on the planet that he could not get a story out of.

He bought himself a small orange juice and Robin a third pint of Guinness and a packet of nuts. The poor lad was really hungry. All he needed was someone to talk to.

16

Drugs
Enjoy but handle this issue with extreme caution.
The "war on drugs" which, fortunately, we can never
win is one of our strongest suits with Mr. and Mrs.
Average.

- The New Labour papers

The noise woke her up. It was a persistent repetitive thudding – like the bassline of rap music. Suzy looked at the bedside alarm clock. It was 4.03. Jesus Christ. She clicked on the light.

Phrases formed in her head, as she searched for her slippers. It wasn't good enough. Didn't Barry know that she had a job to go to? He was a selfish bastard, and so on.

Suzy was tolerant, up to a point. It had been a shock first and then a novelty when her husband had started waking her up in the middle of the night, to listen to music and to "fool around", as he put it. Now it was a pain in the arse.

As a special needs policy officer (adults) she had to be pretty sharp and clued in. It was no good trying to function at work on four-hours sleep. She reached for her dressing gown. She was tall and well built, with straight black hair, cut off at the shoulders. She went onto the landing. Frazer, their six-year-old son, did not seem to have woken up, thank goodness. She went downstairs.

She noticed the smell halfway down. It was a sickly herbal aroma. It would soon fill the entire house. Then it would creep down the road and tap on their neighbors' windows. People would begin to talk and they would be in big trouble. She sniffed. There was something else mixed in with the marijuana – sandalwood or juniper.

Barry was resting against a beanbag in the lounge. Dozens of night-lights and candles had been placed around the room. Joss sticks released incense into the semi-darkness. The music was not rap – it was more middle of the road – and it was not that loud. The television was on, but the sound was down. It was an Open University program, about physics.

He turned his head as she came into the room. "Hi babe, I'm really sorry, did I ..." Babe! He never called her that. "Barry! It just isn't good enough! You know that Frazer's got school tomorrow and you know that we have to get up early. For God's sake!"

Barry looked hurt. Chill, man, he thought. "Listen, I really didn't mean to wake you up. I'm sorry. I'll turn the music down."

He reached towards the CD player, not wishing to leave his horizontal position.

"That's music, is it?" She was in a fierce mood. She saw what he was wearing combat trousers and a faded T-shirt with holes in it. He looked like a tramp.

Next to him was a coffee mug, a half-eaten bag of tortilla chips, and the detritus of joint making. He had been rolling reefers on the closest object to hand, the Labour party manifesto, 1997. There was also an empty CD case. It was the Red Hot Chili Peppers

"Is that better? I'm sorry. I just couldn't get to sleep."

He looked different. His face was softer. And he had washed his hair. Suzy perched on an armchair.

They had bought it at MFI, just after they were married in 1989. She had been working as a secretary then, taking her degree. They met in Camden library.

"You never can get to sleep, Barry."

"Yeh, I know. There's a lot of stuff going round in my head, at the moment." He inhaled deeply on his joint. He offered it to Suzy. She declined.

"Barry. I'm really not happy ..."

She was glaring at him. He looked into her face. His eyes were warm.

"You were happy the other night."

She remembered their lovemaking. Barry had gone on forever.

At Prae Wood, Dennis, Barry's controller, was smoking a joint of the same grass. He saw Suzy through Barry's eyes. Her dressing gown was exposing a long white thigh. She was quite tasty. There was a little puncture in her nose where a stud had once been.

Dennis' loins started to stir. He knew all the secret places on her body – the nape of her neck, her feet, the inside of her thighs – and he had carefully guided Barry's fingers there the night before, when they had made love, focusing all of his attentions on enhancing Suzy's pleasure. That's why their lovemaking had been so mind-blowing.

"Yes, well. The other night was different." Suzy sat back in the chair. The dressing gown flopped back, covering her legs. Dennis cursed to himself.

She looked at her husband – an overgrown teenager, lolling on a beanbag.

"I'm worried about you, Barry."

"Why?"

"Because you have changed."

"Have I?"

"Look at yourself."

He reached for the manifesto. Tony Blair's fresh face had a beard of weed. He began to construct another joint. The Chili Peppers were playing "Californication." He really liked that track.

"I have been looking at myself, Suzy. And I don't like it." He moistened the cigarette paper with a flick of his tongue. He was quite good at rolling joints now.

"I mean, look at the people I see in my surgery and what they tell me. Hospital waiting lists as long as your arm, crappy schools. I have to pretend that things are getting better, when I know that they are not. Shoveling the same shit, day after day."

"You used to be proud of your job, Barry."

"Yeh, but I don't see the point of it, Suze. We sit there in the Commons, voting like obedient little children. But we know that we don't matter. We're just making up the numbers. It's just like a nursery school, with alcohol."

Barry gesticulated with his small, tightly rolled joint. "The stuff that I used to believe, has either been abandoned or it has been put on indefinite hold. And look at the things we have done. Freedom of information. The House of Lords. Top-up fees. Foundation Hospitals. The Iraq War. It was illegal, for Christ's sake, under the terms of the UN Charter."

Suzy's interest stirred. This was like the Barry that she had known when they had first met – campaigning for the local old people's day center to remain open, organizing protests in front of the library.

He was warming to his theme. "The streets are full of alienated kids. We've wrecked most of the inner city schools. The hospitals are a disgrace. Everyone is filling in forms to cover their backs. There is no trust any more. We're ruled by fucking performance indicators. And as for reducing inequality. Do you think that we have? Just look around you."

"Barry?"

"Yeh?" Suzy looked into his eyes.

"Please don't tell me that you are becoming a Liberal Democrat."

"Why, would that be such a problem?"

"You hate them Barry. It is one of your most long-standing and deeply-held beliefs."

"Really?" Barry looked confused. Strange things were happening in his brain. Emotions, memories and volitions were concocting in new, peculiar ways. His temples were throbbing.

"Why would I hate anything, Suze? I mean, hatred is so, negative."

He tugged on the joint, almost finishing it. His lungs expanded. He held in the smoke, feeling its fingers reach deep into his brain. A lightness came, a bright white light. He looked at Suzy. Her eyes were shadowed. He touched her hand. She was pensive and tired. She smiled.

"Come back to bed, Barry. Please."

Barry looked around living room. How on earth had they ever chosen that maroon three-piece suite, the pale brown wallpaper, the china ornaments, the mushroom-colored carpet. The effect was horrible.

"OK babe, I'm coming."

~ ~ ~

Later that morning, Rick Gilliver woke up in Walthamstow. Stacia was beside him. She was still asleep. Things were going brilliantly for Rick. It had given him enormous pleasure to resign from Planning Today. He had done so directly to the eel, the previous week. She had threatened to sue him for breach of contract, if he did not come in to serve his notice. He had told her to fuck herself. She had slammed the phone down.

After his meeting with Bob Clack in Leicester Square, he had discussed moving into a hotel with Stacia. But they had decided against it. The fear of what could happen was the only shadow over their lives. They locked and bolted the doors carefully each night. They also had sensor alarms fitted at the front and back of the house.

Carol and Gina had been moved by the Sunday World to Croydon's Holiday Inn. Gina was OK. It was a novelty. But Carol was really pissed off. She could not understand what was going on and she had little sympathy for Rick's explanations. In their last conversation Carol had screamed at him and he had reciprocated. He had thrown down the receiver, in a rage. They had not had an argument like that for years.

Rick had been busy recently, helping Sunday World reporters to piece together a picture of Emma Henderson – her family background, her education, her relationships. To his surprise, he liked the paper's reporters worked – they were bright, quick and straight-forward. They did not speak in code. Perhaps, he realized, this because they did not have a liberal mind-set. Such a mentality held that all people were basically nice, that the police were awful and that society's victims were never bad and never cheated the system. It was a soggy, pious way of thinking. Bullshit.

Things were on hold. He still felt as if he were on holiday. But the Henderson story would come out soon. Then he would have do decide what to do with the rest of his life.

Stacia murmured something. She rolled over and reached for him. He touched her face. Hungrily, they began to kiss.

Later, they had their usual breakfast, toast. Rick had tried to wean himself off coffee. He couldn't but he was down to only two cups in the morning. Stacia left the house at ten o'clock. She was working for a housing association in Hackney, writing and designing their annual report.

This afternoon, he was going to be interviewed by the Sunday World's Sarah Lucas. They would meet somewhere safe, in the West End.

For the rest of the morning, he would lounge on the blue settee, in tracksuit bottoms. On page two of the Guardian was a story about Emma Henderson. It was quite small.

It said: "The prime minister gave his unqualified backing to the minister for London yesterday, while opening a new cardiac unit in Sheffield. 'Emma Henderson is one of my best ministers,' Mr. Blair told journalists, 'and, I can assure you, she has my full support.'

"Ms. Henderson is suing Private Eye magazine for an article in which ..."

His mobile rang. It was on a table on the other side of the room.

"Hi. It's Bob here, Bob Clack. You all right, Rick?"

"Yeh, I'm fine. How can I help you?"

"Have you seen the latest on the Ice Maiden?"

"Do you mean the Tony Blair thing? Or do you mean that nonsense in the Daily Mail, where she's a cross between Martin Luther King and Joan of Arc?"

"Both. There was also a story in the Telegraph yesterday. It said that the police are re-opening an investigation into the death of that union leader, Reg Harris, the guy who topped himself. But that is not why I am ringing, Rick."

"What's up?"

"Well, something amazing. You remember the reference to the cyber project in the New Labour papers? Well, it's happened in real life. It seems that our friend, Emma, has taken over the mind and body of a Labour MP."

"What?"

"I know it sounds bizarre Rick. But it's gospel. She's controlling this poor little man, like a fucking puppet."

"Do any other journalists know?"

"Don't think so."

"Who is the MP?"

"Barry Triffit."

"Never heard of him."

"No-one has, Rick. He's a complete nonentity. That's why Henderson chose him. The thing is this, Rick, he's going on a telly program, tonight."

"Who is?"

"Barry Triffit. It gets better. Yesterday I met some people who can over-ride Triffit's control system. And they're going to jam his signal, when he's on live TV. I'd like you to meet them, Rick. They live in Luton. I want you to go drive up there this evening, with Sarah Lucas, after she has finished with you. Is that OK?" He did not wait for an answer. "Good."

Clack seemed out of breath. "In case you were wondering, we're going to blow the gaff on Henderson this weekend. It won't just be a few pages. It'll be virtually the whole paper. I wanted to wait but the lawyers are champing at the bit. They're worried about an injunction. I've got loads to do. You must not, repeat not, tell anyone about any of this. Do you understand?"

"Of course."

"Good. Oh and Rick?"

"Yeh?"

"You should also know that Emma Henderson is giving a press conference tomorrow morning, on the London elections."

"Is she?"

"Yes and it should be very interesting. There are bound to be questions about the New Labour papers and her legal action. I shall be there, in the front row, staring her out."

"Does she know that the Sunday World is on to her?"

"Maybe. But there's not much she can do about it. By Monday morning, she will be history, believe me. She'll be a political leper. I've seen it happen."

"That's fantastic."

"It certainly is, Rick. And it's all down to you."

"Thank you."

"No worries. Good luck this afternoon, Rick, with Sarah Lucas. And remember, be gentle with her."

Rick said that he would. Clack had already put the phone down.

17

IT
A mixed blessing. It allows you to do all kinds of extraordinary things – in theory. The larger the project, the more likely it is to fail, especially if fuckwit consultants are involved.

- The New Labour papers

Chris Drake was worried. For one thing, Barry Triffit was not properly up yet. Normally, when Drake started his shift at eight o'clock in the morning the MP was already wearing his work gear – a parchment-colored shirt and grey slacks. After shoveling down some tea and toast, he would whip on his jacket and head for the M1 in his Ford Focus, leaving Suzy to take Frazer to nursery.

This Wednesday, Triffit was taking his time. He was guzzling coffee, not tea, and, good grief, what on earth did he have on? Drake could see the sleeves of a baggy grey garment. Triffit seemed to be wearing jeans. He never wore jeans, except at weekends, for polishing the car, or clipping his hedge. It was now eight forty-five. Suzy had left the house ages ago. But Triffit did not seem to be going anywhere.

It was time for the upload. It was Chris' job to zap Triffit with his daily dose of Blairspeak from New Labour HQ. It was a simple process. All he had to do was to click onto an icon and drag a file across the bottom of the screen. A horizontal bar filling up would indicate that Triffit's neuro-linguistic programmer, and his brain, were being supplied with political bullshit – statistics and data, buzz words, dirt on the other parties, sound bytes.

This morning, it wasn't working. Twice now, the data had failed to transfer. Houston, we have a problem. Drake clicked his mouse on the Blairspeak icon for the third time. The band stopped halfway. There was a sound like a duck farting and a little red cross flipped onto the screen. That meant, 'you're screwed' in any language. If the link from Prae Wood to Triffit was down, well, it didn't bear thinking about. They would lose control of the cyborg.

The phone rang. It would be Derek Foxton, asking him how things were going. Drake had to admit that everything was not OK. Two minutes later, Foxton was peering over his shoulder at the monitor.

"Try again, Chris." He sounded annoyed. It was the first time that the system had failed in two years. The computer emitted a loud raspberry.

"What do you think the problem is?"

"I've no idea. There's lots of things it could be. We can shift to the back-up system. If it still doesn't work, chances are that something's shaken loose in his brain. Oh Christ ... "

They had both noticed something, at the same time. Triffit was looking down, as he filled a cigarette paper with little green twigs. He brought a Rizzla up to his lips for a lick. They both knew what was going on. Cued by what he was seeing, Foxton sniffed. There was no mistaking the faint odor that lingered in the control room. It was as if he was back in the dorm at Fettes, messing about after lights out.

"Chris," he said. "People have been smoking cannabis in here, haven't they? Please tell me it isn't true." Drake turned his head. "And don't tell me that it's the cleaners, because I won't fucking believe you.

They are strict Catholics. It's the night controllers isn't it?"

Drake started to sweat.

"No wonder our man here is skinning up. He's being controlled by dope-heads. Do you realize how serious this is?"

The back of Drake's neck had gone red. He was a dope smoker himself – computer nerds often are. He had tended to choose people a bit like himself when recruiting for the controller jobs. Anti-social geniuses with degrees in astrophysics, who were willing to work through the night. He had suspected that some of them were on drugs. But he had done nothing about it.

"Two things, Chris. No, three." Foxton was heading for the door. "One, no-one takes any drugs in this room again – ever. Is that clear? Two, you get sonny Jim here washed, shaved and on the road, ASAP. And three ... "

Chris looked at him. "If you haven't found out what's wrong and got it sorted by midday I will, personally, tear your fucking head off. Do you understand?"

Chris nodded.

"Good. I'm glad that we are speaking the same language."

The door closed. Drake heard Foxton's footsteps echo down the corridor. He tried to clear his head.

He fiddled with the cyborg in the control room all morning. To his relief, he finally got Triffit's brain to accept the Millbank data. It gave him great pleasure to fire Dennis Johnson and three other suspect controllers. In Dennis' case, he left a message on his answer machine. Drake knew that he was merely passing a bollocking down the chain of command. But it made him feel better.

Barry Triffit left his house at eleven o'clock, after he had smoked three skinny joints of powerful skunk. He was dressed in baggy Levis and a flannels shirt.

Triffit took his Focus out of the garage. He put on a CD by the Orb in the car – normally, he listened to crap – middle of the road rock or Radio Northamptonshire. He didn't drive as fast as usual and he didn't take the motorway. Instead, he selected the pretty A509, which would take him slowly to Newport Pagnell and then London.

Really, he should have been at the House of Commons ages before, like a good little boy. There was a debate this afternoon, with a three-line whip. Drake wondered whether Triffit would get there on time.

The midday deadline arrived. Foxton seemed to have calmed down a bit. When Drake told him on the phone that Triffit was now responding to the control system again he seemed reassured.

"I think it was an overload. That was quite a big file from Blair central this morning – four megabytes. It was a policy paper on the benefits of genetically modified food. When I broke it down into smaller sections, the transfer went through. I'm not sure, but there might be a problem with the neuro-linguistic programmer. Maybe we should to get him back into the lab and whip it out."

"Possibly," said Foxton. They could grab the MP at Tesco's again, if they had to. Poor sod, mugged twice in exactly the same place.

"Do you think he will be OK for the TV program tonight?"

Drake sucked on his teeth. "Yeh, he'll be fine. He's not wearing his normal gear. But it's a late night show, so that could be kind of appropriate. In any case, no one will watch it, apart from a few saddos."

Foxton laughed. Emma Henderson would be one of them. Should he tell the minister for London that her pet MP had gone wobbly and was in need of a 10,000-mile service? She always over-reacted when it came to small problems and she had a vicious temper. For these reasons, he decided not to. It was a mistake.

~ ~ ~

Rick sat in a small room, off the lobby of a hotel near Oxford Street. It was quiet and semi-private. An annoying tape of tinkling cocktail piano was playing softly in the background.

He was sitting on an uncomfortable settee, which looked a like a chaise longue. Sarah Lucas was in a chair opposite, fiddling with her digital tape recorder. She was a young woman with short brown hair and hazel eyes. She was wearing tweed trousers and a well-cut black jacket. No nail varnish but red lipstick. She looked sensible, but playful.

"So Rick." She was ready to begin now. He hated the room – the velvet drapes, the chintz-covered furniture, the annoying low-level lighting.

She looked at him earnestly. "Tell me what happened, from the beginning."

He did.

"So, how do you feel, Rick?"

"How do you mean?"

"Is it scary, being on the run?"

"Well, yes. Because I know what these people are capable of. They kill their enemies. Now that the story is out in the open, I feel a little bit safer. I still feel concerned, not so much for me but for Gina." He was choosing his words carefully. Sarah was taking notes. He knew that her article would be written in clichés.

"Gina?"

"My daughter."

"Oh, I see." She tilted her head to one side. It was a trick he also used, when he was interviewing people, to make them open up. "How old is she, Rick?"

"She's thirteen."

Sarah Lucas smiled, remembering when she was thirteen.

"She lives with her mum. We separated when she was nine."

"Do you see her very often?"

"Oh yes. Every other weekend. I mean, it's difficult at the moment. Obviously."

"What do you do together?"

He thought. "Shopping, mainly."

"What does she like?"

"Apart from shopping?" A picture of Gina formed in his mind. Her sulky scowl. "She likes clothes and music, same as most thirteen-year olds. Drum and bass mainly at the moment. She's always on her mobile, texting. She's incredibly stubborn, like her mum." Sarah was nodding.

"You're pretty stubborn yourself, Rick."

"Am I?"

"Well, single handedly taking on the British establishment?"

"I didn't have any choice. Once the New Labour papers fell into my hands, I just did what I thought was right." He knew that this phrase would end up in the story, in big letters. "I mean, New Labour is hollow. It's a sham, like Blair's smile."

"In what way?"

"Well, it pretends to be about empowerment and democracy and so on, but that's only froth. There's something a lot nastier going on – and it's not very far beneath the surface. You see, Labour has always been nasty in the way it operated and it has never been democratic. Only before, the nastiness was done by trade union barons, in smoke-filled rooms. Of course, there is also the fact that Blair is a war criminal."

Sarah was looking away. This was not exactly Sunday World territory. "I see what you mean, Rick."

There was a pause.

"You and Stacia?"

"Yes?"

"Do you?"

"Have sex?"

"I was going to say live together."

"Yeh, at the moment."

"How did that happen?"

"Well, I moved to her house, didn't I, the night they came after me, in Sainsbury's." He paused. "For Christ's sake don't say where it is, will you?"

"As if Rick." She frowned at him. "So you moved in and you found that you were, soul mates?"

"I suppose so."

"Your situation brought you together."

"Yeh." He feared that was going to be a dreadfully corny article. Prurient too.

"What are your feelings for her Rick?"

The piano music was still playing in the background. Stacia would hate that.

"What do you mean?"

"Sorry, Rick." She smiled. "You probably think I am being far too intrusive."

"No, not all." He laughed nervously.

"God Rick, of course not. You must think I'm really terrible." She paused. "Unless there's something that you want to tell me."

Now they both laughed. He looked at her face. It was hard to assess her age – early thirties he guessed. Her clothes looked expensive. She was wearing a faint, floral perfume. "Are there any more questions?"

"No. I think that's about it, Rick. There's one or two little things. Maybe we could finish this off in the bar?" I know your game, thought Rick. He knew exactly what was coming. This was where she got him a bit tipsy, to loosen him up.

"Do you want to get me drunk?"

"Why would I do that?"

He did not answer.

"Rick, really. You must think I'm terrible. I'm not like that... But, as I said before, if there's anything you want to get off your chest."

The bar was as bland as the rest of the hotel. It was empty, apart from an American couple.

It seemed too early to drink. But that did not normally stop Rick. He had a pint of fizzy hotel bitter. Sarah had a glass of white wine.

In the next hour, he learned that she lived in a small flat in Southfields, near Wimbeldon. She had recently split up from her partner, who worked as a creative director in advertising. Sarah's first job had been on a local paper in Surrey. She loved being a journalist. She had been with the Sunday World for about six months.

She agreed with him that nepotism was rife on the nationals and that a lot of reporters were privileged kids who had drifted into it from Oxford or Cambridge. But she wasn't like that. She had always known what she wanted to do and it had not been handed to her on a plate. She had left school after A-levels, to work on the Guildford Advertiser. On the other hand, it hadn't hindered her career that her uncle used to be a sub on the Daily Mail.

They chatted comfortably. Rick had another beer. Sarah switched to coffee because she was driving. He said that he would love to work on a national paper, but thought that he was too old. Also, he wasn't sure if he could write about soap stars' sex lives. Sarah said he wouldn't have to and she offered to put in a word for him where she worked.

She said that Bob Clack, the senior reporter, was really nice, but that Steven Brown, the news editor, was a creep. He had only got his job because he was married to the publisher's niece. His nickname in the newsroom was "brown nose".

By the time they left the bar at five o'clock they had almost become friends. That was a relief, because they would have to spend quite a bit of time together. The Americans looked across at them and smiled, thinking that they were a couple.

Sarah's blue Ceat Ibiza was parked beneath the hotel. They drove out of London through the rush hour feeling warm and relaxed, talking about journalism and politics. Sarah linked up with Bob Clack on her mobile. He gave her directions to where they would meet Dennis Johnson, in Luton, where the pirate radio transmitter was set up.

18

Council housing
Drab, dreary and damp. Council housing promotes an unhealthy kind of proletarian solidarity, which is not very us, and it gives local authorities a powerbase. We should get rid of it as quickly as possible, preferably by transferring it to private landlords, or, where that is not possible, by giving it to the poor bastards who live there.

- The New Labour papers

Elmwood Park used to have a bad reputation. It was a sprawling estate on the outskirts of Luton, made up of tower blocks and council-built maisonettes, arranged in crescents and cul-de-sacs. Once, it had been a sink estate, where crack dealers barricaded themselves into fortress flats and fought battles that often ended in stabbings or shootings.

Today, things were different. There were few burnt-out cars. The dull, flaking buildings had been freshly painted and the strips of mud with concrete in between them had been landscaped and planted with shrubs. An old warehouse next to the estate had been turned into a community center. As well as meeting rooms, there were shops there, a not-for-profit launderette and a recording studio, where local bands made CDs.

A few million pounds from a regeneration scheme had transformed the environment. The money had captured the imagination of the tenants and residents and focused their energies. It was they who now ran Elmwood Park. They grew their own produce and sold it in a food co-op. They even collected their own rubbish.

Rick and Sarah Lucas had swung off the M1 at junction 9. They found the estate quite easily. They were now on the eleventh floor of a tower block. It was called, un-ironically, Nightingale Point. All of the blocks had the names of birds.

Dennis Johnson, who, until recently, had worked at Prae Wood, rented the flat with his girl friend, Sandra. Dennis was tall and skinny, with hollow cheeks and a mop of dark hair. There was something a bit insect-like about him, Rick thought. It was hot in the flat, which added to the impression, and there was a funny smell, like locusts. On the plus side, Dennis was cheerful and friendly.

There was an abbreviated balcony outside the living room. It was just big enough for a couple of plant pots and a bicycle wheel. The three of them were squeezed onto it and Dennis Johnson was showing Rick and Sarah Lucas the estate. It was dusk. The air was sharp and crisp, with a bouquet of damp leaves and burning garbage.

"You see over there?" There was a roll-up in Dennis' nicotine-stained fingers. "That's where we grow veg. We've got goats and chickens as well."

At the edge of the darkness, they could just make out a wooden, grass-roofed building, surrounded by vegetable patches. The earth was still barren, except for some winter cabbage and translucent red chard. They could see the faint outlines of an ornamental bridge, made out of railway sleepers, and a grass amphitheater. This, Dennis said, was used as a performance space, when they held festivals or fun days on the estate. A clump of silver birches separated the allotments from a patch of scrubby wasteland. No one owned that land. It was ideal for car boot sales, mountain bike racing and grazing horses. Beyond, in a blazing aureole of orange light, was the town of Luton.

"We call it the farm," said Dennis, "I'll show you some time, if you like. The cabin is powered by solar panels. We want to put wind turbines on two of the tower blocks, to provide electricity for the estate. But we can't get planning permission." He smiled. There was a gap between his front teeth. Rick sensed that Dennis got his way on most things – eventually.

"That's amazing," said Rick, "isn't it, Sarah?" Sarah wasn't particularly interested in chickens, cabbages and alternative energy. She was inspecting the flat, with the cold eyes of a reporter. Headlines were forming in Rick's head. It was a habit he had. But they were very different to Sarah's. "Activists create utopia on housing estate". No, that was too long. How about "Eco squatters' high-rise heaven" or, even better, "Heaven on floor eleven".

He looked around the living room. He had lived in a flat like this, once, with Carol in Kentish Town. The walls would be made from reinforced concrete – impossible to drill into. There would be an asthmatic central heating system, which breathed warm air through vents, constant scalding water and a smelly rubbish chute, emptying into a huge metal bin, that would be a target for juvenile arsonists. Tower blocks were full of inexplicable noises and strange odors. They were machines for living in.

The room was done out in squatter chic. Rick's eyes flitted around the cheap rugs, the skip salvage and the mismatched furniture, haggled from second-hand shops. Someone had begun to decorate the flat but had abandoned the job halfway through. Why did hippies never finish things? On the partially painted walls were posters for bands and demos.

By the threadbare settee he saw an electric guitar and a practice amp. There was also an electric keyboard. It was a good guitar, a cream-colored Fender. There would be an estate rock band, Rick guessed. And Dennis would have a hand in it.

"Tea?" Dennis' partner, Sandra, and Robin Atkins had come into the room. Sandra was showing an expanding belly through her plumber's bib and brace. She was pregnant. Her hair was plaited into braids. Robin wore a denim jacket over a white tee shirt. His dark hair was liberated from its ponytail.

Robin looked at Rick and Sarah Lucas suspiciously. There was an awkward silence.

"Dennis has just been telling us about the estate," said Rick. "It's brilliant what you guys have done."

"For a bunch of crusties, you mean," said Robin.

"I wasn't going to say that."

"But you were thinking it."

"I wasn't, actually," said Rick.

"Fuck off, Robin." Sandra had sharp thin features and a Bristol accent. "Don't be so bloody rude. "I've made some tea." She handed Rick and Sarah their mugs.

Rick's mug had no handle. He had lived this way once. He had worn the same clothes for days and not brushed his hair. He had sat round fires made from broken pallets and smoked endless joints, rolled from emptied out cigarette ends. It had been a long time ago. He felt to old for all that stuff now. These days, his lifestyle was more Ikea than squatter.

Sandra had a trusting face, like Dennis. "Don't worry about Robin," she said. "He's a vegan." They all laughed. "Would you like to eat with us tonight?"

"Yeh, we'd love to," said Gilliver. Sarah Lucas gave a worried smile. She was wondering how clean the cutlery would be and if there would be anything to sit on. Once, she had covered an outdoor pop festival in Berkshire, for the Sunday World. It had been Bob Clack's idea. It was supposed to be an expose of drug taking, nudity and frolicking in the woods. It had rained all weekend, turning the fields into a freezing quagmire. Sandra had seen nothing more shocking than a few people skinning up and a woman breast-feeding. To put the lid on it, she had gone down with food poisoning.

Dennis looked anxious. He was standing in the entrance to the bedroom. There was no door, just a bead curtain. "I'd like to show you the equipment," he said. "There isn't too much time. The program starts at seven-thirty. Would you like to see it?"

Sarah shook her head. She said she would have a look later. She went into the kitchen with Sandra. Rick followed Dennis into the bedroom.

It was dark in there, even with the light on. There was a smell of stale socks with a sickly trace of joss sticks. Beige paper with a nasty pattern had been half scraped off the walls. Someone had scribbled some poems and epigrams onto the pitted surface – the writings of Oscar Wilde. It was Dennis's Rick guessed. The books on Dennis' side of the bed embraced Eastern mysticism, cybernetics and erotica. Sandra's area focused on self-development, Celtic mythology and childcare.

"Sorry about the mess." Dennis picked a weaving path, through newspapers and paperbacks, coffee mugs and discarded clothes. "It's all gone a bit mental since Sandra got pregnant. I'll have more time to sort stuff out, now I'm not working. I'm quite glad that I've lost my job, actually."

The equipment was beneath the bedroom window. It looked like something that you would see in a minicab office – a large, heavy-duty radio, with a microphone. An array of green lights blinked at them. Dennis checked that there was a CD playing. He had selected a stack of them that morning.

"Is it broadcasting now?"

"Yeh, it is. I've been giving it short bursts since this morning."

"How does it work?"

"Easy. Basically, we are beaming music straight into Barry Triffit's brain on radio frequency, piggy backing on microwave transmitters used for mobile phones. It's like pirate radio, yeh?"

Dennis smiled. Rick echoed it back, although he hated pirate radio. It gave him a headache.

"At first, we were using UK garage and hardcore, but that made him a bit edgy. Trip-hop and trance seem to work best. They chill him out. They seem to mask out all of the garbage coming from Prae Wood."

"Isn't it making him a bit spaced out?"

"No, not at all. He's cool and easy-going, not in such a hurry. But he's still focused. And it seems to carry on working, even when we're not transmitting."

Dennis pushed a button. Needles flickered like miniature windscreen wipers.

"His personality is definitely changing. But that could be the effect of all of the dope he's smoking." He gave a wheezy laugh.

Dennis turned up the volume. A looping drum and bass pattern filled the room. The music had been made in the recording studio on the estate by a bedroom-based musician.

"Is that what is going into his head now?"

"Yeh."

"It's nice," said Rick. "But it would make it awfully hard for him to concentrate on fishing quotas."

"That's the idea."

Dennis reached forward to turn on a TV. It was a battered ex-rental model. But it did the trick. EastEnders was on, a scene in an upstairs room in the Queen Vic pub. Dennis left the sound down. A woman sat at a table, crying, her head cradled in her hands. Behind her, a mean-mouthed man with a shaved head was delivering an inarticulate soliloquy.

"This political program, 'Round the Houses,' comes on at seven-thirty," explained Dennis. "When it starts, I'll jack up the strength of the signal."

"Should be interesting," said Rick. "How do you think it will go? Will he sit on the floor and start chanting?"

"Nah, he will make contributions to the debate, I'm sure. Interesting ones, hopefully."

They went back into the living room, leaving the television on.

Rick could smell brown rice cooking. It would be mixed with stir-fried vegetables. He was familiar with this kind of food. Sarah looked comfortable, for the moment. She was sitting on the settee with Sandra. They were going through a photo album. The pictures showed the miraculous transformation of the Elmwood Park Estate from a drab hellhole into a successful community.

Dennis picked up the guitar. He turned on the little practice amp and began to play riffs, in time with the music that was coming from the bedroom. He seemed to know what he was doing. Rick sat on the settee, next to Sandra, and shared the photographs. They showed happy kids constructing an adventure playground. In other pictures, jugglers and fire-eaters did their thing, next to smiling children with painted faces.

"Look at this one." Sandra handed him a picture. "It's Dennis playing in his band." He was on a stage, wearing a white shirt and leather trousers. His hair half masked his face as he bent over his Fender. "He looks ridiculous."

~ ~ ~

They ate the rice and vegetables in various postures on the settee and the floor, since there was no table. Sarah looked uncomfortable, nervously brushing animal hairs from her trousers. Already, her ankles were itching. She knew what that was. Cat fleas. She could hear herself telling the story back at the office. God, it was absolutely filthy. And the food!

"Does anyone know what the time is?" asked Dennis. Sarah looked at her elegant little watch.

It was twenty-five past seven.

"Right," said Dennis. "It's almost started."

They went into the bedroom. It was a curious scene. Four adults lounging on bean bags on a double mattress, with no bed beneath it. Sandra leaned into Dennis, who cupped his hand on her belly. Rick and Sandra were next to each other, not too close. Radiance from the television screen covered their faces with a curtain of flickering light. It was cool in the bedroom because one of the windows was broken and repaired, ineffectually, with a piece of cardboard.

Rick wondered about covering himself. But there was only one duvet and he could hardly snuggle under it with Sarah. He could sense a tautness in her body. How ironic – a Sunday World reporter in bed with three adults. He still felt stoned from the joint that he had shared with Dennis on the balcony. God, that skunk stuff was strong. He wasn't used to it. If Triffit was smoking this stuff, he must be off his trolley.

Dennis explained that it had been grown on the estate. It was not exactly legal to cultivate the stuff. But the police did not seem to mind much these days. In fact, they were more liberal on cannabis than the government, which could not make its mind up whether it was for it or against it.

With dope like this, either you lay back into it, like an armchair of smoke, or you resisted. Then you ended up like Sarah. Tense. Rick had chosen the first option.

Bright light danced on their faces as the opening credits of Round the Houses, came on. A camera dipped and weaved around a model of the Houses of Parliament, lit luridly in orange and green. There was a full moon behind it. It was all a bit amateurish, like something made for Blue Peter.

The presenter's smile was just as contrived. She was a young black-haired woman in a pea green jacket. Across from her three people sat on a pale blue settee. A smug man with a yellow tie, another with bulging eyes and bad skin and Barry Triffit. Triffit looked self-possessed. He was sitting on the edge of the sofa, between the two other guests.

It was a medium shot. They saw Barry Triffit scratch his head. Slowly, the camera moved towards the presenter, until her head and shoulders filled the screen. Her hair was sleek and well brushed.

Obviously, they needed to hear the program. There was some confusion because Dennis could not find the remote control – it was lying beneath a heap of clothes – so they missed the first couple of minutes of the program.

By the time the volume was turned up, the presenter was finishing her introduction. You could tell from her voice and her clothes that her social milieu was bounded by Kensington High Street to the north and the King's Road to the south. Her attitudes would be shaped by the Daily Mail. Having the right carrier bags and labels would be tremendously important to her.

The camera moved back into a medium shot. Every so often, the producer was careful to show the presenter's long, tanned legs. They were the program's main attraction. Otherwise, it was dull stuff – verbal muesli for the chattering classes. They could see that the presenter's eyes were following an autocue. "We know what the government thinks. But what about ordinary backbench MPs, the parliamentary foot soldiers. Well, we have three of them here tonight ..."

Rick adjusted his position on the beanbag.

19

Liberal Democrats
Strange, gnome-like people with bad skin who, for whatever reason, have failed to integrate with society. Don't have anything to do with them. In the first term, we can pretend to be looking into some proportional representation thing, to string them along a bit. Then quietly bury it.

- The New Labour papers

Triffit's skin crawled with sweat, beneath the hot studio lights. The scar at the top of his head was itching. He scratched it again. There was something weird there, just under the skin, a hard patch. It bothered him sometimes. There was another problem. The front of his head was throbbing. Smoking a joint in the toilets just before he had come onto the set had not helped at all.

One his right was a Liberal Democrat and on his left a Conservative. The floor manager for Round the Houses had given the three guests a little pep talk – be natural, be concise, don't look into the cameras. Since it was a live show, there was always the danger of a guest behaving weirdly or becoming abusive. Not MPs, though. They were normally as docile as Laboratory rabbits, unless they were drunk.

The program's presenter, Caroline Kirkdale, was a Cambridge graduate. Svelte and long-legged, she knew all the right moves. Combining brains and beauty, she was Channel 4's most potent weapon, as sleek and well targeted as a Cruise missile.

There were only fifteen seconds until they were on. She looked round at her guests. The Labour guy was sweating badly. He didn't seem nervous though. His dampness had provoked a long debate between the producer and the floor manager, leading to some emergency dabs of powder.

"Everyone ready?"

The Liberal Democrat nodded, looking blank. The Conservative, a louche double-chinned fellow, with floppy hair smiled weakly at Caroline. Triffit's head was itching like hell.

Five, four, three. The producer in the control room counted Caroline in, through her earpiece. Two, one.

With practiced casualness, she followed the words on her autocue.

"Hi, I'm Caroline Kirkdale and welcome to 'Round the Houses.' It's a new and, we hope you'll agree, irreverent look at British politics. On today's show, protecting the public from terrorist attacks. We know what the government and the home secretary think. But what about ordinary backbench MPs, the parliamentary foot soldiers. Well, we have three of them here tonight ..."

Triffit was not listening to the preamble. If he turned his head at the right angle, he could see into Caroline's blouse. He could also smell her perfume. It was nice. She finished speaking, addressing her first question at the Conservatives.

The Conservatives were in trouble. How could they say that New Labour were soft on the country's security when, obviously, they weren't? The home secretary, a sour, joyless man with a lazy eye, was the most illiberal in living memory. He believed that anyone with a beard or a foreign accent should be banged up indefinitely.

Blah, blah, blah. Triffit vaguely heard the Tory trotting out this week's bullshit. He was subliminally aware of the man's moist chins quivering. The Tory was not perspiring much, considering his thick jacket and his tightly knotted silk tie.

"Barry, what do you think?"

"Sorry?" Her eyes pierced him.

"About the point that Gerald has just made. You, presumably, back the new legislation. What do you think it will achieve?"

"Nothing."

"I beg your pardon."

"Nothing good anyway. I think that the idea is total crap. That's why I voted against the bill this evening."

Caroline was blinking.

"Please tell us more"

"That's right, and I was of only three Labour MPs who had the balls to do so.'

"Why do you ...?"

He interrupted her. "I think, basically, that the Civil Protection Bill, which had its second reading today, is an unprecedented and unjustified attack upon or civil liberties. It will mean that emails can be spied on, that people can be locked up and held without warning that the government can take over the broadcasting system on a whim, if a state of emergency is declared. I think that we have made a big mistake and I cannot, in all conscience, support it. I mean, what are we going to do, shove everyone who we don't agree with in jail? There just aren't enough prisons, Caroline."

He looked at her. She stared back. The producer was jabbering through her earpiece: "This is good. More, more." She invited him to continue.

"I see. You think that the measures go too far then."

"Of course not. And I think that we can connect this paranoid over-reaction and these flagrant abuses of power with other issues – the abolition of the Lord Chancellor's office, the creation of a Supreme Court, the attempt to impose a non-elected Upper House. The executive has got out of control. It is riding roughshod over the will of Parliament, let alone that of the British people.

"I see." She blinked.

"I have never been a particular fan of the judiciary, or the Lords. But I would rather have them than grey-place men who are in the pocket of the government. We are reverting to a form of monarchial patronage that we had before the Restoration – our system is not even as democratic as the American presidency. At least they have a written constitution."

"Surely the idea is to ..."

"Increase accountability?" He looked at the presenter. "That's the rhetoric Caroline. But who believes it? When our friends, the Liberals, curtailed the powers of the Lords early this century, at least they were putting something better in their place. They were for the people. But this lot are not for the people, they are for themselves. And look at their use of ..." he felt a stabbing pain in the front of his head.

"But surely you have been a keen supporter of previous government policies – on fox hunting for example."

"I was, but only under duress."

"What do you mean?"

Triffit hesitated. A shaft of pain, like a bright light, stabbed through the front of his head.

"I, er ..." The pain squeezed his eyeballs. He felt nauseous. "Do you really want to know?" Caroline nodded. Yes, yes, buzzed through her earpiece.

"It was sheer funk, Caroline. Because I was aware of what the whips could do. They would give me a slap if I did not toe the line. They would brief journalists and spread rumors that I was interfering with little boys, in the tearoom. They are despicable, Caroline, bullies and ball breakers. Especially that bitch Alice Wilmslow. Quite frankly, it is repugnant. I joined a party which encouraged debate. It was a broad and welcoming church. It has become, I am afraid, a nasty little fan club. Ouch ..."

Triffit clutched the side of his head as a shaft of pain sliced into his brain. Chris Drake, who had been watching the program with horror, had been steadily increasing the strength of signal from Prae Wood.

Dennis at Elmwood Park suspected as much.

"They're fucking with him. We'll have to block their signal." He got to his feet. There was one thing that he knew might work. Somewhere, in his collection, was an album by a band that he used to love – Linkin Park. He placed it in the CD caddy.

Needles twitched dramatically, lights flashed. A cleansing process was taking place in Barry Triffit's brain. He felt the pain subsiding. His face was white and filmed with perspiration. His pupils were like deep, dark pools.

His mouth began to move. "The genetics revolution it is already underway and it is changing the world in which we live – holding out the potential for new drugs and therapies, new means of preventing ill ..." Whoops, what the hell was he saying? He had no idea. He stopped. Caroline leaned forwards.

"Would you like a glass of water, Barry?"

"No, I'm fine. Sorry about that. Now, where was I? Ah yes, er ... bullying. You know, I think that we have become more like the Taliban than a modern political party. We are paranoid and old-fashioned. We are intolerant of people's views and lifestyles. And, of course, we blindly followed the Americans into an illegal war. We are even worse than those old fossils, in some ways." He jerked this thumb towards Gerald Jones, the Conservative. "At least they have a tradition of upholding freedoms."

Jones tried to butt in. Caroline blocked him out. She knew that the program had already become a national news story. It would be on front pages. But she wanted a bit more.

"Go on."

"I mean, take our drugs policy. It's all over the place. I smoke dope, like a lot of people. It makes me a nicer person. People who are stoned do not pick fights with strangers; they do not sexually molest workmates or break the speed limit. I think that politicians could learn a lot from that. Don't you?"

She laughed. There were only four minutes to go. "I don't know, Barry. Many people will agree with you, many won't. Your views are certainly different to those of most of your colleagues. Gerald, any thoughts on what Barry has just said?"

She turned in her seat, revealing her long, shiny thighs.

The Conservative was unsettled. He used the adjectives outrageous, irresponsible and appalling all in one sentence.

~ ~ ~

Alone in her Kensington flat, Emma Henderson had put down her drink. She was jabbing the keypad of her phone. This was supposed to be a gentle canter for Barry Triffit – a televised demonstration of his total obedience, giving him a gentle shove up the ladder of preferment.

"Hi, is that Derek?"

"Yeh."

"Are you watching this?"

"Of course I am."

Initially, at Prae Wood, Foxton and Chris Drake had been diverted by Caroline Kirkdale's long thighs and her tanned bosom, seen through Barry Triffit's eyes. Their pleasure had quickly turned to panic.

"What on earth is going on?" said Emma, coolly.

Foxton took a breath. "We've lost him, I'm afraid. I don't know why. We think that someone must be blocking our signal."

"What?"

"Someone must be transmitting on the same frequency."

The minister was watching Triffit gesticulate, as he made some point. The Tory MP was smirking. The Liberal Democrat was looking the other way.

"You've got to do something. Push the kill button – anything!"

"Tried that." Derek Foxton sighed. "Listen, we're doing everything we can. We're trying to re-load the ..."

"Don't baffle me with bullshit, Derek. Just stop him for Christ's sake!" She slammed the phone down.

The program was ending. Triffit was sipping from a glass of water. Caroline thanked her guests, then the credits came up. Thank Christ, thought Derek Foxton. He wondered what would happen now. It was no use doing anything rash tonight. The damage was done. Tomorrow, they would calmly assess the situation.

"I thought you told me that there wasn't going to be a problem. Jesus, Chris!"

He looked at Drake with pure hatred. Drake said nothing.

~ ~ ~

It was eight-thirty. At Elmwood Park Sarah Lucas decided to drive back to Southfields. Dennis said that Rick could stay the night, if he wanted. He could have a look around the estate and the farm in the morning. Rick agreed. The two of them drank beer and smoked another joint, standing on the balcony. It was drizzling and cold. The air smelled faintly sulfurous. Music and laughter drifted across the estate. Someone was having a party in one of the tower blocks. They usually were. Afterwards, they went inside and listened a CD of Dennis' band, The Vibrators. Rick liked the music. It was RnB in the old sense, with guitars.

Later, he phoned Stacia, from his mobile to hers, to tell her that he would come home tomorrow afternoon. He asked her if she had seen the program.

"Yeh." Her voice sounded flat.

"What's wrong?"

"There's this van right outside the house, Rick, watching my windows. It's a white Astra."

"And?"

"There's a gorilla in it. He's been sitting there all evening, reading the Sun and picking his nose."

"Does he have a scar on his face?"

"I don't bloody know." It was the first time he had heard Stacia sound irritable. "I'm not going to go out there to chat to him, am I?"

Rick paused. "Listen, don't worry about it. He's just trying to spook you."

"Well he's succeeding." She was anxious but controlling it. "Do you think he'll stay there all night Rick?"

"Yeh, he's bound to. That's the drill. He'll wait to see if I come out of the house in the morning."

"And then what?"

"I won't obviously."

"And then?"

"I don't know. But you could come here. This guy, Dennis, has already offered me a flat on the estate.

Some of his friends are away. We could hole up for a while."

"But it's in Luton." She sounded horrified.

"So?"

"The place is hideous. Anyway, I'm supposed to work in Hackney tomorrow."

"You'd like it here, honestly."

There was a silence.

"No I wouldn't."

"You would. You could come here now. I don't think you'll be followed. Well, probably not."

She was breathing heavily. "What you're saying is, come to Luton, in the middle of the night, in the pissing rain, dodging a psycho who is probably armed."

"Yes." The word came out like a question. "We can meet you at the station. Dennis has got a car."

"Oh, thank you so much. That is so kind of you."

"Stacia ..."

She had turned off her phone. She called back two minutes later, to apologize and to say of course she would come.

20

Spin
A friendly American term for lies and propaganda. Suggest we adopt it.

- The New Labour papers

"Do you smoke cannabis, Ms. Henderson?"

"What?"

"Do you smoke cannabis?"

She was losing control of the press conference. In fact, she had never had control of it. And it was annoying her. She peered ahead. The question had come from a bald reporter in the second row. All the familiar faces were there – the red-faced one from the Telegraph, that tart from the Times, Roger Coverington from the Guardian. There were many other faces she did not recognize and loads of cameras.

This event was supposed to be devoted to her policies on tourism for London, hopefully, with a couple of friendly questions tacked on at the end about her libel action against Private Eye. Tourists were being scared from London by fears of terrorist attacks, so the minister was announcing a ten-point plan designed to bring them back. She was joined on the platform by a theatrical impresario, a museum director and an orange-skinned actor from EastEnders.

The Mayor of London, Ken Livingstone, who was now a Labour party member had been invited. But he had failed to turn up. Emma, who had been disgusted when he was readmitted into the Labour party, was relieved that he was not there. She despised the man. Now, she would not have to smile when he laid out his stupid plans for the capital, in his whining nasal voice.

It was all going wrong. Thanks to Barry Triffit's disclosures the previous night, the journalists were pursuing another more interesting story, like a swarm of flies licking blood from a carcass.

Did she smoke cannabis? Normally, the question would not have fazed her. It was Howard Harris from the Express.

"No, I do not. I have always thought that soft drugs can lead to ..."

Her answer was lost in a melee of voices. Each person in the room was competing for her attention. Camera and sound people fought for position. Boom mikes with furry tips were waved around. Hands strained for the ceiling.

"Ms. Henderson," James Buffin's imperious voice broke through. Buffin, the Telegraph's home affairs man, was bred from generations of hunters. His larynx had been adapted by natural selection, so that his commands would carry a long way across grouse moors.

He was flourishing a copy of that morning's Daily Mail. A lot of the others also had Mails. They were being handed around, like porn mags at a scout camp.

The paper had abandoned its original front-page story and written a new one the previous night, in an inspired last-minute rush. It was the editor's idea. He was at home watching Round the Houses, nodding off to sleep with a brandy and soda. As soon as the contents of the program had sunk in, he phoned the night news editor and told him to stop whatever he was doing and watch Channel 4.

The show had only been on for about five minutes. The paper had already gone to press but they could re-make the front page. The night news editor sighed.

The Mail's new lead story was simple. It needed to be, because it was scrambled together in twenty minutes. The headline was brief – Dope head, in huge letters. There was a large picture, a fuzzy screen grab, of a disheveled Barry Triffit in the Round the Houses studio.

Triffit's face stared blearily from the picture. His eyes were red, with half-closed drunken lids. He was jabbing a finger to make a point. Behind him, out of focus, was the Conservative MP, Gerald Jones. The Tory was merely a dark, blurred shape in the background.

The story began: "Labour MP Barry Triffit launched an astonishing attack against the government last night". It was dotted with extended quotes. One had been pulled out and run, in bold type, beneath the picture: "I smoke dope, like a lot of people. It relaxes me and it makes me a nicer person."

Triffit, said the story, thought that New Labour's Civil Protection Bill was "crap", that the government's whips were "despicable" and "ball breakers" and that the prime minister's inner circle was a "nasty little fan club". The article, although it had no evidence for this assertion, said that the prime minister was "fuming" at this outburst from a previously obscure backbencher.

It was a quiet week for real news. The next day, all of the tabloids would follow the Mail and run stories on the outspoken MP. Triffit's disclosures would also be covered in the broadsheets. The Guardian and the Independent would place them on their front page. Radio and TV bulletins would have a good go at the story too.

~ ~ ~

At this moment, Triffit's house in Northampton was under siege from a rowdy mob of caffeine-fuelled reporters, paparazzi and film crews. The photographers bristled with aluminum stepladders and long lenses. They clanked as they walked, like a terrifying medieval army. Notes offering large sums of money for "exclusives" had already been thrust through the MP's letterbox. He had taken his phone off the hook but his doorbell was now ringing about once every two minutes. The frequency was increasing in proportion to the journalists' desperation.

Triffit was lying in bed with Suzie, in a curtain-darkened room. Frazer was with them. He had been crying. Now, he was sucking his thumb. They could hear a babble of conversations, as the journalists compared notes and talked into their mobiles. Triffit dreaded what was happening to his little patch of lawn. They were like a herd of cows. In London, their colleagues were digging out background on the obscure little man who had been thrust, suddenly, into the limelight.

A few minutes before, a helicopter had hovered, apocalyptically, just above the roof. It had almost shaken the tiles loose. That was what had set poor little Frazer howling. Soon, a police car would arrive, following a complaint from Triffit's neighbor about a reporter who had urinated against his wheely bin. One officer would try to push the media scrum back and another would hammer on the MP's front door.

When the time was right, Triffit would go downstairs and talk to the press, from a trampled flowerbed. He would be wearing jeans and a blue baseball cap. He felt light-headed, almost feverish. But at least the vicious headache, which had plagued him for the past three days, had gone.

~ ~ ~

"Mr. Buffin." Back at the press conference, Emma picked out the reporter in a green Barber jacket, with a voice like a foghorn. "You have a question."

"I do indeed." Buffin cleared his throat. "Can we expect a statement from the prime minister, later today, on whether smoking cannabis is a good or bad thing? I think we are all a little confused. And should one inhale?" Buffin gave a throaty laugh. To use an analogy from cricket, the question was meant to be a gift to the minister, a soft lob that she could swing to the boundary for an easy four.

What happened next took everyone by surprise. The minister had been looking uncomfortable for the past few minutes. Her words came out in a snarl.

"We are here to talk about London, not some stupid non-story. If you lot have nothing better to write about than this, nonsense then, quite frankly, you are wasting everybody's time." She looked fiercely around the room. "Any more questions?" There was no response. "Right, that's it!" The minister stood up. "I do not have to put up with this any more."

Her eyes fixed on Jackie Jones, from the Times. She was wearing a red jacket, her usual short skirt and far too much makeup. She had a big perm and large grey eyes, fringed by thick flaps of crusted mascara. She looked like a small girl, corrupted by evil. The woman was as hard as nails. She had reported on several wars and had held her own in newsrooms against the biggest ball breakers on Fleet Street.

Emma stared menacingly into her face. Without another word, she turned and left the platform. She had disappeared before many people had realized what had happened.

Her press secretary, Linda Plaskitt, had seen her boss have tantrums many times before, but never in public. The reporters were looking at each other incredulously. They could not believe that such a brilliant story had fallen into their lap. Variations of the same clichéd intro had popped into each of their heads: "The embattled minister for London stormed angrily out a press conference ..."

Linda Plaskitt knew what would happen. The papers would all say that her boss was a "liability", that she was "accident prone" and "not a safe pair of hands". It was hard to put a positive slant on an outburst of petulance.

Her staff knew better than to speak to Emma when she was in this kind of mood. The black Jaguar whisked her straight back to Eland House. She did not say a word to her press secretary or her assistant, her pps or the driver. They sat in total silence. Politics is a cruel business. If a person is drowning, you do not cling to their body. You swim into clear water.

~ ~ ~

Emma set pensively in her office with a large drink. She was waiting for the Standard to arrive, before she made her next move. Often, on a big story, the Standard would give you a steer on how the nationals would play it the following day.

Her press secretary brought it into her office at half past two. Linda Plaskitt stood by the desk, saying nothing. There was a cheesy picture of Barry Triffit in his baseball cap on the front page and a large headline: "Cannabis MP has 'no regrets'".

The story began in a similar way to the Mail's, with the same quotes from Round the Houses. It continued that the day before, Triffit had defied a three-line whip to vote against the government on the second reading of the Crime and Public Order Bill. Triffit had never voted or even spoken against the government before.

Next, there were quotes from Barry Triffit's press conference that morning. The story said that he had announced his attention to leave the Labour party. He had told reporters: "I stand by literally everything I said last night. I now think that the party I once loved has gone too far. It is out of touch and it risks becoming an elected dictatorship. The problem is, it distrusts the people and it believes its own bullshit."

The minister turned to the editorial: "In the past few hours, a previously obscure MP has become an unlikely national figure. To some, he is a degenerate, to others, a hero. We believe that the Mr. Triffit is a sincere but misguided man. He has been wrestling with his conscience for some time and had no option but to air his views.

"The prime minister would do well to take note of Mr. Triffit's words. MPs are not merely robots and sometimes they speak their minds. His outburst could be a sign that the cracks in New Labour are beginning to show. It is now falling apart."

"Fucking hell!" Emma Henderson threw the newspaper across his desk. She glared at her press secretary. "How could this have happened?"

Linda Plaskitt shrugged.

"Just go," said the minister, "we'll talk about it later."

The press secretary left the room. Emma called up Prae Wood.

"Is that Derek?"

"Yes."

"Have you seen the Standard yet?"

"No, why?"

"Triffit is on the front page. He's becoming a national bloody hero. This was not supposed to happen, Derek, not this way. What are you going to do about it?"

"Nothing we can do."

"Sorry."

"I'm afraid that we have lost contact with him. The system crashed last night, when he was on TV. We have no visual or audio contact. We're looking at a blank screen here."

He heard her breathing.

"We can't terminate him. Do you want us to reel him in?"

"What?" Her mind had skipped to something else.

"Shall we bring him back to Prae Wood and have a poke around in his head? Because, the thing is, that's going to be tricky. He's got reporters all over him, like flies around a dead hedgehog. We won't be able to get near him for a while. And he's stopped going to Tesco's on Fridays, so we can't grab him there. He buys his groceries on the internet."

"He has the patience for that does he?"

"Yeh, apparently."

Triffit went up in the minister's estimation. She knew, from personal experience, that on-line shopping was next to impossible, unless you had the iron will of an SAS man, unlimited spare time and a computer with a planet-sized memory.

"We are in the shit then, aren't we." Even as she said these words, the minister was making a plan. They could pretend to be a production crew, for a cable TV company from Norway or somewhere. Foxton could be the director, Trevor Jones could be a gaffer – he looked right. They could grab Triffit from behind while he was talking to camera and shove him into the back of a van.

Back at Prae Wood, they could mess up his brain a bit and turn him into a vegetable. When they had done the business, they would toss him back. He would be useless now, as far as politics were concerned. He could become a DJ on Radio 2. Everyone would say that Triffit's mental condition had been caused by drugs.

They could easily pick some other hapless drone from the backbenches and make a new cyborg. Start again.

"On second thoughts, Derek, there is something that we can do." She felt almost cheerful again. "I'll give you a ring later and take you through it. I'm a bit busy at the moment. Ciao."

Next, she phoned her press secretary's extension and called her in. Emma was smiling when Linda came into the office.

"Right," she said. "The mess up at the press conference this morning. Made a complete tit of myself. What are we going to do about it?" Linda Paskitt sat down. The minister was listening as she spoke, but also writing. She had already had some ideas and was scribbling them down on her yellow legal pad.

~ ~ ~

On the morning of the press conference, Rick and Stacia were at Elmwood Park. Stacia had packed a few clothes in a small rucksack. She had also brought some items for Rick, including his razor. She did not know how long they would be staying.

They slept on a mattress on the floor. It was damp, because the flat, in Blackbird Point, had not been lived in for some time. The last occupants had been squatters.

At nine o'clock in the morning yellow stains of sun streaked across a dirty grey sky. They lay awake, listening to traffic and airplanes. There was a filthy piece of sheet tied across the window and they were staring up at a bare light bulb.

Rick felt guilty that he had dragged Stacia away from her warm, comfortable house. The funny thing was, they were really happy. They could not stop giggling.

He got up and rustled around in the kitchen. Making breakfast would be difficult, unless they wished to dine on cold water. There was a grease-encrusted electric oven, but no food.

Dennis Johnson had told him that there was a cafe on the estate. They could go down there to eat. Before they did, he needed to check in with Bob Clack on the Sunday World, to see what was going on.

The newspaper's number was stored into Rick's mobile. He got straight through to the editorial secretary.

"Hi, is Bob there?" There was a silence. "Bob Clack please."

"Didn't you know, love?"

"What?"

"I'm afraid that Bob is dead. He was killed last night."

"Sorry?"

"Bob has been killed. It was a car crash."

A sick feeling rose into Rick's throat. He said nothing.

"They say that he skidded off the road, into a wall, in his Clio.'

"I see."

"Shall I pass on your condolences to his wife?" the secretary said.

"Of course. I'm so sorry."

"We all are."

Rick felt empty. He ended the call.

21

BBC

England dreaming. Warm as coco, soft and fuzzy as socks on a radiator. The BBC are generally on our side and they won't bite the hand that feeds them – especially when a new director general has done his work. He will fragment, demoralize and confuse the whole network, lose sport to the competition and reduce the quality threshold. By the time he has finished, the BBC will be wall-to-wall crap.

- The New Labour papers

Rick's next call was to Steven Brown, Clack's boss on the Sunday World. He got through to a distant and irritable secretary (the kind that are used as gatekeepers on national papers). With bad grace, she put him through to the man himself. Brown was in a foul mood. He usually was.

"Rick who?" he said.

"Gilliver."

"Do I know you?"

"No, you don't. I was working on a story, with Bob Clack?"

Brown went quiet. From his large, glass-walled office was a panoramic view over docklands. The other way, he looked over the newsroom. Thursday was a busy day on the Sunday World. The room was full of movement.

Brown had been working in or near newsrooms for years. They were the world that had formed him – the fingers clattering across keyboards, the jokes and curses that relieved the tension, the murmured conversations, the bollockings, the phones cradled beneath reporters' chins.

In his present job, he was separated from the coalface by his glass wall. He was expected, by convention, to have temper tantrums, to drink whisky and smoke cigars in his transparent office, to have meetings there with important people from upstairs and to wear red braces, as badges of his authority. He was also expected to guide, in a presidential way, the paper's daily news conferences.

If Brown was the news desk's head of state then Bob Clack, the senior reporter, was its prime minister. Clack ran the news diary. He knew what was going on in the world, which soap star had just had her breasts enlarged, where the paper's reporters were at all times, exactly what they were doing, even the state of their love lives.

The reporters liked and respected Bob Clack – he was the salt of the earth, they all said, and a bloody good journalist. But they all thought that Steven Brown was a tosser.

He was the product of a minor public school and Cambridge. He had barely managed a desk before becoming news editor. He had only got the job because he was related by marriage to the publisher. To make matters even worse, his wife was a snooty bitch. She swept imperiously through the office, flaunting her expensive shopping and treating the staff like serfs.

Brown had assumed a certain coarseness, in an attempt to blend in. But it did not come naturally to him. His efforts to adopt the reporters' idiom came across as either patronizing or sneering.

The symbols of his power – the neatly pressed shirts, the cigars and the braces – meant nothing. He had nothing to back them up with except his arrogance. They meant less than nothing.

It was because Brown did not have the respect of any of his staff that he would frequently lose his temper. He would bully people in public, sometimes sacking them, on a whim, in his glass kingdom. Watching, his staff would snigger nervously, hoping that none of them would be next.

Sometimes, they would see Brown and Clack arguing. In the office, Clack would always support the decisions and tantrums of his boss, however stupid, from a sense of loyalty. But in the pub across the road, when his tongue was loosened by a few drinks, it was a different story.

Brown would normally follow a sacking with a glass of whisky, to steady his nerves. Afterwards, he would walk around the newsroom, spreading a brittle bonhomie. Only his secretary, Jean, was loyal to him. She had worked on newspapers for decades. A crabby, pretentious woman she was disliked by most of the reporters, who regarded her as a spy.

This morning's news conference had been strange, without the presence of Clack. Initially, the senior reporter's deputy, Sandra Thomas, led things along. It was an uneasy occasion. Brown lost his temper. He said that the meeting was a shambles and that he would have to take over. Sandra protested. He called her a moron. She fell silent.

That day, everyone tiptoed in a hush around Clack's empty desk. It had become a kind of shrine. Clack's mess was still there. His working methods were shambolic, which had always been a bone of contention with Brown. On the desk were tottering mounds of coffee-ringed press releases and junk mail, post-it notes embellished with his spidery handwriting that would never be followed up and decomposing food.

Clack used to buy fruit almost every day from a little stand across from the office. He had good intentions. The problem was, he hated fruit. So he never ate it.

Tomorrow, his desk would be tidied up by a secretary. His old notebooks would be put into cardboard boxes, to be stored for legal reasons. The rest of his stuff would be scooped into black bin bags and thrown away. Sympathy cards and bouquets of flowers were accumulating where he had sat.

The following week, they would be sent in a Sunday World car to his widow, Audrey. Clack also had two daughters. Their photographs were hidden in the clutter on his desk. They were lovely girls – auburn-haired and with toothy smiles. He had been enormously proud of them. The oldest, Charlotte, had just started at Bristol University. Neither of them was remotely interested in becoming a journalist.

Clack had been born on a council estate in south London and had left school when he was sixteen. He had clawed his way onto the nationals like a man scaling a cliff-face – crap jobs on local papers, a toehold on the Daily Mirror and, finally, the Sunday World. Approaching fifty, he had known that he would get no further. He had a beautiful house, private health insurance, two great daughters. He knew that he did not have the education or the contacts to work on the posh papers. It was just a question of coasting to his retirement

Steven Brown stood up. He was in a hurry to end this conversation.

"The thing is," said Rick, "I was working on the Emma Henderson story with Bob Clack." He waited for a response. There was a pause.

"I don't know what you are talking about."

"Sorry?"

"I don't know what you are talking about. Don't you understand English?"

"You know, the minister for London. She wrote this document, the New Labour papers and ..."

"I know who she fucking is.

"I was the one who got hold of them first and ..."

"Hold on my friend." The phrase was like a stop sign. "One, Bob Clack is dead and two, two, I have no idea what you are talking about and three I am not remotely interested. Do you understand?"

Rick started to say something.

"Yes? Good. And, by the way, I don't know who gave you my number but never phone me again. Now fuck of."

Brown threw down the receiver. From the other side of the glass, he could be seen mouthing an insult. The reporters wondered how Brown was going to scramble together a newspaper in less than two days without Clack. The clever ones would keep their heads down and rejoice silently as he screwed up. It was going to be interesting.

~ ~ ~

The morning after the press conference, Emma Henderson was scheduled to give a phone interview, on radio. She was appearing on Friday's Today program on Radio 4. Today was the big one – it both reflected and set the news agenda Normally, Emma took these things in her stride. Even at the height of the Digitrunk crisis, when she had been on Today several times, to good effect. To help her, Linda Plaskitt was nearby. Her job was to nod in the right places, to encourage her boss and to rescue her, if she appeared to be drowning.

Emma was finding it hard to concentrate. It was seven o'clock. She had drunk too much coffee and she had a headache. Her body was screaming out for more caffeine. She had been waiting to be contacted for the past twenty minute to do a short recorded interview that they would run later on.

The previous afternoon, Emma had been contacted by an anonymous caller, who had told her something extremely worrying. He had said did the minister know that she had been bugged, that she had been filmed and photographed in compromising positions and that the Sunday World was going to splash on her (it was an unfortunate phrase) on Sunday?

The minister said no and thank you. She made a call, immediately, to the Sunday World's publisher. The publisher, a former pornographer, had good connections with New Labour and was now angling for power and influence. They had met a couple of times, at parties. After a brief conversation, he told Emma that she could have all of the tapes – everything.

He would talk to the Sunday World's news editor, and get it sorted. She asked him who had been working on the story. He said that it would have been the senior reporter, Bob Clack. Emma asked for some personal details about Clack.

The pornographer spoke calmly and reassuringly, like a family solicitor. Don't worry, he said, no one will ever know. He did not tell Emma that he had his own copy of a videotape of her having sex at his home, that he had almost worn it out from fast forwarding and rewinding and that, at that moment, he was rubbing his stiff member through his shiny grey trousers.

Later that afternoon, a fat padded envelope had arrived by courier. In the envelope was the video. Emma gripped it delicately, between her shiny red fingernails. There was also a mini-cassette from a tape recorder and a flash card, containing digital photographs.

One thing had troubled Emma, when she had opened the package. The New Labour papers, the most incriminating piece of evidence, were not there. She was annoyed. She phoned the publisher but he was not there. She left his secretary a message.

This problem was at the back of her mind as she spoke to Today. Linda Plaskitt sat close to her boss on the white settee. She was holding a sheath of notes.

The interviewer, in the BBC's studio at White City, was Alistair McNulty. McNulty's, a frustrated lawyer, favored long-winded and convoluted questions. His florid interrogations were more designed to showcase his brilliance than to elicit an interesting response. Being interviewed by him was generally a doddle, like playing tennis with a blind man

"But things are getting better in London," said Emma. "They really are." She smiled at Linda Plaskitt. It was the first of the three points that they had decided to get across. The second point was the Mayor of London's extensive powers on traffic management. The third point was ... Oh Jesus, what was it? She could not remember.

The previous morning, two simultaneous accidents during the rush hour, combined with a simultaneous terrorist alert, had caused virtually the whole of London, from Hammersmith to Bethnal Green, to gridlock. Some people were stuck in their cars for seven hours. There was a riot in Shepherd's Bush.

Do you really think that traffic conditions are getting better?"

"Oh yes."

Emma was holding her hands as if she were praying. Linda Plaskitt had taught her to combine short answers with long ones.

"Go on, minister."

Linda smiled at her. "Well, I think that you will find that the congestion charge has made a significant reduction to traffic volumes since February. In fact ..."

"Hang on minister." McNulty was a master at the art of interruption.

"You were once opposed to the congestion charge, weren't you? Did you not say, in August 2003, that it would be an 'utter disaster' and that it would 'squeeze the life' from central London."

"So, I ..."

"You are not a big fan of the mayor either, are you, Ms. Henderson?" McNulty was warming to his theme.

"Didn't you once describe Ken Livingstone as a 'squalid little Marxist' and, on another occasion, as having 'the intelligence of a reptile'? You said last year that having him back in the Labour party would be like inviting Michael Jackson into your child's bedroom ..."

"Shut up!"

"Excuse me."

"I said, shut up."

Emma's lips were trembling. Linda Plaskitt leaned forward. She placed a hand on Emma's leg.

"For once in your life, why don't you fucking listen!"

Linda Plaskitt was shaking her head. Emma talked to for another forty-five seconds. McNulty did not interject again. After she had finished, he politely thanked the minister and terminated the interview.

Frantic phone calls were made, including from the prime minister's office. But Linda could not get the interview pulled. It was run, for the first time, including her rude remark, (although the f word had been bleeped) at eight fifteen, in between items on Libya destroying its weapons of mass destruction and a late February cold snap that was sweeping the country.

As soon as Today broadcast the item, another story was up and running, like a hare streaking down a dog track – F****ing minister loses her temper on radio. The following day's the newspapers would relish

Emma's outburst. They would run her quote prominently, some as a strapline – "For once in your life, why don't you F****ing listen!"

Immediately afterwards, neither of them said anything. Linda Plaskitt felt depressed. This was not going to make her look very good.

She realized that Emma was staring at her.

"Thanks," hissed the minister.

"What?"

"Thanks for helping me when I needed you." Emma's blue eyes were fixed on her victim. "Of course, I was making the assumption that you knew what you were doing."

Linda did not respond.

"You were not there for me, Linda, that was unforgivable."

Linda started to speak. "I don't think ..."

Emma's brow furrowed. There was one deep line there.

The press secretary squirmed in her seat. Emma looked out of the window, not registering the view.

~ ~ ~

While Linda Plaskitt tried to minimize the disaster, Emma brooded in her office. She removed the padded envelope from the Sunday World from her desk and fingered it. How was she going to get rid of the tapes? She could try to burn them in the barbecue on her little patio. The plastic would melt and make a terrible mess. It would smell bad too.

She remembered a time management course that she had once done. She must prioritise her actions. Deal with it now, delay, or do nothing. First, she called Derek Foxton at Prae Wood. She needed an update on Barry Triffit. Foxton's phone was on voice mail. It was eight-thirty. He would normally be at work by now.

Maybe he was avoiding her. She left him an anxious message.

Her next call was more personal.

"Hi, is that TJ?" It was her soothing, beguiling voice. There was a muffled reply. "Did I wake you up? I'm really sorry." Of course she had woken him up. He worked in a nightclub.

Trevor Jones was wearing tracksuit bottoms and a stained white sweatshirt. He had stumbled into the living room with his eyes half open when he had heard the phone. Trevor lived in a two-bedroom flat on the South Circular Road, in south London, at Tulse Hill. He had bought the flat five years before when he was flush. It was modern and sparsely furnished, a bachelor pad. Parked on the courtyard at the front was Trevor's black BMW. It was his pride and joy.

Next to Trevor's building, four lanes of traffic congealed from different directions into a single stream. He did not mind the noise, the periodic curses, the traffic fumes, the splenetic honking of horns. He found these things strangely reassuring. His car and the area around it were sacred. If he caught anyone messing with it, or parking in his spot, they would be lucky to escape with all of their limbs intact.

Trevor burped. He hoped that Emma could not hear the noise. His living room smelled of unwashed gym clothes. This was because he used it for exercising and lifting weights.

"How are you sweetie?"

He half suppressed a yawn. "I'm all right, cheers."

"Trevor." She went straight business, as usual. "Did you do that little job for me. You know, the journalist, Clack?"

Trevor smiled. Clack the hack.

"Yeh," he said. "It's sorted. Code nine."

"That is excellent." Emma touched a paperweight on her desk, a plain cube of Italian glass.

"Trevor," she said, tentatively, "you know Nigel?"

Of course he knew Nigel.

"Did you know that he has been filming me, secretly?"

"What do you mean?"

"He has been filming me in his office ... making love."

The phrase lingered in Trevor's mind. It sounded curious, like a foreign phrase. Making love.

"He has made videos of me, Trevor. He has also been recording my personal telephone calls. What do you think about that?"

"I don't know." Trevor rubbed his thigh contemplatively.

"Nigel has been also talking to the press. He has been stitching me up. Big time."

"Yeh?" It was funny when Emma spoke in slang. It was like the queen using plastic cutlery.

"It was Nigel who did a deal with Clack. He sold me out, Trevor." She sniffed, as if she were about to cry. Trevor knew that they would be crocodile tears. But, still, he felt an urge to protect her. He always did. "He's a little cheat Trevor. I can't believe that he has done this to me."

"So?" Trevor massaged a thick bicep.

"I don't know. Do you think we could ... Do you think that you could?"

Kill Nigel? Of course he could. He was as weedy as a girl. But Trevor had worked for him for eleven years.

"I know that you are loyal, Trevor, I admire that. It is one of your best qualities. But the bottom line is this. I know that he is your boss. But if I go down, he goes down, and then you would go down too. Do you follow me?"

Trevor would have to think it through.

"Don't worry about your job. I will make sure that you keep it, whoever takes over the club."

She paused. "Would you do this one teenie weenie little thing for me, just as a favor? Please?"

How could he refuse a request like that?

"OK." He did not sound certain.

"Are you sure?"

"Yeh, of course."

"You darling. You absolute darling. I love you."

Trevor felt himself puffing up with pride.

"You'll need to do it in the next few days. I shall phone you again next week. I think that we should meet soon, so that I can give you a present. Maybe we could have dinner? Does that sound nice?"

Dinner. He was staggered.

"Yeh."

"Good. That is absolutely super. Listen Trevor, have a smashing weekend and we'll talk soon. Bye now."

"Bye."

Trevor heard the phone click. He wondered what he should have for breakfast.

Emma did not need to look up the next number. It was lodged in her head. She knew that she would have to wait for ages for the phone to be answered and that the person who spoke would be wheezing.

"Hello, Birdsall here."

"Uncle Paddy?"

"Hello, my darling. Are you all right? What's wrong?"

Emma felt sadness welling up inside her.

"Oh, Paddy, I am in such a mess." She sniffed. She explained to him what had happened – the press conference, the Today program. She did not, however, tell him about Barry Triffit.

He listened, murmuring in the right places. He told her not to worry and that worse things happened at sea.

"Why don't you come and see me?" he said.

"Could I?"

"Of course"

"When?"

"You can come tomorrow. Betty is having a day off. I can look after you, poppet. Will you come?"

"Oh yes, uncle." He voice sounded bright.

"Splendid. Remember, take deep breaths. Don't worry. Paddy will sort everything out, like he always does."

"Oh, thank you. Thank you so much."

"Think nothing of it. I shall be expecting you my sweet. Love you."

"Bye."

She put the down the phone, smiling. Uncle Paddy always cheered her up. Tonight, she would have a nice dinner with one of her girl friends. She would spend the following afternoon at Paddy's house in Chertsey.

22

EU
It's undemocratic, its incomprehensible and its inefficient. In other words, it's the ideal form of government. Public position – hang on matey, we're British. Private position – yes, please, give it to me! Now!

- The New Labour papers

"Hi Tracie."

Tony walked into the room.

She looked up from her writing pad. He told her not to get up. He was carrying a mug of coffee. It was a red and white Arsenal mug.

The prime minister enjoyed these Saturday mornings. They were a chance to catch up with things that he had not seen or heard, to chew over who was bitching about him, who was coming up and who was sliding down. Tracie Parsons, his personal secretary, had taken on a pivotal role since the departure of his director of communications. She filtered what was coming in, and helped him to spin and nuance what was going out.

In the center of the living room in 10 Downing Street was a large coffee table. It was not aggressively modern. It blended in with the embossed wallpaper, the oil paintings, the brown leather settee and matching armchairs. The table was scattered with broadsheets and tabloids and magazines.

It was OK magazine that Tony tended to take away after the meeting, saying that it was for Cherie. Sometimes, he would take The Economist too.

Tony was wearing faded, recently washed Levis and a pale blue shirt, open at the neck. Tracie was in a dark blue Marks and Spencers suit and a white blouse. She had coppery hair, almost red, and green eyes. She always wore scarlet lipstick. Her skin was smooth and creamy.

Tony had known her since they were teenagers. She was a bright, inquisitive woman who laughed easily. Professionally, she was an optimist, but she was not afraid to speak the truth.

Tracie was siting on the settee with a pad on her knees. She had made several pages of notes, in her dense italic handwriting. Some of the newspapers and magazines had been marked with highlighter pen. She had also photocopied a couple of things for him to read.

Tony eased himself down, looking for a spot on the table for his mug. In the background, a boy's voice could be heard. It was a small child, whining for attention.

"For God's sake, Leo. Not now. Go and see mummy!"

He was not normally so irritable. It had been a tough few days, what with the furor over the bugging of the headquarters of the UN Secretary General, Kofi Annan.

Where should they begin – Iraq, top-up fees, foundation hospitals? Tracie glanced down at her list. They usually tackled the big topics first.

Tony was scanning the papers on the table. Something had caught his eye. It was a two-page feature in the Daily Mail. The headline was Truth is the best drug. At the center of the spread was a portrait of Barry Triffit, with his wife Suzie and his son Frazer.

They were arranged on a chintz-covered settee, in the MP's living room in Northampton.

Barry was wearing a blue baseball cap. He was smiling, with one hand on the shoulder of Frazer, who had a mischievous expression. Suzie posed stiffly, in a cotton print dress. There was a wary look in her eyes. Only Barry seemed happy.

Tony read the intro: "Barry Triffit used to be a stressed-out, 24-hour-a-day MP. He was tired and bad-tempered. Even when he was sleeping he was working. He barely saw his wife and his four-year-old son.

"Now the controversial back-bencher, whose revelations have rocked New Labour, has vowed to slow down and will spend more time with his family. But he has also promised not to give up on his political trademark – speaking the truth."

Tony's pupils flicked back to the picture. Triffit certainly looked at ease. He was a family man, dressed for the weekend in his little suburban castle.

He spoke his thoughts.

"They seem to like him."

"They like his honesty."

"But the drugs thing ..."

Tracie looked up from her notes. "Let's face it, Tony, who hasn't smoked a bit of dope." She paused, unsure of his reaction. "He says in the article that he doesn't really want to leave the Labour party and that he hates the Tories. He just wants the party to change."

"Change?"

Tracie had already come up with some phrases – New New Labour, grown-up politics, social Socialism.

"You know," she said, "be more tolerant, admit when things are going wrong."

He looked at her. Was she mad?

"But, Tracie ..."

"I know that things are tough. I think that you have won most people over on the war. I actually think that they should see more of your human side. See you worrying about things. Thinking about issues, wrestling with your conscience."

"Like Clare Short?"

They both laughed. The joke was that when Clare Short wrestled with her conscience, she always won.

"I know it's a bit risky."

"What does this have to do with Triffit?"

He studied the photograph.

"I think that you should invite him in for a little chat in Downing Street. We can tell the press that you would like to talk about his worries – if he accepts of course."

Tony frowned. He remembered asking Noel Gallagher and his rock star chums round to Downing Street back in 1997. The Brit pop thing. Some very rude graffiti had been scribbled in the lavatory. Tracie picked up his uncertainty.

"Just informally. I just think that you should be seen to be listening to what he is saying."

The PM laughed nervously. "Maybe I should make him minister for youth culture. Or I could ask him to rewrite the manifesto."

Tracie shrugged. She took a sip of tea, from a white bone china cup. She could see that he was impatient to end the session. He wanted to spend some time with Leo, his five-year-old.

"Right, next," he said.

"Emma Henderson."

"Oh." Tony looked troubled.

"On Thursday, she behaved like a petulant prima donna at a press conference. Yesterday morning, on the Today program, she used an expletive." Tracie paused.

"I think you know all about that." She looked down. One of the papers had led on the minister's outburst.

Tony looked down disapprovingly. Sometimes, he could be surprisingly prudish. Tracie placed her notes carefully on the table.

"What about her libel case against Private Eye?" he said.

"She's determined to fight it. But the press is starting to dig up more and more stuff on her, and some of it is sticking. She is looking vulnerable."

"What should I do?"

She studied his face. He looked tired.

"Dump her. I don't think that you should have given her another chance. If you front out this one, you're going to regret it. Look at Jeffrey Archer. You're lucky, because it's not too late. Pull the plug now."

He nodded.

"I would put her on a tight leash until the London mayoral elections – no statements, no press conferences, no nothing. She can bask in some of the glory when Ken Livingstone is voted in as Labour's candidate. At least she can say that she backed him. If she decides to fight her trial, she will resign first, like Aitken did. Then events will decide things for you. But I wouldn't have her back, even if she wins."

Tony knew what to do. He would not say anything officially. If pressed, he would defend her. But he would put the word out, through the usual channels, that Emma Henderson was about as welcome in Downing Street as herpes. The press would understand. The Ice Maiden had screwed up too many times.

It was a shame. She was so talented. Perhaps the script of failure was written in her perfection.

"Right. That's settled then."

Tony looked at his watch. Saturday morning was his only chance to kick a ball about in the garden with

little Leo, Arsenal's star striker of the future. He liked
doing that, far more than squeezing people's hands or
smiling inanely for the cameras. Sometimes, he would
catch a sight of Gordon Brown's pale, wistful face in a
back window of number 11 Downing Street, next door.

"What's next?"

"The European constitution."

Tony groaned. The right-wing press was violently
against it and they were clamoring for a referendum on
the subject. This was embarrassing. The referendum on
economic convergence had already been put on
indefinite hold. What was wrong with the Mail and the
Telegraph? Didn't they want people to have more
rights?

~ ~ ~

Trevor Jones had been having bad dreams. They
were coming more and more frequently. And they were
merging with memories which were like hideous
flashbacks. Increasingly, he could not distinguish
between what had really happened and what he
imagined.

In one nightmare, he saw the eye socket of Clive
Exley the first man that he had killed. Snakes and
maggots were writhing there. There was blood and
puss in the space that his knife had gouged. In another,
a man begged for mercy as concrete was poured over
his broken legs. The grey sludge slowly enveloped him.
The last thing to be covered was his face. Sometimes,
Trevor saw his own face.

Often, he heard Spider's voice inside his head –
whining on the playground when they were kids,
urging him on, as he kicked in a poof. What cut him up
most was Spider pleading for his life. Please Trevor,
please don't, please mate ... please Trevor ...

He remembered playing with Spider in his mum's
flat in Stockwell. Two little lads making model

airplanes. Eating fish fingers made by his mum. Nearly every day, he heard in his mind the front door click, on the day that his mum had left him and never came back. She had told him he should be at school. He had grunted, not looking up from the TV. He always wished that he had said goodbye.

Last night, Trevor had had a terrible dream. He had seen a contorted white face peering through a car window. The car was burning. The man was screaming in agony, as fire consumed him. Their eyes locked together. The man's face turned red as it blistered and melted. The man's hands came up and flapped against a window. They left smears of blood. His body slid back into the flames. He became a shadow and then nothing, as the fire ate him up.

Trevor gripped his sodden duvet cover. It was an ill-defined time, halfway between darkness and light. At first, he was relieved that he was lying in his bed. Then he remembered. This had really happened – to Bob Clack.

~ ~ ~

On Saturday morning, the day after Emma Henderson phoned him about killing De Vere, Trevor was walking up Brixton Road. Brixton was the center of his world. He could not remember anything before he had known this landscape – the grey skies, the joss-stick hustlers mingling around the tube station, the dark-clothed people, like football crowds, grimly waiting for buses in the rain.

Trevor was heading towards a pub in Electric Avenue, where he was to meet one of his mates. He was feeling very sad. He knew that when he had downed a few lagers, his mood would intensify. He would remember bad things and little tears would stream down his cheeks.

In front of the tube station, the usual weirdos were colliding with shoppers. They were toting used travel passes, chanting through megaphones, waving their proxy petitions around. A record shop boomed out drum and bass from a shop across the road.

Suddenly, someone thrust a pale blue flyer into his hand. Normally, Trevor did not accept shit like that but, for some reason, today, he took it. The piece of paper was headed Sunday of Decision. There was a list on it – Everything Gone Wrong. Nightmares. Can't sleep. Depression.

Trevor perused the words, his lips moving, mentally ticking each category. The flyer quoted the Book of Solomon. "I am the rose of Sharon and the lily of the valley. As the lily among the thorns, so is my love among the daughters." It invited him to a service on Sunday. There was a message across the bottom – Kiss your old life ... good-bye!

He folded the piece of paper and placed it carefully in his breast pocket. In the pub, he touched it every so often, to check that it was still there.

The next morning, whether by accident or design, Trevor was in Brixton Road again. He had been thinking a lot the previous night and studying the leaflet. The church did not look like a religious building. It was more like a shop.

Through the window, he could see neat rows of chairs and a polished linoleum floor. A few people were already inside. They were all black. At first, he was far too nervous to go in. He looked in through the door and walked past, quickly, towards Stockwell Road.

When he went back, the church was full. The people inside were milling around, smiling. Trevor looked through the door. He did not know whether his heart was thumping from excitement or fear. Music beckoned him. It was not like the hostile, pounding noise in the nightclub. The people were beginning to clap and sing. Trevor clenched and unclenched his fists. Then he went inside.

~ ~ ~

Rick was depressed. He and Stacia were living in a shabby room halfway up a shitty tower block. They had been there for four days. It was not safe to go back to Stacia's house. It was not safe to go anywhere, now that Clack was dead.

He had been trying to get hold of Sarah Lucas since Thursday. But she was always busy, or her mobile was turned off.

It was Saturday morning. Stacia was still in bed. He stood in the living room and punched a number impatiently into his phone.

"Sarah Lucas?"

"Yeh." Christ, it was her at last. Her voice sounded distracted. She had decided to be in a bad mood. But she changed her mind when she realized who it was.

"It's Rick here, Rick Gilliver."

"Oh hi Rick, how are you?"

"Fine. What the hell is going on?"

"What do you mean?"

"I've spoken to Steven Brown. He treated me like a piece of dirt under his shoe. He said he didn't know anything about the Emma Henderson story."

"Rick." Sarah Lucas looked around, the newsroom. "It's not a good moment. I'll phone you back in about ten minutes. OK?" She hung up.

He did not think that she would call back. It was all over, he told himself. His life was ruined. He stared through the window. The view from the north-facing window was miserable – tower blocks and a grey sky sagging with clouds. He had no job and no home. Now there was no physical evidence of Emma Henderson's wrongdoing. It was all word of mouth. What would happen to him? And what about Carol and Gina? He thought about phoning Sarah Lucas again. But there was no point. She would just blank him. The bitch. He felt sick.

His mobile played a little tune. He pushed the receive button.

"Hello."

"Hi, Rick." She sounded more positive but she was in a hurry. "That's better. I'm out outside now, so I can talk. You were asking me about Emma Henderson?"

"Yeh."

"What's happened is this." There was a rushing sound in the background, a lorry or an airplane. "Someone made Steven Brown pull the story. Brown has got rid of all of the evidence, Rick – all the stuff that was in the safe. And nobody is allowed to mention Emma Henderson in the office. If they do ..."

"Shit." Rick could imagine what would happen.

"But don't worry."

"What do you mean?"

"Clack was a sly old devil. He knew that something like this might happen. The day he was killed he told me that he had made copies of all of the evidence – everything. He told me where it was. He said that if anything was to happen to him, I should take it to another paper. I told him not to be so stupid." She paused. "I didn't think ..."

"Do you still have it?"

"What?"

"The evidence."

Sarah sniffed. "Yeh, I have some micro-cassettes, a copy of the New Labour papers, a video and a flash card with pictures one it."

Rick smiled. Bob Clack was a genius. He thought of something.

"Where is the original?"

"The original of what?"

"The New Labour papers."

She thought for a second.

"I don't know. They weren't in the safe.

Believe me Rick, we've got more than enough to crucify the bitch. We don't need them."

"What are we going to do?"

"You don't have to do anything. I know this reporter, Rachel, who works on the Guardian. I was at journalism college with her. I'm going to give all of the stuff to her. I'm seeing her tomorrow morning, in Clapham. I don't think that Emma Henderson has any influence over The Guardian. She won't be able to stop them."

The Guardian would wet itself when it realized what it had, Rick thought. It would love this story. The only danger would be an injunction.

"Do you reckon it will work?"

"Rick, I can't talk now. We're incredibly busy. I'll phone you in a few days. Are you still, you know where?"

"Yeh."

There was no furniture in the living room. The walls had not been painted papered or painted since the seventies. They looked like a skin disease.

"The Guardian will want to talk to you, Rick. But it will take them a while to get everything legalized. The good thing is, we're back in business. We've got to do this, Rick. We owe it to Bob."

"I know we do."

"Bye then. Talk soon."

Sarah had gone before he could tell her to be careful.

He slid the phone into the side pocket of his combats.

Rick could hear Stacia in the bedroom. She was getting dressed. He looked out of the window. A 747 loomed over the next tower block, dangling from the sky like a bird of prey. It would be making its descent into Luton Airport. Maybe they could fly somewhere when this was all over. Amsterdam or Nice, on Easy Jet. Rick did not feel sick anymore. He was cheerful again.

"Stacia." He tried to put some optimism into his voice. He would tell her the good news, then they would have a huge unhealthy breakfast, in the greasy spoon cafe on the estate. His stomach started to rumble in anticipation.

23

Failure
Remember, failure is only a state of mind. As such,
it does not exist, in politics or in life. A person who is
mentally fit can recover from any disaster. It is when
you are on your uppers – dodging bullets and wading
through shit – that the greatest opportunities will
come. But it takes a real hero to see that.

- The New Labour papers

Uncle Paddy's study was exactly the same as she
remembered it. She had not been in this room for
two years. But his smell was there. She recalled the
pungent, masculine aroma from her childhood. It was
a combination of old leather, moth-balls and pipe
smoke, with a hint of something spicy, like snuff or the
old-fashioned hair oil that he used to use.

When she was a little girl, her uncle had
encouraged her to explore his library. She had
developed a tactile relationship with his books. She
thought that the aromas of exotic places came from
their pages. There were the memoirs of civil servants
and military men, tales of pig sticking in the raj and of
doomed military campaigns on the Northwest frontier.
There were complete sets of Victorian novels and
antiquated works of reference, orange-jacketed
volumes from the Left Book Club, blue-spined Pelicans
and elderly Penguins, their spines now cracked and
faded to umber.

Uncle Paddy used to talk to her about politics. He would tell her about the rivalry between Stanley Baldwin and Ramsey Macdonald, "the loon from Lossiemouth" in the 1920s, as he puffed on his old briar pipe. He would dilate upon Winston Churchill's curious living arrangements and Anthony Eden's nervous breakdown after the Suez crisis. Uncle Paddy would talk of the battle of wills between Harold Wilson and Tony Benn and of George Brown's half-hearted fight with the bottle. Paddy brought their whisky-breathed ghosts into the room, as if he had known them personally. In many cases, he had. He spoke of their visions and vanities. Of how their ideas had been compromised by squabbles and frailties.

Some children would have found Paddy dull, or even repellant. But Emma did not mind her Sunday visits to his house in Surrey at all. In fact, she looked forward to them. Emma liked the mischievous look in her uncle's eyes. She liked his stories, the scratch of his chin on her cheek and the peppery smell of his clothes.

The house had a long garden, sloping down to the Thames. There was a tennis court and an ancient, ramshackle boathouse. Every summer, Paddy held what he called his garden party. In her first year at Oxford she attended the gathering with a group of pals from the Socialist Workers Party. They had wandered around, trying to shock Paddy's friends with their roll-ups and their donkey jackets. Emma had sex in the shrubbery and emerged with twigs in her hair. Paddy was not scandalized at all. He found it all rather amusing.

They had always got on. Her father was the complete opposite to Paddy. He was a naval man, cautious and unimaginative. He would have been happy for her to marry and to quietly disappear into the

Home Counties, an invisible stalwart of the Women's Institute and jumble sales.

It was really because of her uncle that she became a politician. Paddy visited her at Oxford – her father never did. He was delighted when she became an MP and, as she climbed the Parliamentary ladder, he followed her progress, scouring the newspapers for stories about his golden niece and pasting them into scrapbooks. Paddy said that the day that she was made a minister was the proudest of his life.

Throughout her political career, she would phone him to ask his advice. Paddy was never dogmatic but always on the mark. He was upset when she got into political scrapes. But he knew that she was resilient and that she would bounce back – look at Aneurin Bevan, thrown out of the Labour party in 1939.

Paddy had grown up on a farm and had been educated at Winchester School and Oxford. He was a tall, red-haired youth, shy but very funny. His gifts were almost uncanny. He came down from Oxford with a first in Persian and Arabic. He was also fluent in French and German. There was only one place for him to go – the Foreign Office.

But he was bored and frustrated in the job. He was delighted to join the Guards regiment in 1939, just before he was due to be called up. In May 1940, he was seconded into the Special Operations Executive. He spent most of the war in Egypt and Palestine. In 1945, after his secret work with the Arabs, the thought of going back into some dingy office in Whitehall horrified him. Then he had a stroke of luck. His father knew Stafford Cripps, also a Winchester boy, who was President of the Board of Trade. Cripps took on Paddy, as his private secretary.

He retired from the civil service in 1976, the year that Harold Wilson resigned as prime minister. He was sixty, so it seemed the right time. James Callaghan made him a knight. He went to Buckingham Palace to get his gong. Arise, Sir Patrick William Birdsall. Emma was eleven then. She had just started at St Paul's School.

Paddy hated Margaret Thatcher, the next prime minister after Callaghan. Not because she was a Conservative, but because, in his eyes, she was small-minded and vulgar. His scorn for Thatcher was something that he shared with Emma as she grew up.

In his retirement, Paddy wrote a memoir of the 1930s and the war. There were four copies of the hardbacks, still in pristine sky-blue dust jackets, standing to attention on his shelves. He had wanted to call it Bombs and berets but the publisher would not let him. It was titled A Word in Your Ear.

When his wife died, he was desolate. He compensated by taking a keen interest in Emma and by working on the scrapbooks that followed the twists and turns of her career.

By 1997, when Blair got in, arthritis had crippled Paddy's joints, his lungs were weak and his sight was failing. Weeds had grown up through the tennis court. He now restricted himself to one pipe a day. A part-time housekeeper looked after him. He moved around the ground floor in an electric wheelchair, which he called his chariot. His parties had become diminished affairs – a little cluster of friends with glasses of Pimms, chatting wistfully about the latest obituaries in the Daily Telegraph.

~ ~ ~

Emma stood in the conservatory that led from Paddy's study. It was Saturday afternoon, too late for lunch but too early for tea. She had come out to Chertsey on the train from Waterloo. She was wearing a Lanvin dress, the color of forget-me-nots. She always tried to look smart for her uncle.

She heard a whirring noise from the wheelchair as he approached. There was a spot in the conservatory where Paddy always parked himself in the afternoons. He liked to enjoy the evening light, as the sun dipped through the trees by the river.

Paddy's face was pale and freckled. There was a trace of ginger in what was left of his hair. His skin looked too big for his face. It hung down from his chin in loose folds.

He beamed at her. He loved seeing Emma.

"You look wonderful, darling. Can you stay for dinner?"

Emma seemed uncertain. She glanced away. "I'm not sure uncle. I've got rather a lot on."

"I see. I quite understand." He squeezed her hand. He was always surprised how beautiful she was – her porcelain skin, her cornflower blue eyes.

"Well, poppet, how can uncle Paddy help you?"

Emma described how her ministerial career had gone off the rails. She explained how she had been stressed out at the press conference. How she had been terrible rude to a Radio 4 presenter. She would have to apologies to him. Paddy nodded. The lurid cuttings, which had bigger headlines than usual, had been carefully collated. They were waiting to be pasted into his latest book.

When she had finished, he was silent for a moment. "You're just going to have to ride it out," he said.

"I don't know if I can."

"Why not?"

"It may be too late for that." She looked through the window. They used to play croquet out there. "I think that Tony has turned against me. That bitch Tracie Parsons has been pouring poison into his ear."

"I see." He paused. "But the libel case. That will vindicate you?"

"I'm not so sure, uncle. It started well. The problem is, it's not just Private Eye that I'm dealing with. There's this little creep who works on a trade magazine. He has been telling horrible stories about me to the nationals ..."

Her words trailed off. Did Paddy know about the rumors? The cocaine. The killings. The sex with strangers.

"What's next then?" He moved his chair fractionally, so he could get a better look at her face. The conservatory's windows were smeared with lichen. Some of the panes were cracked.

"On Tuesday, I am seeing my lawyer, to go through the case. He's sure that I can win."

"Well, he would be, wouldn't he?" Paddy had had a lot of dealings with barristers, including the Attorney General, who was a close friend. "You must be sure, Emma, absolutely sure. Because if you lose ..." His watery eyes looked straight into hers. Emma sniffed. She felt tears coming. She bent awkwardly over the wheelchair. He cradled her head in his arms.

"Oh, poppet. Don't cry. Remember what I used to tell you. Politics is like a playground. There are the bullies and there are the quiet, clever ones, who bide their time. The quiet ones usually win. It just takes longer."

Emma pulled herself back. She was embarrassed that she had let herself go. He checked her face. "You're in a dip at the moment. But, you mark my words, this time next year, everybody will love you. And soon, you'll be in the cabinet, I'm quite sure of that."

"Do you think so?"

"I know so."

She looked down at her feet. "What about the libel case? I mean, should I go through with it?"

"Are any of the allegations true?"

Her gaze pierced him.

"No."

"Then you must fight it. It's the only thing you can do."

"OK." She felt better.

He pushed a small button and re-aligned the chair.

"I know things aren't going well for the government at the moment. But Blair has got the next election in the bag. London is just a stepping-stone for you, Emma. You've just got to keep your options open for when Blair goes down, as he certainly will." He paused.

"You know what." Paddy pushed a button on the arm of his wheelchair. He whirred slowly back into the shadows. "You are going to the top. The very top."

"Oh, Paddy." She laughed.

"There's something I have to show you." She could not see him now. He had turned the chair round and was rummaging in his writing cabinet.

"Someone sent me this weird thing. Don't know who. It came in a plain brown envelope." He moved forwards. "It's this." He offered her something. A sheaf of A4 paper. His fingers were red and swollen.

Emma took it. She gulped. It was the New Labour papers. The original copy, covered with her handwriting.

"Who sent you this?"

"I have absolutely no idea. It arrived yesterday morning. There was a London postmark."

"Have you read it?"

Paddy frowned.

"Oh yes."

"What is it?"

His eyes met hers, then flicked away. "It is remarkably cynical document, a kind of warped political primer, an update on Machiavelli, for New Labour. Whoever wrote it is a sick individual, I would say, a sociopath."

Emma laughed.

"Who do you think did write it?"

"I don't know. It's curious because some of things described here have happened, in real life, as it were. Some haven't. It reads to me like the work of a frustrated junior minister. Someone who has the morality of an alley cat and who knows some pretty unsavory characters in the East End. It's an insider, because they know all about the Language Generation Unit. Either that," he twisted his chair through forty-five degrees, "or it is a complete work of fiction."

"Of course, there is the handwriting. Looks like a lady's to me. One who went to a good school, where they teach you how to write properly. She is someone quite fastidious and well off – it's written with a fountain pen. Of course, I'm no expert."

Paddy moved past her. There were some geranium leaves on the conservatory floor, close to the back door.

"What are you going to do?"

He bent down to pick up the leaves. She heard him gasping for air. Paddy had weak lungs, from years of smoking. Chronic obstructed airways disease, the nurses called it. He kept a cylinder of oxygen in the kitchen.

"I'm going to send the papers to Sir Colin Hargreaves, head of the Civil Service. He'll pass it down to MI5, I should think. He'll want the handwriting boys to have a look at it. And forensics. I'm also going to send a copy to the prime minister's office."

"I see." She laughed again to cover her anxiety. Paddy reached out for the document. She handed it back.

"I know, you think that I am a silly old fool, my love. But I have to keep myself busy. I am still a public servant you know. It's in the blood." He chuckled. "Would you like some tea?"

Emma did not hear him. She was choosing the hymns for her uncle's funeral – We plough the fields and scatter, Oh come all ye faithful. There was a lovely little church in the village. Not that Paddy ever went to it. She would have to buy a new black outfit.

"Would you like some tea?"

"Sorry. Oh, yes please."

The task was quite straightforward, because he was so frail.

While her uncle was in the kitchen, Emma went into the living room. She selected a large silk cushion. It was peach-colored. She knew that he would place the tea service and a bowl of biscuits on a tray and bring them out to the conservatory, balanced precariously on the arms of his chair.

Emma waited for a couple of minutes and then went to the ground floor lavatory. She crept back into the conservatory, with the cushion hidden behind her back. Uncle Paddy was looking through the windows, surveying the dilapidated tennis court. He had been quite a good player once. When she had been a teenager they had tried to have a game. They had spent more time laughing than playing.

He did not hear her until the last few seconds. But it was too late. She placed the cushion over his face and, with two hands, jerked back his head, bracing the wheelchair against her body. At first, Paddy wriggled and groaned. He wet himself. She watched a dark stain spread across his trousers. She kept the cushion over his face long after he had stopped struggling. She bent down, to see if he was breathing and took the cushion away.

Paddy's head lolled to one side, his neck limp. His face was white and his tongue was protruding from his mouth. There was a blood on his chin. Emma whispered goodbye to her uncle. She took one of the cups and some of the biscuits and replaced them in the kitchen. Then she pushed his body forward from the chair, using her knuckles. He slumped onto the floor. They would think that he had died trying to pick up geranium leaves.

She took only two things from the house, the cushion, which was stained with her uncle's saliva and blood, and the New Labour papers. She burned the papers at the end of the drive, allowing herself a faint smile as their ash blew across the gravel. The cushion was a problem, because of its size. She went round the side of the house and made her way to the bottom of the garden. Next to the boathouse was a damp, wild place where water slapped into tangled roots.

There were always bluebells there. The smell of wild garlic reminded her of when she was a little girl. As she threw the cushion into the river, she began to cry. She watched the cushion float away, like a giant orange leaf. When it had disappeared, she wiped her face and walked back up the garden.

It was a bore. But she had to pretend to the police that she had gone to the house and that no one had answered the door. She had to watch as the police broke in and to gasp when they told her about the body. Then she had to shiver as if she were cold. The two policemen were extremely sympathetic. One of them was quite hunky, in a working class kind of way. He kept looking round at her in the back of the police car, driving to the station in Slough. Her blue skirt was quite short and, clearly distracted by her grief, she did not stop it riding up her thighs.

Emma made a statement in an interview room, sipping hot sweet tea and fighting back her tears. When she had finished, the police arranged for her to be taken back to London by a government chauffeur. It was eight o'clock when she turned the key in her front door. Emma was back just in time for Casualty.

24

The Big Issue
A magazine about rich people sold by poor people,
all budding capitalists. How cool is that! It hits the
zeitgeist spot on – voyeuristic consumerism combined
with economic aspiration.

- The New Labour papers

On Monday afternoon, the day after he had gone to church, Trevor sat in an interview room in Brixton police station. It was a gloomy room on the first floor, with no real colors – only beige and grey. It was not Trevor's first time in Brixton nick. He had been in the same room fifteen, years before. Then he had had been sullen and un-cooperative. The blinds were closed. There was a plastic cup of tea in front of him. It was untouched.

On the table was a three-page document. The witness statement had been taken down in longhand that morning and typed up at lunchtime. Trevor started reading.

Statement of: Trevor Raymond Jones. Age of witness: over 18. Occupation of witness: Security Manager. Address of witness: 23 Hardel Rise, Tulse Hill, London SW2.

He looked up. "Carry on?". The policeman nodded.

Trevor worked his way through the page, like a heavy man plodding through snow.

"I, Trevor Raymond Jones, am employed by the Think Tank night club, at the Elephant and Castle,

London SE1. I have worked at the Think Tank since 1993. My employer's name is Nigel De Vere. I hold the British Federation of Inn Keeper's door supervisor certificate. I also hold a brown belt in judo.

There was some stuff then about being in care and his first convictions for thefts and criminal damage. He skipped over it.

"In February 1994, I murdered Clive William Exley, known as 'Lucky', at a private party in Agar Grove, Camden. Mr. Exley was deputy manager of a drinking establishment in Brewer Street, London W1. I stabbed Mr. Exley with a bayonet in the face.

"I killed Mr. Exley on the instructions of Emma Henderson, the member of parliament. The body was disposed of, at a location known to me, near Chigwell, in Essex. I have also carried out robberies and assaults on her behalf

"In July or August, 1995 I was asked by Ms. Henderson to murder Reginald Harris, general secretary of the GMB trade union. I hanged Mr. Harris with blue synthetic fiber rope, in a garage premises off York Way, close to King's Cross railway station.

"On 17th February, 2004, Ms. Henderson instructed me to kill Adam Baker of Brixton. I strangled Mr. Baker with electrical flex, after torturing him in Ms. Henderson's presence, in my office.

"Two days later, I murdered Darren Philips, a door supervisor, also known as Spider, at my place of work. I shot Mr. Philips in the forehead, with a small caliber pistol. The bodies of Mr. Baker and Mr. Philips were disposed of, by me, at locations in Kent.

"On 25 February, I was responsible for the death of Robert Clack, journalist, in a road traffic accident."

Trevor read carefully, his lips moving. At the end of each sheet, he licked his index finger and looked up. There were a couple of small mistakes. He wrote on the document in ballpoint pen and initialed the changes. When he had finished, he signed and dated each page of the statement.

The young Detective Constable had grown up close to Trevor in Stockwell. Sarcasm came easily to him but he was trying to rein it in.

"Well, you have been a busy boy haven't you," he said. "You've done it all really, haven't you, crimewise?"

Trevor nodded.

"Except armed robbery."

"No, I've done that too." Trevor was offended.

"Is that right?"

The detective scooped the statement off the table.

"This Emma Henderson, you know her well do you?"

Trevor sniffed. "Very well."

"On a social basis?"

"What do you mean?"

The policeman noticed that Trevor was wearing a Rolex'

"How does she ask you to do this stuff? I mean, do you hear voices in your head? Or does she send you messages?"

Trevor looked into his eyes.

"She phones me up usually."

"What, regularly?"

"It depends. I done nothing for her for a few years and then she contacted me about three weeks ago."

"Go on."

The policeman listened carefully. Trevor was not a schizo. There was a name for people who claimed to have committed violent crimes. They were seeking a macabre kind of celebrity.

"We're having dinner together this week."

"Sorry?"

"Miss Henderson is coming round to my place."

"I see."

Trevor knitted his fingers together. He looked into the policeman's face.

"Ain't you going to arrest me then?"

"What for?"

Trevor pointed at the statement.

The policeman smiled.

"Look, Trevor. We've got to go through it first. Then we will have to make inquiries, to corroborate what you have said. If we do require you further, I can assure you, we'll be in touch straight away."

Trevor looked hurt.

"When?"

"I can't say. It depends."

Trevor looked crestfallen. OK then. The policeman decided to give him something.

"Mr. Jones, I am not formally cautioning you or charging you at this time, but I would ask you to remain where we can contact you for the next few days, because we may need to interview you, in connection with your statement."

Trevor looked happier.

"So I can go."

"Yes, Mr. Jones."

"But you'll be in touch with me."

"That's right. We'll be in touch, as soon as we have made further inquiries. I must ask you not to leave the country and to refrain from, er, killing anybody in the next forty-eight hours."

The policeman winked. But Trevor did not notice. The previous Trevor had hated policemen. He had never been polite to one before.

A door was opened for him.

"Thank you so much for coming in."

"It was a pleasure, mate."

Trevor walked through.

The policemen wondered whether to bin the statement. It was more of a psychiatric case study than anything else. He decided not to.

~ ~ ~

Everybody noticed a change in Trevor in the club that night. There was lightness about him and he smiled a lot. On his way in, he gave some money to a Big Issue seller. Before, he had always regarded them as scum. Why don't you get a fucking job mate? In the club, he was not rude or aggressive. He settled a disagreement, over the ownership of a drink, with tact and diplomacy.

It was a normal Monday. Office girls swayed together in groups in their uncomfortable shoes. Young men got into disputes over perceived slights. Their friends held them back. Girls in tight clothes watched as the young men spat insults at each other.

Most nights, some people drank themselves to oblivion. They vomited copiously in the dark alleyway at the back of the club. The young men urinated there. The most drunk and reckless of the women urinated in the alleyway too.

Trevor had seen it all before. He knew what people did and how they reacted. He knew who was dangerous and who was not. That night, he learned that it was possible to do his job in a new way. He did not tell anyone that he had been born again. But his little secret made him feel happy. He was a righteous man in Sodom and Gomorrah. He decided that night that he would leave the club and pursue another career.

The next night, Trevor was sitting in his office at nine o'clock, when the phone rang. Nigel De Vere kept a low profile at the beginning of the week. It would probably be him, giving instructions.

"Hi TJ." It was Emma. She sounded out of breath. "How are you?"

He frowned. "I'm fine."

"Good." She hesitated. "Have you done it yet?"

He didn't say anything.

"Have you, you know ..."

Killed Nigel. He thought for a second.

"Yeh, boss."

"When?"

"Last night." His brow furrowed. "What I done ..."

"I don't need to know the details, sweetie."

Even though she was not there, Trevor sensed her perfume. It was weird. Whenever he was hurting or killing she would squeal a little to urge him on. And he could always smell her.

"Listen, you know coming round for dinner ..." Good, he thought. She was going to cancel. "I think we should do it tonight. I know that it's ridiculously late. But I need to talk to you about something. Is that OK?"

"Of course it is." He wondered what they would eat.

"That is so sweet of you."

His face became flushed.

"I shall meet you at your little flat, at say, ten o'clock?"

Trevor gave her instructions. Emma could not follow them. But she humored him. She liked his south London accent, with its slurred elisions and ritualized phrases. It was almost like a foreign language.

"Thanks, TJ."

"You're sure you know where you're going?"

"Oh yes."

"Cheers then. See you later."

"Ciao."

Trevor put the phone down. He would have to leave early. He would put Spoons in charge of the club. When he saw her, he would explain that he had not killed Nigel and, also, that he had let Jesus into his life.

Trevor took a Bible from the drawer of his new desk. It was already book-marked, with bits of torn paper. He turned to Psalm 56. When I am afraid. I will trust in you. In God I trust. I will not be afraid.

~ ~ ~

At twenty past ten, she stood on Trevor's doorstep. It was a wet, miserable night. She was wearing a plain black coat and black leather gloves. Cars streamed by, illuminating the rain. Trevor has always liked the South Circular Road. The smell of it, its rhythms and noises made him feel secure. Now he lived virtually on top of it.

Emma had not wanted to use a driver or taxi tonight. She had arrived at Tulse Hill using a train and a strange little bus. It had been an interesting experience. She pushed the doorbell. She wondered what kind of food Trevor ate. Microwaved mush probably.

There was no response. She felt irritated because she was cold and wet. On the bus, she had tried to think herself into the role of a drab south London woman. Emma knew, vaguely, that working class people shopped from catalogues. They ate stewed greens and watched Coronation Street.

She had not known, before tonight, that poor people waited in the rain for hours for buses that did not come, that bus time-tables were ludicrous works of fiction and that bus drivers responded to polite complaints by being rude and sarcastic. She had been outraged. She had already decided to look into the scandal of London's failing transport system.

Just before she pressed the bell for a third time, Trevor came to the door. He had shaved, including his head, and had changed into a fresh lilac-colored shirt. The top button was undone, revealing a thin gold chain. He had an astringent, chemical smell, like anti-freeze.

Trevor did not say anything. He kissed her awkwardly on the cheek. He helped her out of her coat, almost swooning from her scent. Afterwards, he led her through a narrow hallway and up some stairs. She was wearing a silk Gucci dress, tight across the back.

Trevor's decorative style was minimalist. He had never bothered to paint the magnolia walls of his flat. Most of the things he needed, he kept on the floor. There were a few holes in the walls, where Trevor had vented his frustration by pounding the plasterboard with his fists.

Earlier, he had swept up newspapers, pizza boxes and piles of clothes and dumped them in his bedroom. He had turned up the central heating. It was oppressively hot and there was also a slightly rancid smell. Trevor had put on a CD. It was a collection of Ibiza anthems. The music thumped softly in the background.

He removed her coat.

"It's nice to be warm TJ. That awful bus."

Trevor looked blank. He did not use buses.

She sat, gingerly, on the settee. She turned her blue eyes on him. "Don't worry about food, sweetie, it really doesn't matter."

He seemed offended.

"I've got some lasagna."

She was surprised that he pronounced the word correctly.

"That sounds lovely."

"Would you like a drink?"

He was standing in front of her. She realized how bloody big he was. And strong.

"Yes, please."

"What would you like?"

She was studying the walls.

"White wine?"

"Oh yes, lovely. It's so sweet of you to cook for me, Trevor, at such short notice."

"I didn't cook it myself."

"No, but still." She smiled, placing a hand to her wet hair. "Would you like any help?"

"No. It's all right. Are you OK?"

"I am fine, TJ, sitting here. You do what you have to do."

"Right."

He went into the kitchen. She looked around. There were no books in the room, no photographs, no decorations. What on earth did Trevor do with his time? The wide-screen TV and DVD player in front of the settee were clues. And the gym weights.

She heard clanking. Trevor was foraging for glasses. She opened her handbag and removed something from it – a silver canister, with a plastic top. She hid the canister behind her.

Trevor removed the wine and a ready-cooked meal from the fridge. He placed the meal in the microwave. Then he opened a drawer for a corkscrew. He was muttering something, under his breath. It was a prayer. One that he would say over and over again.

"Lord Jesus, come into my heart now. I believe that you died on the cross to save me. Forgive me and wash away my sins. You are my Lord and savior. Thank you Jesus for saving me, amen."

The words reassured him. Trevor had popped a can of Stella. He had almost finished it already. A warm feeling was spreading through his body. What would she do when he told her about his new life? Should he tell her?

His large frame filled the doorway. There was a glass in his hand. She touched the canister, now warm. This was her opportunity.

"Oh thanks, TJ, that's lovely."

He approached, stretching out his hand. When he was close enough she pulled out the canister and depressed its plastic nozzle.

Trevor did not register what was happening at first. He had clocked the canister as a little can of hairspray. The gas chewed at his face, like a swarm of bees. Jesus, his fucking eyes. He raised his hand to rub them. He had also swallowed some of the gas. His throat stung.

Emma hoped that she had bought the time that she needed. She fumbled in her Gucci handbag for the knife. It was her sharpest kitchen knife, bought in a special offer from a color supplement.

She gripped the knife with two hands and plunged it upwards, towards his stomach. She was lucky. The blade entered Trevor just beneath his rib cage and punctured his left lung. Air hissed from the narrow wound as she removed the blade. A saucer of blood spread across his shirt.

Trevor folded in half, groaning. Emma stood up. She knew what to do next. She brought up her knee as hard as she could into his groin. He fell back onto the carpet.

With his left hand, Trevor felt the warm liquid seeping from his wound. His right arm was stretched out across the floor. He was blind. His eyes were burning. He thrashed at first, as he tried to breathe. Sweat had broken out all over his face, which had turned white. He began to make a noise. It was a weird sound, like people speaking in tongues.

Emma feared that it would take him a long time to die. She did not want to take any chances. A strange exaltation gripped her. Her crotch was wet now. Straddling his stomach, she grasped his right wrist with her left hand. With her free arm, she plunged her knife into his face. She stabbed and twisted the knife in each eye. Soon they were like strawberry jelly and ice cream, mashed up by a child's spoon.

Next, she pinned Trevor's hand to the floor with the knife. She had seen this done in a gangster film. The blade sliced through his skin and tendons and penetrated a few millimeters into the Victorian floorboards. She left it there. The local paper would love that – "Crucified man found in burnt flat".

A peculiar wheezing noise was coming from his throat. His face had turned parchment-colored. Blood was trickling from one corner of his mouth. The sight reminded her of her husband, lying on the garden path when she had pushed his ladder over. But Jonathan had died quickly.

Emma put her gloved hand over Trevor's mouth. She felt something stiffen beneath her. It was his cock. The little devil was getting an erection.

"It's too late now, Trevor."

He heard her voice. And he could smell her. He remembered now what the smell reminded him off. It was his mother's hair, after she had had a bath. He wanted to tell her. But his throat was tight. There was a wall between his brain and his mouth.

"Goodbye, Trevor."

Emma gave his testicles a valedictory squeeze. He felt the pain, dimly, as if through layers of gauze. She looked down at his ruined face. With no eyes, it was hard to relate to him as person. He was like one of those dreadful beggars in India. Soon, the noises from his throat ceased. She was pretty sure that he had stopped breathing. She decided to check with a little compact mirror in her handbag. It was next to the settee.

At that moment, she heard a sound. A door opened behind her.

25

Fame
It is the spur. But personal ambition is not enough.
There must be something else – something bigger than
you are, like a political party. Otherwise, you might
just as well be a presenter on daytime television.

- The New Labour papers

The day started brilliantly for Barry Triffit. It was the first Tuesday in March and there was sunshine, which was a bonus. It streamed through his bedroom window, as yellow as egg yolk. Suzie was still asleep when he woke up at eight o'clock. He watched her face quivering as she breathed. Her skin was white – too white, they needed a holiday – and she was getting a double chin. Underneath, was the woman he had met in Camden library, the sparky, bangle-covered feminist? He still loved her.

These days, Barry nearly always got up first, made some tea and toast and served it to his wife in bed. Since he had stopped going to the House of Commons, he was amazed how much energy he had. He still saw his constituents and dealt with their problems. In fact, he was seeing more of them – he was holding an extra surgery on Thursday nights. But he was spending his mornings at home, he was picking up Frazer from nursery and making dinner in the evenings. He had become a househusband. He liked his new role. He wished that he had changed his life years ago.

He had explained to his constituents that he had stopped following the Labour whip. But he was still in the party and it had not thrown him out. He might stand at the next general election as an independent, like George Galloway. He had not made up his mind yet.

In the past six days, since the television program and the features about him in the papers, Barry had become a minor celebrity. When he walked through Northampton town center, people shouted after him in the street. Others stared and pointed but did not say anything. No one had ever given Barry a second glance before. He always wore his blue baseball cap when he went out. Suzie had bought him another one, in case the original got lost.

Barry's postbag had also increased dramatically. Some letters just had his name on the envelope, plus Northampton, or MP. There were notes of support from people who wanted cannabis to be legalized – eccentric crusaders, stick thin soap dodgers in grimy denim.

Terminally ill people, who depended upon the drug, embellished their letters with smiley faces and impressions of cannabis leaves. Barry had become their hero

People who were worried about the direction that New Labour was going in wrote him long, earnest notes. Usually, they had just resigned, with regret, from the party. Other correspondents thought that Barry should be ashamed of himself. One, who had served in the war, had threatened to kill him. He had passed that letter to the police.

Barry went downstairs, humming to himself. He was wearing black tracksuit bottoms and a pale green T-shirt. Making love with Suzie the previous night had been brilliant. He smiled, thinking about it. Their roles had reversed. Now, he was the one who wanted to. She was too tired.

Barry heard a noise when he was halfway down – a load of letters cascading onto the doormat. It was taking longer and longer to open his mail. Soon, when the office day began, the phone would start ringing. He had changed his number at home. But it had made little difference. Newspapers and magazines were asking him to do interviews. He had been phoned by researchers from a couple of TV shows. One was a late night show that he and Suzie really liked. He had agreed to go on it, the following week.

Barry surveyed the puddle of letters on his doormat. He had always received lots of them, even when email had partially taken over – misspelled sagas of misfortune, peculiar trade magazines and unwelcome invitations, which he politely declined.

Today, hidden among them, was something special. In an expensive, lined envelope was an invitation to Downing Street. It was a short note, dictated in a few seconds, with a friendly confident signature – Tony Blair. Barry would have felt shocked and excited as he read the letter. He would have stored it for his grandchildren to read. But he was never to see it.

He went into the kitchen. The rear of the house trapped the morning sun. There was a little patio by the back door, where he and Suzie left out scraps of bread for the birds. There was also a water bowl, for the hedgehog.

Barry was still humming as he filled the kettle and slotted bread into the toaster. He turned the radio on, softly, so as not wake up Suzie. He still liked to listen to the Today program in the mornings. There was always some new crisis. It was like an aural blanket, attempting to protect the middle classes from the nastiness of the world. Sometimes, the voices talked about him.

The windowsill was crowded with cyclamens with purple, red and white flowers, like a gaudy banner. Suzie had green fingers. He looked out at his little suburban garden – the conifers, the shed for his tools, the yellow forsythia bush, the carefully mowed lawn. Since his personality had changed, he had hated the garden. It was far too formal, too rigid. Now he had plans. He was going to cut down the conifer trees and let the grass grow. There would be stepping stones in the lawn and patches of wild flowers. The garden was far too straight-laced. It needed to be much more, what was the word – funky.

The kettle clicked off, bringing his mind back into the kitchen. Pouring water into mugs, he reviewed his day. He would drive the car into town and drop off Suzie, then Frazer. He would spend the morning opening and answering letters and emails at his office at home. Frazer would have to be picked up at half-past three. He would play with the boy in the afternoon. Suzie would arrive home at half-past six, stressed from her meetings. He would massage her shoulders. They would eat tea and watch some television together.

The doorbell rang. Strange, it was only twenty past eight. Barry wiped his hands on a tea towel. He felt irritated. He was probably being door-stepped again by that young journalist from the local free sheet. It was too bloody early.

As he walked down the hall, Barry heard a metallic clunk from the toaster. It was sod's law, he thought. The toast would be cold by the time he got back to the kitchen.

Suzie heard the sound too. The doorbell had woken her up. She reached for Barry and murmured something when she did not find him. Frazer would be awake second, heading for their bed. She turned over to catch a few more minutes' sleep.

Barry saw the top of someone's head, first through the glass fanlights in his front door. He opened the door. The man was in his thirties, blond-haired and stockily built. He was wearing a black leather coat and carrying a clipboard.

"Delivery, mate."

"Delivery of what?"

"Brochures."

"What brochures?"

The man looked at him quizzically.

"The ones you ordered."

"But I didn't order any ..."

Barry felt exposed, standing outside in his tee shirt and slippers. The sun was bright but there was no warmth in it. His skin tingled.

"Better see 'em then, yeh?" The man glanced down at his clipboard. There was a small white van behind him, a Renault Kanga.

"OK."

The doors of the van were open. The man with a clipboard moved to one side.

As Barry leaned over, two hands shoved down hard on his back. There was another man crouching in the darkness inside. He grabbed Barry's T-shirt.

There was a brief, confusing struggle. The man outside pinioned Barry's legs to the floor. Barry felt only a slight sting as a needle was jabbed into his arm. It was hard to hold him. His body writhed convulsively, as the injection of potassium chloride did its work.

It took about ninety seconds for his heart to freeze. When Barry was still, the man with a clipboard cursed softly and pushed the legs inside. He looked around the quiet street. Then he shut the rear doors and got into the van.

~ ~ ~

Derek Foxton slotted the gear-stick into first and pulled off smoothly. He was very calm, Chris Drake thought, considering what they had just done.

Drake twisted round in the passenger seat. Barry was lying on his back. There was a red mark on the inside of his left arm where the needle had gone in. It was becoming a bruise. The worst sight was Barry's face. The head was bent back at a strange angle, as if his neck had been snapped.

Barry's eyes would have been staring straight up at Drake, if his pupils had not rolled back into his skull. The whites of the eyes were sallow. So was the face, as if it was made from wax. There was fresh blood on the mouth. It had dribbled down the tilted-back face, towards Barry's eyes, like a weird upside-down mustache.

On the moist yellow forehead Chris Drake could see a tiny white scar. This was the spot were they had inserted the neurolinguistic programmer into the MP's forebrain, down at Prae Wood, two years before.

"Jesus, he's ..."

"He's what?"

Foxton did not look back from his seat. He had to concentrate on turning into a main road.

"He's fucking dead."

Foxton did not say anything.

"Don't you understand? We've just killed somebody."

"Somebody?" Foxton accelerated into a clear space. There was a stiffness between second and third gears. It was annoying him.

"Aren't you forgetting something, Chris?" he said.

"What?"

"He was a cyborg. We made him. We terminated him. He wasn't human."

"But ..."

"Yeh, he had a wife and a kid and a nice little house with net curtains. So what? If anything, Chris, it was two years ago, when he had the brain implant, that was when we killed him."

"Yes, but ..."

"He lost his free will. That is what makes us human, is it not?" Foxton tutted to himself as he checked his wing mirror. He was stuck behind a lorry.

Drake looked down at the head. It was lolling around, as they went over bumps. It was like a tacky mock-up of something that had dropped off a guillotine.

"Yeh, I know, tell that to his grieving widow. OK Chris, it's sad. It's very fucking sad."

Drake opened his mouth. "I still think ..."

"Listen, it wasn't our fault. If we hadn't lost control of him, we would never have had to do this, would we? Blame those fucking hippies, not me."

"So we did kill him," said Drake.

"What do you mean?"

"When the neurolinguistic programmer broke down, he got his free will back. So he became human again."

Foxton decided to overtake. He changed down into third, to get some revs into the Kanga's engine.

"The programmer broke down intermittently, so, in that sense ..."

"It broke down completely. You know it did. Anyway, it's just semantics."

Drake did not respond. His face was pale. He was starting to feel sick.

Foxton slid neatly into a space in front of the lorry.

"OK," he said. "It's a shame. He was a great dad. He dug his garden. He went to Ikea. But these things happen. He's fucking dead. End of story."

He looked at Drake to check his reaction. They were silent for a few seconds.

"He was pretty crude, you know, poor old Barry," said Foxton.

"What do you mean?"

"I've been doing some thinking on how we could improve on him."

"Yeh?"

Drake always checked his work in progress with Chris. He was great to bounce ideas off.

"I've been thinking about a haptic interface, linked to the endocrine system."

"Go on."

"You wouldn't control the cyborg through a screen, with a mouse. You would be inside it. You would feel the same things that it did. If it was cold, you would be cold. It would be like..."

"Virtual biofeedback."

"Exactly."

Foxton had recently attended a conference on cybernetics. Ever since, he had been full of this stuff.

They were driving through Collingtree, close to junctiont 15 of the M1, when Foxton noticed something in his rearview mirror. There was a black van with mirrored windows behind him. It had been there since Northampton. He ignored it.

"You know," he said, "we've only just scratched the surface of this thing. And the thing is nobody else has done the work. I mean, on a human subject."

Foxton was scanning the side of the road, looking for somewhere to stop. The black van was keeping a steady distance.

"Imagine old Barry here, rigged up with some enhancements. He could leave the Terminator standing. He could make Stephen Hawking look shabby."

Chris Drake smiled.

"Take it one stage further. Imagine a bio-robot, a roborg, with artificial intelligence and servo-prosthetics, linked to a controller through a haptic interface. You could do anything you liked with it. You could jump over houses.

"Now imagine a warehouse, or a biodome, with tropical forests, or a lake, or deserts. It's full of roborgs. And they are interacting with each other. Controlled by you. You are sitting at home, with this virtual reality helmet on."

"Games, yeh?" said Drake. It sounded a lot more fun than the House of Commons.

"Exactly, Chris. That's where we should go with this. Fuck politics."

Foxton had a little secret. An American company had recently sent him an email and he had written back. It was a defense company but there were just as many dollars in making games as there were in killing. They wanted Foxton to be the scientific director of their new leisure division. He had already said yes. And he wanted Chris Drake to go with him.

Foxton slowed down. He had spotted a restaurant. The last one before the motorway.

"Coffee?"

Chris Drake smiled. Color had returned to his face. "Yeh." He glanced back at the body. It was just meat now.

Foxton delayed before indicating, for as long as he could. He glanced back to see if the black van copied his maneuver. It did. It was probably only a coincidence, he thought, dismissing his anxiety. Ahead was a neat little building with a red tiled roof. A Wimpey restaurant.

The black van, a Mercedes Sprinter, drifted along behind the Kanga. It came to a stop as Foxton searched for a parking place.

He and Chris got out of the white van at the same time. A fraction later, the rear doors of the black Mercedes swung open. Two men jumped out. They were wearing black trousers, polo necks and balaclavas.

The Heckler and Koch MP5 submachine gun can fire up to 600 rounds per minute. Each man emptied one 30-round magazine in three-round bursts. Foxton went down first. The bullets chewed up his chest. Drake managed to cover some ground. He was hit first in the back of the head. His brains splattered onto the car park.

The two men did not hang around. They had one more job to do. They opened up the back of the Kanga and pulled out Barry Triffit's body. The Mercedes reversed up close to them. Quickly, they bundled the body inside. Then they drove off.

26

Benefits
Keep 'em complicated, bureaucratic and labor intensive and add tax credits to the brew. Creates work for paper shufflers and encourages the black economy, which, of course, keeps down labor costs.

- The New Labour papers

There was a curious aroma in the Elmwood Park social club – a sickly combination of vinegary old wine and beer, mixed with cigarette ends and disinfectant. It was the kind of aroma that lingers in living rooms, like the last guests, the night after a riotous party. The smell reminded Rick of his student days. It was almost giving him a hangover.

He was sitting on a plastic covered bench, close to a shuttered-up bar. This was a night place, etiolated in the daytime. Morning light drifted fitfully through the grilled windows. It slithered across a grey linoleum floor, scuffed with black marks from a million stiletto heels.

Rick had already flicked through that morning's Guardian. He had lost interest when he saw that there was nothing in it about the crisis of Emma Henderson – Tony Blair's accident-prone minister. Now he was skimming the pointless bits of the paper – features on wannabe celebrities and the brittle gossip of columnists. On their picture by-lines, the female columnists looked fresh-faced and perky, with a hint of irony. Appearance was obviously a factor in their recruitment. Stubble and deeply shadowed eyes were de rigueur for the male versions. They wrote about the tribulations of living in Wimbeldon.

A startling sound crashed into Rick's brain. It was a chord played on a Fender Telecaster guitar. There was a small raised platform at the other end of the social club. Dennis Johnson was sitting on a plastic chair on the stage, next to Stacia. She was leaning against a speaker cabinet.

He played some jazzy chords on his guitar, looking at Stacia. She began to sing. When Dennis smiled, she grew in confidence. It was amazing that so much noise could come from such a small person.

The previous night, when they were drinking in the estate pub, Dennis had told Stacia that his band was looking for a singer. Why didn't she have a go? Stacia said that she was more new wave than R and B. Dennis said no problem. Why didn't they have a try out the following morning?

Stacia would have been horrified about singing to jazz chords when she was a punk. But she was a lot more tolerant these days. She smiled as Dennis played. This was fun.

Something began to wriggle like a ferret in Rick's coat pocket. It was his mobile. He removed it with his left hand, cupping his right around his ear.

"Hi."

"Hello, Coverington," the voice said.

"Coverington who?"

"Roger Coverington." The voice sounded slightly annoyed. "From the Guardian."

"Oh, I see."

It was the man who dressed in corduroy. The journalist with wire-rimmed spectacles who asked complicated questions at press conferences.

"I can't hear you very well. You seem to be ..."

Rick stood up. He went through a door next to the bar. The music was still loud, but it was muffled.

"Is that better?"

"Yes, it is."

"I'm in a toilet now."

"Oh." Coverington did not laugh, which was a bad sign. He sounded embarrassed. "We would like you to come in to see us. Could you do that, do you think?"

"Yeh, I suppose so. Why?"

"Something's happened."

"Is it Emma Henderson?"

"Yes."

"What?"

"Listen, I can't really ..."

"Has she been arrested or something?"

"Yes."

"Fantastic. Why? Where?"

"I'm afraid I can't give you the details."

"Is she still in custody?"

"Um ... yes."

"It must be pretty serious."

Coverington did not say anything. Rick disliked people who used silence tactically.

"You still haven't told me what she's done."

"I can't do that."

Something inside Rick snapped. "What do you mean you can't tell me? This is my fucking story."

Coverington started to stammer something. He was not used to being sworn at, even by his news editor.

"I don't think ..."

"Listen. You need me. And if you want my co-operation I suggest that you start being seriously civil and polite. Starting from fucking now." You pompous twat, he thought. Fortunately, he did not say it. He turned off his phone. He took some lungfuls of air to calm himself down. He went back to his seat, trembling. He decided to wait for a few minutes, before turning his mobile on again. Coverington would phone back ... he knew that.

Dennis and Stacia were playing a cheesy song from the '80s. Rick was pleased to see her happy. Also, something had just occurred to him. What with Emma Henderson being banged up, he was safe. The Ice Maiden had melted.

The day before, he had signed on for the Jobseeker's Allowance. It had been Stacia's idea. He wouldn't get any cash for weeks, because he had made himself unemployed. A question on the form had asked why he had left his last job. Because someone is trying to kill me? He had left the space blank.

He did not want Stacia or Dennis to see him misting up. He decided to go outside. He stood by the door of the social club and sat on a grass verge. After a while, he turned on his mobile. Thirty seconds later, it chirruped.

"Hi."

"Hello. Look, I'm sorry if we got off on the wrong foot. Can we start again, Richard?"

Rick took a deep breath. At least Coverington was trying.

"Yeh, why not. Please call me Rick. There was a pause. "So, what's happened?"

"Well, Emma Henderson was arrested last night. It's rather an amazing story. She was in a flat, in south London. The chap in the flat upstairs had a key, because he was mates with the guy who lived there. At about half past ten, he let himself into the flat after he heard some noises."

"And?"

"There was a blonde, well-dressed woman sitting on his neighbor, clutching his testicles. The man's hand had been pinned to the floor with a dagger. Apparently, she had ... gouged his eyes out. There was blood everywhere."

"What happened next?"

"He was a bit concerned, naturally, so he locked her in and called the police?"

"Didn't she try to escape?"

"She couldn't. The flat was on the second floor."

"Where is she now?"

"She's in Brixton police station, remanded in custody. According to our contact, she's already been charged with murder. The chap she killed was head of security at the Think Tank night club."

"Fucking hell."

"Exactly. She was carrying lighter fuel. The police think she would have torched the building if she hadn't been caught. She could have burnt everyone in there to a cinder."

"Jesus, the evil cow. Do they know about any of the other murders?"

"Don't know. Apparently, this guy from the nightclub had made a statement to the police, just before he was killed. So they must know quite a lot. They'll know a lot more when they've seen tomorrow's Guardian."

The police don't read the Guardian, Rick thought.

"So you're running the story tomorrow?"

"Yes, we have to. The other papers will lead on the murder but they won't have much detail. Some rather interesting documents have come into our possession – audio and video tapes, and photographs."

"The stuff from the Sunday World?"

"I'm not sure where it came from."

Coverington sounded unconvincing. He was at it again. Being evasive. Still, at least the story was going to come out.

"Are you going to use the pictures?"

"Some of them." Rick could sense Coverington blushing.

"You'll have to be careful. It will all be *sub judice*, now that she's been charged."

"We do know that. But it partly depends on what she is being charged with." Irritability was returning to Coverington's voice.

"Sorry," said Rick. He waited.

"Look, I'll lay my cards on the table. We need you. I am aware that other newspapers may make you offers. Perhaps they already have. As you know the Guardian does not generally wave checkbooks around. However, in this case ..." He paused. "Could I just ask you not to talk to them, until you have seen us?"

Rick had been reading the Guardian for his entire adult life. There was no way that he would even consider going to another paper. For all its foibles and absurdities, it was as familiar to him as a family member.

Coverington breathed heavily. "There isn't much time. How about it?"

"Yes, I will talk to you."

"Good. I'll tell you what, we can send a car to pick you up. How does that sound?" It sounded great. There was a train direct from Luton to Farringdon, where the Guardian was based. But Rick was not going to turn down an offer like that.

"Where are you, by the way?"

Rick told him.

"OK, just hang on then. Our car will be there in about an hour. And thanks ... mate."

The term of familiarity did not come naturally to Coverington. He only used it when he was talking to plumbers or other tradespeople.

"My pleasure. Bye."

"Ciao."

Rick smiled, trying not to feel smug. Tomorrow, on Thursday, his name would be all over the Guardian. After that, the story would rampage its way across the planet. He would be famous. Maybe he would be able to get a new job on the back of it. But not on Widget World or Caravan Monthly. He had finished with trade magazines.

The media would whip themselves into a frenzy about Emma Henderson, the minister who had lied to the House and nailed a man to the floor. The saga of the Ice Maiden would run for years. There would be innumerable editorials and features, TV documentaries and, later, books.

Rick doubted that it would bring the government down. The PM would go into his pious and puzzled mode. The existence of the Language Generation Unit would probably come out. But not the E Squad or the cyber project. Blair probably didn't even know about them.

He peered through a metal grille into the social club. It was like looking into a cave. Dennis and Stacia had paused between songs. Dennis had lit a cigarette and clamped it into the machine head of his guitar. They were laughing.

To fill in some time, Rick decided to go to the estate cafe to indulge himself with a full English breakfast – sausage, egg and bacon, with tomato, fried bread and a huge mug of sweet tea.

Smiling like a kid, he set off across a big patch of grass the size of a football pitch – the kind where ball games are not allowed. It was a bright but cold day. The sun was dipping in and out of the clouds. Ahead of him was Blackbird Point, the block where he and Stacia had been living for the past week. They had thrown out all of the rubbish and acquired some lampshades and curtains. The flat was almost habitable now.

A woman was walking her Alsatian towards him. They had become familiar over the last few days, exchanging hellos. Rick was feeling happy. When he had eaten breakfast, he would phone Carol and tell her that she and Gina could move back into their flat. This evening, he would try and talk to Gina. Thinking about his daughter made his heart beat faster.

Rick reached the edge of the grass. He said hello to the dog walker, who murmured a reply. The dog saw it first. A black van had been shadowing Rick, cruising the estate in second gear. Now it was only a few meters away from him. As the van's side door slid black, a dark human form was revealed inside. It appeared to be holding a stick. This caused the dog to bark in excitement. Rick turned.

The man with the gun had been startled by the Alsatian, which is what's what saved Rick's life. For a second, assassin and quarry scrutinized each other. The assassin's finger rested on his trigger. He now noted that the dog's owner, an old lady, was watching him too. She stood stock-still. Should he take her out as well? No, that would be exceeding his brief. The door slid shut. The van drove off.

"Fucking hell."

Rick could feel the blood draining from his face. He was too numb to clock the registration number –not that that would have helped him.

"Did you see?"

"Yeh ..."

Machine guns were not common on Elmwood Park.

The old lady was still frozen.

27

The Guardian

*An irritant, like scabies or head lice. Like them, it
will never go away. Fortunately, its journalists are
gullible and easily seduced by proximity to power.
They can easily be strung along – and you don't even
have to bribe them – which is a good way of keeping
the liberal middle classes on our side.*

- The New Labour papers

Roger Coverington walked across to the window and
looked out. It was lunchtime. Normally at this hour,
he would have been ensconced at his favorite table in
The Eagle, with a pint of real ale and a plate of
glutinous sausage and mash in front of him.

"Where the fuck is he?"

He was panicking. He was not used to running
stories this big.

"Phone the cab firm again would you ..." He called
across the room.

As he spoke, Rick entered the room. He was wide-
eyed. He had never been in the Guardian before. It was
the holy of holies. He was carrying a bulging leather
bag.

"Ah, Rick. Welcome ... mate."

Coverington breathed out.

"I'm glad that you are here."

Rick was studying the room. It appeared to be
terrifically calm. No one was shouting or crying. Just
computers and desks.

"We don't have much time. I want you to read our stories and add some quotes. Then we have to get it legalized."

"Right."

Rick wondered whether to tell Coverington that he had almost been machine-gunned. He would. But not yet.

~ ~ ~

"Come on guys." Tony Blair looked tense. "You will all get your turn. If you could all be a little patient."

The PM had been as scrubbed up as much as possible, but the thick make up on his face did not disguise the worry lines on his brow and the shadows under his tired eyes. He had been through a lot in the past year – Iraq, exhausting rows over Europe and hospitals, the inquiry into David Keeley (which had unconvincingly concluded suicide as the cause of death), then the Barry Triffit rebellion. Now, one of his favorite ministers had murdered someone.

Blair looked defensive. Later, reporters said that he was ill at ease; his attempts at humor were brittle. Would he survive this crisis and lead his party into a general election in 2005? Probably. He was a lucky bastard.

When he opened his mouth, there was a hailstorm of camera flashes.

"As you know, I have called this press conference following the arrest on Monday of Emma Henderson. I have called it following intense media speculation in the past few days about ..."

"Mr. Blair?"

"Yes?"

"Are you still supporting Ms. Henderson?"

"Please, guys, give me a break." Blair shielded his eyes with a hand, like a visor. He peered ahead, unable to locate the questioner. "Ms. Henderson is in custody.

I believe that charges have already been laid. Her behavior is obviously a matter of regret. I cannot pre-empt the results of the police investigation and I am not going to indulge in lurid tittle-tattle about what she may or may not have done, in her private life. We can leave that to the tabloid press, can't we?"

He paused and looked around, sensing the mood of the room. Good, he thought, he was back on track.

"I can, however, announce today a full and independent judicial inquiry, in connection with Ms. Henderson's alleged activities. The inquiry will be conducted by Sir Christopher Millet QC. I cannot tell you when it will start, but it will be as soon as possible. Right …" He stopped. "Are there any questions?"

"Mr. Blair?"

"Good. Yes."

It was Roger Coverington.

"Thank you for talking to us, sir. You will have seen the Guardian's very full coverage of this story yesterday. Can you give us your views on the possibility that a former leader of the Labour party may have died in suspicious circumstances and that Ms. Henderson was involved in other illegal and covert activities on behalf of the …"

Blair blinked.

"As I have said, there will be a full inquiry into these matters. I think that is as far as I can go, at this point, Roger." The prime minister smiled, unctuously. "Incidentally, the government is taking legal advice on your stories. You may be hearing from our solicitor."

The room filled with laughter. Blair basked in it. It was a good reaction shot. There was another flurry of clicks and flashes.

"Mr. Blair?"

"Yes?"

"Howard Harris, Daily Express. Could I just ask, sir, have you seen the New Labour papers?"

"Look." Blair's eyes widened. "Let's get this into perspective. As far as I am aware, this document does not exist. I am aware – we all are – that certain forged documents have been touted around Fleet Street. I am not going to start talking about robots and mind control and other nonsense. If you place any credence in all of that, then, quite frankly ..."

"What about the Language Generation Unit?"

"What about it?"

"Does it exist?"

Blair glanced to the side of the room, where one of his advisers was standing. It was a good job that they had anticipated this question. He spoke slowly. "Yes, of course it does. There is no secret about that. It is simply part of the machinery of the civil service and we er ... inherited it from the previous government. The name, by the way, is something of a misnomer. It may be that the inquiry will look at its terms of reference. And if so, in due course, we will make a decision about its future."

"Mr. Blair?"

"Yes."

"Fiona Wilson, BBC News. Prime minister, do you know where Barry Triffit is, because, according to our information, he has disappeared. He has not been seen by his wife for three days."

"Sorry. Barry who?"

A civil servant appeared from behind Tony Blair and whispered something in his ear.

"You mean, the er ... MP Barry Triffit."

"Yes."

"I am not aware that he has 'disappeared' as you put it, or what this has to do with the subject of this press conference. But, if that is the case, I shall certainly look into it. Thank you, Fiona. Next question."

"Scott Farren, Sky News. Mr. Blair, there are reports that Emma Henderson blinded her victim before she killed him and that she castrated him."

"Yes."

"Also, that she was filmed participating in orgies in a London night club."

"And ..."

"That she had several people murdered, possibly including an eminent London scientist who will be well known to you. And that she planned to assassinate the mayor of London. Obviously, these are very serious allegations and ..."

"Look Scott" Blair leaned forwards. "I'm not sure what you are asking me. If you are asking me, 'have I seen the videos?', then the answer is 'no'. They don't have them down at Blockbusters." He waited for the laughter to die down. "As to the other matters. Well, it all sounds like a rather lurid and improbable paperback, doesn't it? As I said before, there is to be a full police investigation and an independent inquiry. It would be quite wrong of me, here, to pre-empt the work of that inquiry, as I'm sure that you will agree. Now, I don't really see what else I can do. Do you?"

The reporter shrugged.

The prime minister's posture relaxed.

"Right, next question."

The clock on the other side of the room told him that it was nearly over. Thank God. There would be a few more questions, but he knew that he had put up a good performance; also he had done enough to fill the evening bulletins with some fascinating tittle-tattle. From now on, it should be plain sailing.

~ ~ ~

It was Sunday afternoon. Rick Gilliver sat in the living room of a small flat in Clapham. It was Carol's flat – neat, cozy and decorated in bright colors. That morning, She and Gina had moved back from the hotel, where they had been hiding for two and half weeks. Their bags were still in the hallway.

Rick sat next to Stacia, on a settee covered with a russet throw. Carol, his ex, liked autumnal colors – beige, maroon, dark yellow. Stacia was tense. She felt uncomfortable in the presence of Rick's ex. She did not know why.

The floor and table were scattered with newspapers. The same front-page story screamed from all of the tabloids and broadsheets. The headlines were variations on a few themes – "Murder Minister, Red Emma, Ice Maiden ..." The Sunday papers had followed the lead of the Guardian's expose, adding, at great length, their own speculations and details.

More enterprising reporters from the tabloids had besieged the Think Tank nightclub and tracked down current and former employees. One of them had signed up Nigel De Vere, with a large check, and pumped him for details of Emma Henderson's hyperactive sex life. When her trial was concluded, it would have carte blanche to use the material. At the moment, only the Guardian had compromising pictures of the minister. And it was far too prim to use them. But that could change. There were rumors that someone had taken some stills from the infamous porn video and was touting them around for unfeasibly large sums of money.

Rick's name was in all of the papers. He was a hero. He did not have to hide now. In due course, he would be able to sign a contract with one of the newspapers, if he wished to. Soon, greasy publicity agents – the jackals of the media – would be sniffing around him. The previous day, he had moved back into his flat, to find a group of journalists and his cat, who they had apparently adopted, waiting by the front door.

"Sorry to leave you on your own."

Carol walked into the living room. There was a towel on her head. She had just washed her hair. It was a gingery shade of auburn.

"Would you like some tea?"

Stacia murmured that she would.

Carol was short, only a little taller than Stacia. She smiled a lot. Rick called her the Celtic Tiger.

Of course, she had been furious with him when they had spoken on the phone the previous evening. Didn't he realize how hard it had been to live in one room, with no clothes or washing facilities? Didn't he think that it was totally irresponsible for him to have disappeared for weeks on end? And so on.

At least Gina, Rick's daughter, seemed to have enjoyed living in Croydon's Holiday Inn, and being liberated from school. According to Carol, she had spent most of her time exploring shopping malls, spending her generous allowance from the Sunday World on cosmetics and clothes. To her disgust, the hotel's TV only had only provided seven channels.

Rick had listened to Carol moaning for almost an hour on the phone. As usual, he just mumbled something every so often, so show that he was still alive. Then he had suggested that she too might be able to sell her story to one of the papers – "life on the run for ex partner of murder minister's intended victim". It was a bit complicated but that would not put off a good reporter. That had cheered her up a bit.

"I really like your flat."

"Do you? Thank you."

Carol warmed to Stacia's compliment. Stacia had had a good look through Carol's books (self improvement, Celtic mysticism) and her CDs. She seemed to approve of them. This was a good sign, Rick thought.

"We've been living on a really grotty council estate, in Luton," Stacia said. "It was horrible. There was no furniture when we moved in and it smelled of pee. At least you were in a hotel."

Carol smiled. If Rick had said that she would have killed him.

"Yeh, but it was pretty tough," said Carol. "We didn't know when Gina could back to school. We had to wait until Action Man here had finished."

Stacia laughed.

"But aren't you proud of him?" Stacia put her arm around Rick's waist. "I mean, look at all these ..."

She gestured towards the newspapers. In them were half a dozen different versions of how Rick had taken a call from a disaffected civil servant; how he gone on the run; how he had listened while Emma Henderson had threatened to kidnap his child; how he had almost been machine gunned on a Luton estate, in what the police were claiming, erroneously, was a 'drugs war'.

Carol shrugged. She claimed not to have read any of them.

"Look," he said, breaking the silence, "I've had an idea. Why don't we all go for a meal?"

"Are you paying?"

"Course I am."

"Well, that's good." Carol laughed.

"All right then. But I'll have to get changed."

Rick groaned. He knew that it could take an awfully long time.

He left the living room. He could tell that his ex and current partner would get on. Stacia was not naturally jealous. He would tell Carol that she and Gina could come and visit in Walthamstow any time.

He walked down the narrow hallway of the little flat. The walls were painted light blue. He reached a door. Music was softly pulsing from inside. It sounded like hip-hop. There was hand-written sign on the door in felt-tip pen. It said "KEEP OUT" in violent capital letters. Rick tapped softly on the door.

When he heard no response, he slowly pushed it open.

She was sitting on the bed. She looked up. Her hair not had changed. It was still an odd color. Her hoop earrings were a little smaller.

"Hi dad."

"Hi darling."

He looked around the room. On the walls were no references to Pokémon characters. There were some drawings that she had done and a poster of a band that he did not recognize.

"I missed you."

She stood up. She took a few faltering steps towards him.

"I missed you too."

They hugged.

"I love you," he said.

"I love you too."

Rick did not mean it to happen. Tears began to stream down his cheeks.

= = =

Appendix

Introduction

The Labour party began in 1900. But it has only been in government for 23 years during this century. Quite frankly, it isn't good enough. How can we make sure that we win and, more importantly, keep on winning, into the foreseeable future? This document offers some tentative suggestions. What I describe here is an invisible infrastructure that will make us invincible and bury the Conservatives forever. You could call it the Fourth Way.

When we are in power (and we will be, I assure you) it is very important that we don't hurry. I would suggest that we could spend the first two or three years reviewing. After reviewing we can consult (wins brownie points). This can be dragged on for as long as necessary, especially for those policies which we no longer favor and would like to kick into touch.

Near the end of our first term, after 2000, I would suggest a blitzkrieg of overlapping initiatives, each with different boundaries, delivery mechanisms and measurement systems. They will promote confusion while looking good, especially if we associate them with lots of vague and conflicting performance indicators. We will do blah, blah, blah by 2005. This will win us even more time. No one, apart from a few policy dweebs, will ever hold us to account for them.

The following sections are a brief guide to how we can ensure victory and then stay at the top indefinitely. Enjoy!

BBC

England dreaming. Warm as coco, soft and fuzzy as socks on a radiator. The BBC is generally on our side and they won't bite the hand that feeds them – especially when a new director general has done his work. He will fragment, demoralize and confuse the whole network, lose sport to the competition and reduce the quality threshold. By the time he has finished, the BBC will be wall-to-wall crap.

Benefits

Keep 'em complicated, bureaucratic and Labour intensive and add tax credits to the brew. Creates work for paper shufflers and encourages the black economy, which, of course, keeps down Labour costs.

The Big Issue

A magazine about rich people sold by poor people, all budding capitalists. How cool is that! It hits the zeitgeist spot on – voyeuristic consumerism combined with economic aspiration.

Conservatives

They left their clothes on the beach and went for swim when John Major was in charge. We stole them. Now watch the bastards drown!

Constitution

There really isn't one. Only some unintelligible seventeenth-century gibberish and a homoerotic pantomime (men in tights, black rod etc.). Long may it remain so! We must keep this policy area as confusing as possible, while promoting a vague idea of reform.

Problem areas. Freedom of information. No way we can let that happen. Create bill with widely drawn exemptions? Human Rights. We're committed to adopting the European convention into UK law. Barristers will cream themselves with greed. But don't worry. It won't actually make all that difference.

The House of Lords. I have thought about this long and hard. I suggest that we deconstruct the upper house by abolishing most, if not all, of the hereditary peers and then fail to replace it! The situation can then be left in limbo. Obviously, in the longer term, a purely appointed upper house would be best. Appointed by us! Parliament may not be very happy. I think that by 2004 or 2005 we would be able to get away with it.

It is extremely useful that our do-it-yourself democracy has few, if any, internal safeguards. It's a suck it and see kind of thing. As for the British public most of them haven't got a clue. Only those who go to public schools are taught in detail about the Parliamentary system!

Council housing

Drab, dreary and damp. Council housing promotes an unhealthy kind of proletarian solidarity, which is not very us, and it gives local authorities a powerbase. We should get rid of it as quickly as possible, preferably by transferring it to private landlords, or, where that is not possible, by giving it to the poor souls who live there.

Countryside

Green stuff around the towns. Seriously, it's a horrible, smelly place. But we can't ignore it since, on a map, it's nearly all blue. Simply speaking, we have to win over the floaters and divide and demoralize the Barbour-jacketed Tories. I suggest that we release a fast-spreading livestock virus into the countryside, just before our second election victory in 2001 – something potent that will knock the stuffing out of what is left of agriculture. Whining farmers – the few that have not killed themselves – will bleat on about being hard done by while they stuff their pockets with compensation money. NB Farmers are all cheats. I have never met an honest one.

Cyber project

Imagine if we could grow a politician. We could give them the right face, and hair, and fill their head with our language. He or she would always use the right words and hit the right emotional register. I believe that this may now be possible. An MP that we started now could be foreign secretary by 2005 and prime minister by 2009. Think about it.

Diana

Baby-faced ingénue. In the long term, could cause serious inconvenience and embarrassment to The Firm. May have to be dealt with.

Drugs

Enjoy but handle this issue with extreme caution. The "war on drugs" which, fortunately, we can never win is one of our strongest suits with Mr. and Mrs. Average.

Email

What a brilliant idea! The more we can remove the human interface between news gatherers and the news, the better. The key newspapers are safely tucked away in Canary Wharf – that means fewer boozy "off the record" lunches. We should disseminate information by website and email as much as possible and avoid meeting people. The more electronic we are, the more control we will have over "the human factor".

EU

It's undemocratic, its incomprehensible and its inefficient. In other words, it's the ideal form of government. Public position – hang on matey, we're British. Private position – yes, please, give it to me! Now!

Event management

We have to neutralize our opponents, especially those in our own party. MI5 are spineless public school types. Useless. Our own people will take over their role (assassinations, honey traps, blackmail etc.). They are ready for this. All they need is the word.

Some organizations we should infiltrate but otherwise ignore (Trots, animal rights people). They are ineffectual and will simply make us look good, frothing at the mouth outside our conferences. Potential enemies in our own and other parties must be made harmless, won over, or taken out (see appendix).

Assassination versus ennoblement? Both are effective as a means of disempowerment. Assassination is quicker, but should be used sparingly. Misguided fellow travellers (Tribune editors etc.) and senior party figures need to be watched closely and, in some cases, got rid of (e.g. JS).

Executive

The big one! Remember this is where power should be. Effectively it's the Cabinet (which, for public consumption, has only one voice), and the prime minister's Office (which should be greatly expanded).

Our leader should be a president not a prime minister. Not difficult, because Parliament is a poodle.

Failure
Remember, failure is only a state of mind. As such, it does not exist, in politics or in life. A person who is mentally fit can recover from any disaster. It is when you are on your uppers – dodging bullets and wading through shit – that the greatest opportunities will come. But it takes a real hero to see that.

Fame
It is the spur. But personal ambition is not enough. There must be something else – something bigger than you are, like a political party. Otherwise, you might just as well be a presenter on daytime television.

Football
If you support a football team, try to remember a) their nickname and b) the names of the chairman, the manager and at least some of the players. (There are eleven of them by the way.) Turn up every so often. The food is horrible – sausage rolls and warm lager – but you'll keep the proles happy.

Foreign policy
Schleswig Holstein and all that. Sorry, it's not my subject. Suggest that we just shove our head up America's arse and follow whatever they do.

The Guardian
An irritant, like scabies or head lice. Like them, it will never go away. Fortunately, its journalists are gullible and easily seduced by proximity to power. They can easily be strung along – and you don't even have to

bribe them – which is a good way of keeping the liberal middle classes on our side.

Influence

First, find out what a person wants most. It could be sex, it could be fame, it could be the love of their child. Then threaten to deny it them. They will do whatever you want.

Insincerity

Insincerity is the oxygen of politics. However, if you don't believe anything, you can't be insincere can you?

Investigative reporters

By-line freaks with bad haircuts. Tend to espouse youthful causes as they grow old. Contemptible.

IT

A mixed blessing. It allows you to do all kinds of extraordinary things – in theory. The larger the project, the more likely it is to fail, especially if fuckwit consultants are involved.

Language

Language is power. It will form the skeleton and sinews of our success. We should adopt a vocabulary that suggests business-like efficiency, combined with social concern. For example, 'rollout' (verb and noun), 'toolkit', 'empowerment', 'cross-cutting', 'capacity building', 'joined-up', etcetera.

These words will be used in all speeches, consultation documents, white papers and press releases – e.g. 'The DoH has announced the roll-out of a cross-cutting engagement mechanism for community capacity building'. The fact that such a phrase means little, if anything, does not matter. 1) It sounds good. 2) Print has its own authority. 3) Most people are pretty stupid. They do not actually think about what comes in through their ears or eyes.

It is important that we spread our vocabulary as widely as possible. Gradually, it will seep into newspapers, magazines and even daily discourse e.g. 'Mavis, have you rolled out my tool-kit yet?' (joking). This language will seep into the political culture. In time it will become the political culture. As I said, language is power.

We should develop software so that computers can generate policy documents spontaneously from key words – social exclusion, regional empowerment, whatever.

Suggest that Derek Foxton heads the Language Generation Unit. All speeches, press releases etc. must be cleared through him. Derek has invented an instant rebuttal machine. It is capable of monitoring all press stories about us – news stories and features – at all times, in all media.

The machine, Guinevere, can be used to generate an instant response to any criticism – a party line that can be fed to spokespeople and politicians at all levels. It will be indispensable in the lead up to the first election, probably in 1997

Liberal Democrats
Strange, gnome-like people with bad skin who, for whatever reason, have failed to integrate with society. Don't have anything to do with them. In the first term, we can pretend to be looking into some proportional representation thing, to string them along a bit. Then quietly bury it.

Livingstone, Ken

Don't be fooled. He's a reasonable fanatic. Stalin in a cardigan. He wants power, he's as slippery as a condom and he'll use exactly the same techniques as us to get it. Creating a mayor of London could create an opening for him. Watch carefully.

The north

It's grim up there and the food is hideous. (North is anywhere above Muswell Hill by the way.) But it can be very cozy on those long winter nights. Northern people are tribal. They are inexplicably loyal, even to complete tosspots, and our votes are weighed up there, not counted. So it remains our emotional heartland. Tip – don't go anywhere the Durham Miners' Gala (look what happened to Kinnock!).

Pop songs

Useful as anthems, but dangerous. Indie bands have street cred, but the singer will invariably be on heroin and badmouth you, once the novelty has worn off. Queen is favorite (royal associations, transvestism – always popular). Do not, under any circumstances, appear in a pop video!

Poverty

I suggest that we drop this word. It's too scary and, quite frankly, we can't do very much about it, like the weather. How about using a term that is far more neutral and ambiguous, like "social exclusion"?

Press conferences and interviews

TV journalists are the easy option. They are looking for short answers, for people who have the attention span of a mayfly. Radio comes next – radio journalists stick to scripts and rarely ask difficult follow-ups –

then come the nationals and, finally, the trade mags. Trade mags will try to trip you up. If you can, give them short shrift.

If questions are likely to be difficult, ask for them to be grouped into three. That can get you out of sticky situations. Ideally, know what you are going to be asked and what you are going to say. You should bang out about two or three simple points and hold onto them, like a dog with a bone. Never do lifestyle-based interviews. Avoid – like the plague. She is poisonous.

Shopping
The best form of therapy. All those boxes and carrier bags are a soothing antidote to the stresses of life. Fortunately, the rest of the country agrees with me. Shopping has everything. It's an economic, leisure and social activity all in one package. In fact, it's a religion, and big is best. Let's convert the UK into a giant out-of-town shopping mall!

Soaps
Prole pap, *de rigueur* for those with the "common touch." "I never miss EastEnders". Poor production values, pantomime characters and crap stories. Try to familiarize yourself with at least one of them and maybe one or two actors. But not, please God, Emmerdale. Don't go there!

Spin
A friendly American term for lies and propaganda. Suggest we adopt it.

Tabloids
Potty, botty, totty. That's the level one is dealing with. A puerile baby world, on the threshold of consciousness. Unfortunately, the tabloids are

important. If people want to have their genitals tickled and bright dangly things bounced in front of their eyes, there's not very much we can do about it.

Terrorism

Ideal enemy, because it has no boundaries and no fixed source. We could seal the border with the Irish republic. We could introduce ID cards, abolish sectarian parties in Northern Ireland and revoke Irish rights to UK citizenship, unless the IRA stops killing people. I suggest we do none of things. What could be better for us than the so-called troubles? They make good telly and have little danger of seriously escalating. Eventually, the hate-filled mullahs will die and demographics will re-join the six counties to the republic.

Think tanks

The purpose of a think tank is to encourage us to do what we wanted to do already and to show us how to do it. Initially, they will soften up resistance to "unthinkable" ideas – privatizing prisons, abolishing free healthcare. When the time is right, and public opinion has shifted, they will have already prepared the ground for some really wicked policies. Hey presto!

Thank you for reading.
Please review this book. Reviews help others find New
Pulp Press and inspire us to keep providing these
marvelous tales.

If you would like to be put on our email list to receive
updates on new releases, contests, and promotions,
please go to NewPulpPress.com and sign up.

About the Author

William Hatchett is a London-based journalist. Politics are his job as well as his hobby. He works on a trade magazine, writing about how the environment affects health. Many moons ago, after graduating from a UK university, he attended the University of Paris VIII to study American literature: the novels of Thomas Wolfe. He then hitchhiked through the United States and lived for year, in 1983, in New Mexico. He loves American literature – Chandler and Hammett, naturally, and also, in the crime and pulp genre, Jim Thompson, Cornell Woolrich, Elmore Leonard, Georges Simenon (and many more). He lives in Forest Hill, south-east London, sharing his house with a cat and small collection of guitars. He has a grown-up daughter and two wonderful grandkids. His published books include espionage-based thrillers and social history. One day, he hopes to live in a log cabin, next to a lake.

NewPulpPress.com

www.ingramcontent.com/pod-product-compliance
Lightning Source LLC
Chambersburg PA
CBHW070556260626
47161CB00002B/623